# I Ain't Me No More:

## *Book One of the Always Divas Series*

# I Ain't Me No More:

## Book One of the Always Divas Series

*E.N. Joy*

**URBAN CHRISTIAN**

*www.urbanchristianonline.com*

Urban Books, LLC
97 N18th Street
Wyandanch, NY 11798

I Ain't Me No More: Book One of the Always Diva Series

ISBN 13: 978-1-60162-769-8
ISBN 10: 1-60162-769-6

First Printing October 2013
Printed in the United States of America

10 9 8 7 6 5 4 3 2

Distributed by Kensington Corp.
Submit Wholesale Orders to:
Kensington Publishing Corp.
C/O Penguin Group (USA) Inc.
Attention: Order Processing
405 Murray Hill Parkway
East Rutherford, NJ 07073-2316
Phone: 1-800-526-0275
Fax: 1-800-227-9604

# I Ain't Me No More:

## *Book One of the Always Divas Series*

by

*E.N. Joy*

# Other Books by This Author

*Me, Myself and Him*

*She Who Finds a Husband*

*Been There, Prayed That*

*Love, Honor or Stray*

*Trying to Stay Saved*

*I Can Do Better All By Myself*

*And You Call Yourself a Christian*

*The Perfect Christian*

*The Sunday Only Christian*

*Ordained by the Streets*

*A Woman's Revenge (Anthology; "Best Served Cold")*

*Even Sinners Have Souls* (Edited by E.N. Joy)

*Even Sinners Have Souls Too* (Edited by E.N. Joy)

*Even Sinners Still Have Souls* (Edited by E.N. Joy)

*The Secret Olivia Told Me* (N. Joy)

*Operation Get Rid of Mom's New Boyfriend* (N. Joy)

# Acknowledgments

My thanks go to the Urban Books family, Kensington Publishing Corporation, and Charlton "CP the Artist" Palmer. Each of you bring my product to life in so many different ways. You give me a voice, my characters a voice, and the readers a visual to my words and characters. I wish to extend my thanks to the graphics department, the editorial team, right down to the individual who lists my books on every online book retail Web site there is so that my readers have access to my work. No job is so small that it doesn't deserve recognition. I come to you as a person with a story to tell; you clean me up and package me so that the story gets told. I thank God for you!

Dr. Maxine Thompson, the best story development editor in the world, thank you for pulling elements of this story out of me that I didn't even know existed. Everybody has a book in them, but not everybody can tell a story. Thank you for making sure that I didn't just write a book, but also told a story—a good story.

I would like to express my gratitude to you, my readers. If it were not for you, this book would not exist. Those are not just words. In all honesty, if you all had not latched on to the lives of these divas, this "soap opera in print" would have not been renewed for another season. So I thank you from the bottom of my heart for allowing these characters to invade your lives and for your continued support of me as a person and what I do.

# Acknowledgments

To Pastor Maurice Jackson, God gave you a word to deliver during your 11:00 a.m. sermon on Sunday, September 3, 2006. Like you said, people may not know us by our face, but it is up to us to make sure they know us by our story. This is Helen's story, and I'm leaving no stone unturned. . . .

To my auntie Lynne Carson, you'd had a few, so you probably won't even remember the conversation you had with me at Mel's album release party (God rest his soul). But among so many other jewels you dropped, you told me that no matter how high God elevates me, I should never forget where I came from. You told me that no matter how many Cadillacs God affords me, I should never forget that brown Chevy Chevette I used to have to drive around in to get to school and work. You told me that no matter where God takes me in my travels, I should never forget the neighborhood I came from, never forget who I used to be. You told me that no matter how many big names and famous people I'm allowed to connect and break bread with, I should never forget my family. You spoke volumes. I just want you to know that I won't forget those things and I won't forget you. I won't ever forget my Carson family, who to this day loves and supports me and claims me as if my last name were Carson. That's love. That's family!

I can't *not* acknowledge my Davis, Edwards, and Ross family. I am so blessed to have the love and support of you all.

Breakfast Club members, my sister Jawan, my bestie Angie, Carla, Jeri, and Takeeah, the devil tried to break me into pieces during the process of getting this book complete. Thank you, ladies, for being the glue to put me back together with our monthly get-togethers. I must also

# Acknowledgments

thank my sister-in-law, Nicole N. Ross, for her powerful prayers and counsel. And I thank my mother-in-law, Gwen Marsh, and my bestie, Stephanie "Anderson" Davenport.

Dad, thank you for continuing to instill in me daily the importance of family, and, Uncle Dudi, thank you for all the effort you put into bringing the family together for fun, memorable times. Your efforts are not in vain. The people who God wants to be there show up!

Elder Price of Power and Glory Ministries International, I don't know how I would make it through the week without the teachings of your eight o'clock service, in which you have remained steadfast and dedicated to seeing that you share the knowledge and wisdom God has instilled in you with His people. You are an appreciated and a blessed man of God.

Last but certainly not least, I wish to acknowledge my dynamite children and my husband, Nick "Bang" Ross. Wow! What can I say, Nick, besides the fact that it takes one "bleep" of a guy to love me—all of me? The old me, the new me, and the me that is yet to come. Yep, I'm convinced that God chose the right one to be able to deal with me.

*"O keep my soul, and deliver me: let me not be ashamed; for I put my trust in thee."*

–Psalms 25:20

# Prologue

Man, I hate the cleaning guy! Why does he have to do his job so well? Can't he ever leave just one spot, smear, or smudge on this dang stripper pole? Something so that I don't have to see myself, so that I'm not so painfully visible like this? I mean, I could see if the pole was in some studio that offers pole-dancing classes for women trying to keep their relationships exciting. But this is Club Shake 'Em Up, a hole-in-the-wall strip club in Columbus, Ohio. What makes him think I want to be able to see myself twirling around and sliding down this pole like some skilled monkey, caught up in the powerful grip of the almighty dollar, a grip known to have choked the life out of many, while leaving others gasping for their last breath? If that's what Mr. Cleaning Man thinks, he's wrong. Dead wrong!

"That's for you," Damon says over R. Kelly's "Your Body's Callin'."

The owner of the club makes sure the DJ plays the music at a level where the patrons don't have to compete with the music artist. Money talks. The customers are money. Therefore, they have to be heard loud and clear.

With his chestnut brown bald head and his facial hair that is edged up nice and clean, Damon licks his thumb and uses it to flick a twenty-dollar bill off the stack of money he's palming. "That's for you too," he says. "And this is for your mama." He flicks another twenty off the pile. "Anybody who helped make something as beautiful as you deserves to get paid, so on that note, here's a little something for your pops too." He flicks yet another bill.

My hips are like a boat, rocking in an open sea of lust disguised as love. I look Damon in the eyes and say, "I thank you, my mama thanks you, and my daddy thanks you too." I give him a flirty wink and instruct my midsection to do a roll, creating a wave that rocks the boat just that much more.

"You better go, go-go girl," Damon says, cheering me on.

Damon's a regular at Club Shake 'Em Up. He isn't one of my regulars. He's the regular of a fellow dancer named Sky, but she's been off work the past couple of nights. The unconfirmed rumor is that she got knocked up and is recuperating from an abortion. Whatever the reason, her loss is my gain.

I swivel my body down to the floor the way the vanilla and chocolate swirl ice cream at DQ makes its way from the machine to the cone. Dropping it like it's hot is my forte for now, at least until I can learn to work the pole like a pro. Talking smack is quickly becoming another skill I can add to my stripper repertoire.

"Baby, you know it takes gas to keep a Cadillac like myself going," I say to Damon. "So as long as you keep filling up the tank, I'ma go-go, all right." I swivel my body back up to a standing position while adding, "In any direction you want me to go. As a matter of fact, I'll let you drive." I lick my lips. "Naw, you look like the type who likes to ride."

Damon's lips part into that sexy signature smile of his, the left side of his upper lip turning upward, revealing the bling of his diamond-studded capped tooth.

All the girls only wish they had a regular that dropped bills like Damon drops them. And all the girls know that he's strictly hands-off. He's Sky's monthly mortgage on her condo. She's made this fact known to Damon, as well, as the only time he ever steps foot in the club is during Sky's shift. If she isn't there, he keeps it moving, which is what he'd done the past two nights. I guess night number three, tonight, was his breaking point. He'd breached his loyalty to Sky, because this time when he came in and asked for her, only to find that she still hadn't returned to work, he stayed. It was just my good fortune that I was on deck to hit the stage once he'd gotten settled with a shot of Hennessy.

"Whatever you want," Damon says. "It's your caddie. I'll drive, ride. . . . Heck, I'll even be a backseat passenger. Just know that I got you, Ma." Damon begins to flick off bills like he's the dealer in a game of spades.

I'm very much content with the hand I'm being dealt. So much so that I want to drop to my knees and begin scooping like a kid standing under a piñata that has just been busted open. But I don't want to appear too desperate. As if dancing half naked in front of a bunch of horny men and a few dykes doesn't make me seem desperate enough.

Resolving to strip in the first place was out of desperation. At the time I made the decision, which was just two weeks ago, I felt trapped, like Jonah in the belly of the big fish. I was always trying to make ends meet, but neither of my ends were the least bit interested in getting to know one another. Bills were due. I needed fast cash. Not the natural kind of fast, but the "Marion Jones on steroids" kind of fast. World record breaking fast. I weighed some options on my immoral scale of desperation, and stripping was a lighter load to travel with in my mental carry-on. I mean, at least I'm not selling my whole self—just bartering a piece of me.

Needless to say, bills are still due. The notice that my gas had been turned off greeted me at my door earlier today like an ex-boyfriend I had never expected to run into. I almost hadn't noticed it, because of the eviction notice that partially covered it, the new bigger, stronger boyfriend. They were each vying for my attention, wanting to be acknowledged and paid, just like the dancers in the club. I'm sure anyone would agree that would make one act a little desperate.

I was desperate.

I'm still desperate.

Dressed to the nines plus one with my make-up done up like a black Barbie, I'm looking like an angel, so never mind the fact that I'm dancing on the devil's stage. My white sheer lingerie-like robe trimmed in sparkling rhinestones leaves very little to the imagination. It's covering up the silver and white two-piece thong costume I'd purchased at an online exotic dance wear store. It's safe to say not much is being covered up.

"Go on, go-go girl. You know you wanna bend that thang over and pick up that loot." Once again, Damon licks his thumb and lightens his pile of money as he flicks a couple more bills onto the stage, at my feet. This time, though, he'd licked his thumb slowly while staring me down. He looks as though he can see right through me, right down to my bare essentials, even though I'm still wearing my cover-up.

Each dancer in the club does a two-song set. First one slow, then one fast. The cover-ups aren't shed until the second song. Damon's wafer-brown eyes, a contrast to his sable-toasted skin, are soliciting me to abandon the cover-up prematurely.

"Come on. Just show me a li'l sumpin', sumpin'," Damon urges. "Move that thong on over to the side and let me get a little peek." He flicks off another bill. "Surely, that's worth a five-count peek." His eyes peruse my body from head to toe, and he wets his thumb in preparation to keep making it rain.

And this was rain, might I add. Ones being flicked off, that's a chance of rain. Fives being flicked off; that's a little drizzle. Tens being flicked off, that's a scattered shower. Twenties, that's rain. Benjamins, an all-out thunderstorm!

"Come on, Damon. You know the rules. You don't want me to break the rules and get put on punishment, do you?" I ask, making a puppy-dog face.

"Forget the rules," Damon barks like the big dawg he is. "And if all that is worthy of just a peek," he says, referring to all the money he's laid at my feet, "I can only imagine what this will get me."

R. Kelly's vocals are still playing in the background, but I freeze on the stage, which means the bill Damon is now displaying must be triggering some type of ice storm. Until this very moment, I had never even known that such a bill existed.

I gather my equanimity and try to play it smooth, still talking slick. "Boy, don't be bringing no Monopoly money up in here," I joke, an attempt to play off my ignorance of U.S. currency.

"What's the matter, go-go girl? You ain't never seen a five-hundred-dollar bill before?" He chuckles. "Then all that means is that you ain't been with no real man before." He gives me the once-over." So what do you say you make tonight a first for a lot of things?" This time he licks his lips instead of his thumb, making it evident that he is not about to drop that bill at my feet without some type of commitment that he's going to get more from me than just a two-song set, with me sitting next to him, talking smack afterward.

All of a sudden I'm starting to think about church, kicking myself for not having paid my respects or tithes to the house of the Lord in a couple of months. At the same time I'm trying my hardest to recall one of those messages that have to do with temptation, a scripture or something, because to tell the truth and shame the devil, I am beyond tempted to take Damon up on his offer. In my uninhibited imaginings I had never fancied myself standing on stage in a bar, dancing for money, let alone exceeding that act of disgrace.

"A good name is rather to be chosen than great riches. . . ." That isn't exactly the scripture I'm grappling for, but it still seems fitting.

My name . . . Helen Lannden. How much is it worth today? Twenty-five-year-old Helen Lannden. How much will my name be worth tomorrow, especially if I trick for money?

"Only you and I would have to know." Was Damon not only sexy and paid, but he was a mind reader too?

I can feel sweat establishing a nest on my forehead. The fast song hasn't even come on yet, so there is no way dancing is the instigator of my perspiration. Who knew the nonphysical act of thinking, contemplating, could make one work up a sweat?

"You don't scream, and I won't holler. As long as we both keep our mouths shut, nobody will ever find out." Damon sounds convincing as I envision that five-hundred-dollar bill, the husband, trumping both my disconnect and eviction notice, the ex-boyfriend and the new boyfriend.

"So what do you say?" Damon says, placing the tip of the five-hundred-dollar bill between his lips while caressing the bottom between his index finger and thumb.

I gawk at the bill rooted between his lips. My mouth waters as I marvel at it, wondering what it might taste like. Not his lips, the money. The money, coupled with the previous tips I'd netted that night, could get me current on my bills, keep a roof over my head.

Damon slowly removes the bill from between his lips, then suspends it in front of me, which is like waving a fresh-cut sirloin at a pit bull whose master hasn't fed it in days. "So what's it gonna be, Ma?"

# Stone Number One

"I say we convince pastor to kick her tail right on out of this church," Tamarra stood up and said. Thirty-six-year-old Tamarra had been saved for eleven years, New Day Temple of Faith being her only place of worship. Now divorced for one year after a fifteen-year marriage, during which Tamarra had learned her husband had had a child outside of their marriage, it was safe to say that at this moment, she was quite the bitter and unforgiving soul.

"Calm down, Sister Tamarra," Doreen requested as she stood behind the podium in the church classroom. She was born Doreen Nelly Mae Hamilton, then traded in her last name for that of her now deceased husband, Willie Tucker, but members of New Day lovingly referred to her as Mother Doreen. Known as a voice of reason and never one to be in drama or the subject of a drama, this sixty-something treasure chest of wisdom appeared to be nothing short of the perfect Christian.

With the pastor's permission, Mother Doreen, as the founder and leader of the New Day Singles Ministry, had called a special meeting for the ministry. She wanted to discuss a matter concerning one of the newer female members of the church, the woman they referred to as Sister Helen. Helen had joined the church between four and six months ago, and yet she'd already managed to stir up a decade's worth of trouble.

"I really believe something is going on with her," Mother Doreen said, the wheels of concern rotating in

8 E.N. Joy

her brain and in her heart. "Nobody in their right mind would post pictures of church members in what appear to be compromising positions on the church Web site. So there has to be something going on with her."

"I really believe she's just crazy," Tamarra replied. "No disrespect intended, Mother Doreen, but if those pictures on the church Web site had been of you instead of me, then I'm almost one hundred percent certain you'd feel the same way I do."

Mother Doreen had to admit that Tamarra had a point. Those pictures of Tamarra and the man she was seeing, Maeyl, that had turned up on New Day's Web site didn't put the couple in such a holy light. Of course, as it turned out, the photos hadn't been what they appeared to be. The photos had shown Tamarra and Maeyl getting pretty close out in the church parking lot. They came to find, after all was said, done, and found out, that the twosome had merely prayed, then given one another a godly hug afterward.

If it hadn't been for Helen fortuitously revealing the photos to a fellow church member, Deborah, no one might have ever found out the truth. But the truth was out, indeed, and it wasn't setting Tamarra free. It was hardly keeping her free, as she wouldn't have minded doing three to five years in a jail cell for going upside Helen's head.

The photos had been removed from the Web site and the culprit had been found out, but as far as Tamarra was concerned, the damage had been done and Helen needed to pay for such an outright mean and hurtful act.

"I'm with Tamarra," said Paige, Tamarra's closest friend inside and outside of New Day. "Sister Helen is a loose cannon, and we need to shoot her too-much-make-up-wearing, too-much-cleavage-always-showing, skirts-too-short, jezebel-looking behind up on out of here."

"Paige, now you just cosigning for your best friend," Deborah noted, stepping in. "We really don't know what's going on with her." Deborah stared off into the distance. "There could be something deeply rooted in her past that is just eating her up inside, something that's got her hurting so bad, she doesn't know where to direct the pain but at other people." Deborah sounded as if she was speaking from experience.

"Whatever," Paige said, sucking her teeth and rolling her eyes. "We all done been through something. And I know I ain't been saved but a minute, but I know enough to know that we all are going to keep going through things. That doesn't give us the right to take a needle, fill it with all our hurt, pain, and misery, and then inject it into other people's lives. And on that note, I'm still with Tamarra. I say we put her out on that tail of hers, which she's always trying to show everybody with them little bitty ole skirts."

"And then be having the nerve to fall out at the altar in 'em," added Unique, a younger member of the Singles Ministry.

In agreement, Paige high-fived Unique.

"I just can't see ever putting folk out of the church." Mother Doreen closed her eyes and shook her head. She then opened her eyes. "Let's say the child is already hurting, which I'm willing to bet my last bingo chip in a close game that she is. Church hurt is the worst hurt, so imagine what that could do to her. We could be her only hope. The child ain't but what? Twenty-five, twenty-six? She ain't even lived half her life yet. Imagine her having to go through all those years with church hurt." Mother Doreen shook her head again and adamantly stood by her beliefs. "The church ain't where you throw sick people out. It's where a sick person should always be able to come to get healed."

"Amen," Deborah agreed. "Jesus saves."

"Yeah, but that Sister Helen is beyond being saved," Paige chimed in.

"And we can't save nobody who doesn't want to be saved," Tamarra added.

"And just who are you to determine that Sister Helen doesn't want to be saved?" Deborah asked Tamarra with her hands on hips. "You're a caterer, not some psychoanalyst. We have no idea what is in her mind or what she's been through." Deborah couldn't believe this was her talking, seeing that Helen had been her nemesis, a thorn in her side, ever since Helen had joined New Day. But Deborah knew something about past hurt and pain herself. Her life hadn't been a bed of roses, but a cot of dandelions instead.

"And that's why we should let the doorknob hit her where the good Lord split her," Paige said. "We know absolutely nothing about her." Paige looked around the room and pointed at all the women. "Each of us, we pretty much know some of each other's stories—enough to help and enough to know what to pray about. But Sister Helen, we don't even know the first sentence of her story."

"So you want to know my story?"

A hush fell over the room when all the ladies looked at the doorway and saw Sister Helen Lannden herself standing there, posing her question.

"Is that it? Is that why the women of New Day always walk around here like divas with their noses in the air, looking down on me like I'm trash?" Helen asked. "Because you don't know my story? Y'all think y'all are so perfect, huh? Well, isn't there a saying that people who live in glass houses shouldn't throw stones?" Her eyes x-rayed the room. "Which is why I keep all mine in my pocket."

All the women became a little nervous and somewhat discomfited that Helen had been served an unintended and undetermined portion of their conversation.

"Sister Helen, we were j-just t-talking about you," Deborah stammered, standing up.

"You don't say," Helen replied, shaking her head. "So y'all want to know my story, huh?" Helen looked around the room, but no one replied. "That wasn't a rhetorical question. I really want to know if you ladies want to know my story."

"Not me," Deborah was quick to say. She knew from experience that once one person got to testifying, a whole clan of others would be in line next. She was not about to entertain it. "I have to go." She gathered her things and walked toward the doorway where Helen stood. She momentarily looked into Helen's eyes, then cast her own eyes down and exited. Looking at Helen at that moment was like looking into a mirror. Deborah could not stand or face the pain.

Mother Doreen cleared her throat while wiping beads of sweat from her forehead, a trait of hers that revealed itself whenever there was tension that needed to be sliced through like a week-old pound cake. She then lifted her head and with confidence replied, "As a matter of fact, Sister Helen, we would. Us women would like to hear your story." She looked at the other women, silently beseeching them to have her back. Several nodded to show their support. "I mean, we're not trying to get into your business or pull anything out of you that you don't want to share. We just need to know what to pray about concerning you. Because whether you believe it or not, we love you, Sister, and we want to help you. We want to meet you right where you are in life."

Helen stared into Mother Doreen's eyes momentarily before letting out a chuckle. "Okay, old lady," Helen spat as she sashayed over toward the podium.

Mother Doreen backed away, not really knowing what to expect of Helen. She'd watched enough reality shows to know that a grown woman could snap and get physical in a minute.

"Y'all want to know my story? Well, I'm about to give it to you, all of it. Believe me when I say I'm leaving no stone unturned." Helen stared down the women in the room one by one as she prepared to tell them her story, but not before saying, "But trust me when I say that after hearing about my life, it's gon' take more than y'all's prayers to meet me where I'm at."

# Stone Number Two

"Why you so black? Where you from? Africa?" some fifth grade boy said as he walked by. I was playing four square outside on the school playground with three of my fourth grade classmates.

I could tell he was just trying to get a laugh from his friends tagging along with him, which he did. But why did it have to be at my expense? I was just minding my own business, having a good ole time at recess, and then here he came along.

"Did you hear what that boy said? He must be talking to you, Helen," said one of my classmates who was occupying one of the squares. "Because we ain't that black—not as black as you."

Suddenly no one was focusing on the ball anymore. Instead, all the other kids in the squares were laughing.

If I had wanted to, I was sure I could have searched for one of the instigator's flaws to point out and make fun of. My nana, my mother's mother, had once told me that it took at least two people to argue and fight. I didn't want to argue and fight, though. This kid was a fifth grader, and he was a boy. I knew how to pick my battles.

"Y'all so stupid," I said, waving my hand as if I was brushing all the laughter off. "I am black, though." I laughed. They laughed harder. Ever heard of the saying "If you can't beat 'em, join 'em?" Well, over the years of being teased and taunted about how dark I was, that was what I learned to do. I learned to join in with the laughter, even though I was crying inside . . . even though I was dying inside.

There were plenty of days I'd go home from school, go to my room, and cry my eyes out.

"Helen, what's wrong?" my sister, Lynn, who was almost three years my senior, asked one day.

"I'm ugly, That's what's wrong."

"Girl, you being stupid."

"I'm not being stupid. I'm being serious," I cried. "You don't understand, because you're all pretty and yellow," I told Lynn, who was several shades lighter than I was. Both my parents had the complexion of a vanilla wafer. Heck, everybody on both sides of the family had pretty much the same complexion. I was the Hershey's Kiss in the center of the peanut butter cookie.

"You are not ugly," Lynn replied, consoling me. "Besides, you know Nana says God don't like ugly."

I'd heard Nana say that before. And perhaps it was true; maybe God didn't like ugly. But obviously, when it came to me, that certainly didn't stop Him from making ugly.

I stood out in my family, not in a good way and not in a bad way. I stood out in an odd way. It gnawed at me to the point where I started asking grown-ups in the family questions.

"Why am I the only dark one?" I'd question.

"I wish I could be as dark as you," my grandpa on my father's side would say with a smile, pinching my cheek.

"The blacker the berry, the sweeter the juice," my favorite aunt, Lisa, one of my father's sisters, would say.

I never got a straight answer from anybody I posed the question to. Therefore, I could never give a straight answer when the question was posed to me.

It didn't take me long to realize that I was at a disadvantage, not just by being black, but by being the blackest of the black. Not because of how white people treated blacks, either. Other black people were color struck, separating and judging the light from the dark. Not all, but plenty that I encountered. I knew it was 1980, but I used to wake up wondering if that day was going to be the day I'd go to school and see two water fountains, each with a sign hanging above it. One sign would read LIGHT-SKINNED ONLY, and the other would read DARK-SKINNED ONLY.

One time my mother, Genie, took Lynn and me skating. It was always memorable when either our mother or our dad took us places, because it was rare. Although they were married, it never really felt like it. We never did much as a family unit. Usually, one of them was off somewhere, getting high, or our mother was working crazy hours in the strip club so that she could feed their habit. A couple of times when Lynn was at our dad's parents' house and my mom didn't have a babysitter for me, she took me to work with her. Trust me when I say I'd much rather have spent time at the skating rink with my mother than at the strip club with her.

One particular outing at the skating rink was so memorable for me for another reason. Lynn and I were holding hands, gliding around the rink like pros.

"Slow down. You're going too fast," I shouted to Lynn. She was about a foot in front of me, dragging me behind her.

"Come on, girl. Speed up. This is my song," Lynn shouted over the music.

I struggled to both balance myself and speed up at the same time. I eventually managed to be side by side with Lynn. That was when my wheel bumped hers and we went hurling to the ground.

"Helen!" Lynn shouted, giggling after landing on her butt.

"That's what you get for making me speed up next to you," I said back to her as we both struggled to get up. We were holding onto each other, trying to pull each other up, but we kept making each other fall back down.

Finally, some black guy rolled up and stopped. "Let me help you up," he said, staring directly at Lynn.

"Thank you," she replied, extending her hand, and the kind young man helped her balance and rise to her feet.

"No problem," he said.

I lifted my hand, just assuming he'd help me up next.

"You be careful out here," he said to Lynn before rolling away.

I just sat there with my hand extended, unable to amply communicate the feeling that permeated my being. Lightning had struck. Had knocked me out of my skates and had thrown me fifty feet.

"Come on. Let's go get something to drink," Lynn said, grabbing my hand and pulling me up, none the wiser that she was leaving a piece of me there on the floor.

The part of me that Lynn hauled away was this new angry person. This new hurt person with microscopic self-esteem. I was filled with so much pain that in order to feel normal, I needed everyone else around me to hurt too. Hurting, pain . . . it was my normal.

My anger and pain were only nurtured the day my favorite cousin and I were over at my grandparents' house, outside on the steps, playing.

"You know, Rakeem isn't really your father," was what my little cousin said nonchalantly as we played with our Barbies. "So Granny and Grandpa aren't really your Granny and Grandpa, either." Again, there was no spite in her tone. She was simply repeating what she'd heard the grown-ups saying.

Although my cousin was clueless as to the force of her words, they punctured me like a jagged, corroded blade in an unhealed and infected wound. I dropped my dolls, and they plummeted to the ground, sharing salutations with my heart, which had landed only moments prior. My grandpa was the first one I saw, sitting at the kitchen nook in his favorite chair.

I went straight to him and asked, "Grandpa, is it true?" He would tell me the truth. Grandpas always told the truth. "Is my daddy really my father?"

There was a brief pause, nothing to make me think he was conjuring an untruth. Then my grandpa leaned down and looked me dead in my eyes. "You are my grandbaby, and I love you. And don't you ever forget it."

In my nine-year-old mind, since he was confirming that he was my grandpa, then that had to mean that his son, Rakeem, was really my father. Right?

Grandpa's response was an impermanent dose of reassurance. I started mentally scrutinizing things that I hadn't before, like why I was the only one in the family with a different last name. My mom, my dad, and my sister had the same last name. Mine was different. Then, of course, there'd always been the matter of my complexion.

Ultimately, I believed my cousin's words, in spite of how my grandpa had responded to my inquiry. And that day, the day I found out that the man who had raised me as his very own wasn't really my biological father, was the day anger matured into a force to be reckoned with. I think what devastated me the most was that in school I'd always been the butt of jokes. To learn that for all the years of my life I'd been the butt of the joke to my entire family was the ultimate of hurt. I had been practically the only one in my family who wasn't in on the joke, both Lynn and I, that is.

The man who I had thought was my father was really just Lynn's biological father. I didn't find this out by either of my parents being man or woman enough to tell me themselves. I had to find out through my little cousin, who overheard my dad's sisters, one of them being her mother, my aunt Lisa, having a conversation about it. Once word got around that my cousin had let the cat out of the bag, there was a lot of whispering and talking going on. It was one of those things that whenever I walked into the room, all the chatting stopped and I got sideward glances.

"I got in trouble for telling you that Rakeem isn't really your daddy," my cousin said sadly later on. "My mom said it wasn't my place and was none of my business. She said that now that I do know, I shouldn't treat you any differently."

Neither my mother nor Rakeem had the guts to sit me down and tell me the truth, the whole truth, and nothing but. We all just lived the lie silently, and I had to pretend like it didn't matter, like it didn't make a difference, but it did.

I used to wait for the day when my parents would sit me down together and tell me the truth. What had led up to them living this lie? No one ever coming forth to give me answers gave me an inquiring mind that became consumed with trying to figure things out on my own. This was all well and good, anyway, because I figured that since they'd lied all this time, there was no way I'd get the truth if I went to them now. So I opted not to.

When I got older, I did the math and realized that at the time my mom was pregnant and had me, she and my dad were married. So one would have only assumed that the child my mother was giving birth to was my father's. Evidently, that wasn't the case. It didn't take a Chinese math scholar who had graduated first in his class to figure out I was a product of adultery. So who was my real father? Where was he? Would I ever meet him?

I imagined the sit-down between my biological father and me being like an episode of *Little House on the Prairie* or something. All would be forgiven and forgotten, and then we'd move on to the next episode and live happily ever after. That never happened.

At least I had figured out why my skin was darker than everyone else's in my family. So every time I looked in the mirror, I was reminded of who I wasn't, instead of who I was.

# Stone Number Three

One thing my mom didn't have to worry about with her youngest daughter when it came to entering high school was having boy trouble. Boys never gave me a second look, especially when I stood next to Lynn. Although her hair was as thick and as rough as a lamb's wool, it was long and gorgeous and always professionally done. She had these big, beautiful brown eyes and could dress her petite butt off.

I was tomboyish. I figured, why bother worrying about nice clothes, getting my hair done, and trying to be cute? At the end of the day I was still going to be invisible. So in addition to not caring about my appearance, I didn't care much about my body, so obesity plagued me all the way up until high school, at least until after my ninth grade year. It was then when I realized that appearance mattered more than anything to high school kids. So by the time I went back to school for my sophomore year, I was barely recognizable.

"Helen, is that you?" people were asking me to my face.

"Is that Helen?" people were asking each other behind my back as I strolled down the school hallway like my father had been this great philanthropist and the school had been renamed in my family's honor.

"Yep, it's me," I was proud to say, running my hands down my new figure.

"I see you, Miss Helen," this guy named Roman said as he walked by me and a few of my friends.

I watched him walk away and dang near melted. I'd gone to school with Roman since elementary school, and he'd never spoken to me. This was confirmation that all the hard work and dedication over the past summer had paid off.

Feeling like I couldn't fit in anywhere, I had refused to go back to high school overweight. I had stopped running to the store every five minutes to get those twenty-five-cent Little Debbie snacks or cream sodas. I exercised every single day. Back then the music video stations actually played music videos, so I would turn to one of those channels and dance my butt off. So by the time I went back to school, yes, I had danced my butt off literally. I was thirty pounds lighter, going from a size 16/18 to a 10/12.

I started hanging around this girl named Rochelle who had been in a few of my classes in ninth grade. She was always nice enough and spoke to me, but we had never hung out or anything. She had her own little clique of people she already hung around: two girls named Liza and Chelsie and a guy named Chance. But on the first day of school coming into tenth grade, she spotted me getting out of the lunch line and flagged me down.

"Hey, Helen, come sit with us," Rochelle called out.

I didn't hesitate to join her and her crew. For the first time since I started high school, someone had invited me to hang out, and I wasn't going to pass it up. Who knew whether I might get any other offers, and I wasn't willing to take that chance. I wanted to be wanted, and, well, I was wanted.

From that moment on, I basically became part of the crew, as well. Rochelle and I became the tightest of the group. Not only did we hang out in school, but we'd also hang out at each other's house. We didn't have any classes together, only homeroom, so our lockers were side by side.

"Dub likes you. He told me so," Rochelle said convincingly one day, as we stood at our lockers.

"Girl, please." I dismissed her with a smack of my lips and a swoosh of my hand. No way did Dub like me. Back in middle school, he was one of the four cutest boys. Although he was a year older than me, we were in the same grade because he'd been held back a grade. Even though we never had classes together, we still shared lunch periods or passed each other in the halls. He never even once looked my way . . . not even by accident. So it was hard for me to believe that all of a sudden he would be interested in me.

"I swear to God he does," Rochelle insisted with such conviction that my initial icy doubt began to thaw.

I didn't know whether to wholly believe Rochelle or not. At the time, swearing to God didn't mean much to me. Truth be told, after about a couple of months of getting close with her, I had realized she was blood related to Liar. They were first cousins. She played with lying and watched it trigger drama among her peers. Drama was her second cousin. Both biological relatives allowed Rochelle to thrive off of the seeds of discord she'd sow in our clique. Eventually, the other members of our clique couldn't deal with Rochelle anymore and all got together and decided that at lunch one day, when Rochelle came and sat down at the table, they would all get up and leave.

As they all stood, they eyed me, as if to ask, "Helen, are you coming too?"

I heard a voice in my head saying, *Yes.* But my head itself shook the word *no.* So I stayed at the table with Rochelle and remained her true and closest friend, all the while recognizing that blood was thicker than water.

I had asked myself a thousand times why I wanted to be friends with someone so vindictive. Upon asking myself that question once, I realized that I didn't want to be friends with her. I *needed* to be friends with her. Why did I need to then? The half-truth was I figured that since I knew all the dirt she was capable of dishing out, it was better that I was for her rather than against her. Part of the truth was that Rochelle was a shade darker than me even. She was the only person I felt a little bit more attractive than. I figured people would be too busy cracking on her to notice me or crack on me. The whole truth was that Rochelle was the first person to see me. That day in the cafeteria when she invited me to join her, I was no longer invisible. She wanted to be my friend. A bird in the hand was worth two in the bush. How I saw it as a fifteen-year-old high school kid was that being friends with Rochelle was better than having no friends at all.

"Anyway," Rochelle said as she retrieved her books for her next couple of classes from her locker, "I told Dub that you were coming over my house after school today. He's going to shoot through with one of his boys, as if he's just in the neighborhood. So be at my house by four o'clock and play along."

"I wish I might," I spat before closing my locker so I could head to my next class. "How you gon' hook me up without even asking me first? What if I don't want to holler at him?"

She looked me up and down and then twisted her nose, reminding me what I looked like, like her. It was as if I was standing before a mirror. Her eyes were telling me, "You might have lost a few pounds, but you still as black as a bowling ball. You better take what you can get while you can get it!"

All day long I thought about the words Rochelle never spoke. She was right; no matter how many pounds I'd lost, I was still the underdog. So if any boy ever showed any interest in me, then I should jump on the first thing smoking, because who knew if there would be a second. That helped me make up my mind about whether or not to meet up with Dub at Rochelle's house later that afternoon.

"I knew you were going to come over!" Rochelle exclaimed when I arrived on her doorstep at 3:50 p.m., with ten minutes to spare. "Dub and his boy should be here in a few minutes," Rochelle said. "I was just about to make some Kool-Aid. Come in the kitchen with me." Rochelle was acting more excited than I was, and I was the one supposedly getting hooked up.

I followed Rochelle into the kitchen, where she made her famous cherry Kool-Aid with orange slices in it. Ten minutes later we heard a knock on the door.

"That's them!" Rochelle said, putting down the cup of Kool-Aid she had been sipping on. "Come on, girl. Let's go." She grabbed my hand and practically pulled me to the door. She looked through the peephole. "It's them. Yes!" She pumped her fist. "He brought his boy Earl Lee. Come on."

Rochelle and I grabbed our jackets so that we could go sit on the porch and hang out with the boys. The weather wasn't too bad for November. Even if it was bad, we couldn't have invited them in. Rochelle's mother would have killed her if she found out Rochelle had had boys in the house, especially while she was at work.

My legs were shaking, and I could feel the butterflies floating around in my belly as I stepped out onto the porch.

"Dub, this is Helen," Rochelle said, introducing us. "Helen, this is Dub."

Dub held out his hand to shake mine, but my hand was already shaking. No way did I want this boy to know he had me trembling already, so I just gave him a nod and a bump with my fist.

"Oh, it's like that," Dub said and laughed. Earl Lee joined in.

Rochelle shot me an evil eye, so I quickly cleaned up the situation.

"Naw, I'm just playing." I shook his hand so quickly, there was no way he could feel it trembling. Hopefully, the chill in the air had dried up the sweat on my palms, as well.

"So y'all want to take a walk down to the park or something?" Rochelle asked, giving Earl Lee googly eyes the entire time.

Dub and Earl Lee looked at each other and shrugged. Then we all headed three blocks up to the park.

Rochelle and Earl Lee went off to a picnic bench somewhere, while Dub and I sat on the swings and talked. Before I knew it, the sun was warning that it was about to retire for the day. The time had gone by so fast as I sat talking and laughing with Dub. I was smitten with him, to say the least.

"You cool people to hang out with," Dub said as he and Earl Lee walked Rochelle and me back to her house.

"You are too." I smiled.

"Then why don't you give me your number so I can call you up and we can do it again?"

"Okay." I knew better than to hesitate as I gave him the number to the private phone line Lynn had in our room.

Dub called me later that night to make sure I'd made it home from Rochelle's okay and to set up a time to hook up again.

For the next month and a half, the four of us met up at Rochelle's house almost every day. Her house was the best meeting spot because her mother worked from three in the afternoon to midnight, so there were no adults hovering over us and questioning our every move. Besides, my mother would have never approved of me meeting up with boys.

"No dating until you're sixteen," was what she'd repeated over the years. And even though my mother hadn't been raised in the church and had never taken us to church a day in her life, except for an Easter Sunday here and there, not dating until I was sixteen was Bible! Chapter one, verse one, of the Book of Genie.

Well, I was still fifteen, but sixteen was within walking distance. I figured if Dub and I got serious before then, I would just have to hide him for a few months. Little did I know just how serious things were about to get.

# Stone Number Four

"It won't hurt if you just let me do it real quick," Dub whispered in my ear as he caressed his manhood.

At this particular meet up at Rochelle's, we had decided to be bold and allow the boys inside. Besides, it was wintertime and too cold to be out on the stoop or at the park. We had started off just listening to music while we sipped on Rochelle's famous Kool-Aid. The next thing I knew, Rochelle and Earl Lee were in her mother's bedroom and Dub and I were in Rochelle's bedroom.

"I'm scared. It might hurt," I told him, but he promised it wouldn't.

I remember giggling the entire time. Dub wasn't finding too much of anything funny. His mind was stuck on one thing, sticking his one thing into me.

"Come on. Just lay down real quick," he coaxed. "Everybody else is chillin', doing their thang."

Of course, by *everybody*, he meant Rochelle and Earl Lee.

"But I told you I've never done this before." I was still giggling. In all actuality, I wanted to cry. I was so scared.

I had never asked God for much before. Neither side of my family had been raised in the church, so I knew nothing about God's commandments and convictions other than what I might have seen or heard on television. I did believe in Him, though. I did believe that only a higher power could have created the earth and the things of it. Therefore, I barely ever even spoke to Him, being taught from my toddler years not to talk to strangers.

I knew of God. But I didn't know God. Therefore, I figured He didn't know me, either. Even though Nana hadn't been raised in the church and hadn't raised her children in the church, she did start attending right around my freshman year of high school. Sometimes I would join her here on a Sunday or there if I spent Saturday night at her house. But at that time, as I lay there on Rochelle's bed with Dub on top of me, I wanted nothing more than for God to reach His hands down from heaven and scoop me up out of the situation I had gotten myself into. God didn't, though. I guess He figured I had been big enough to get myself into this situation, so now I had to be big enough to get myself out of it. And since God didn't pull me out of this situation, I made a mental note not to really call on Him for others.

How did I even end up in this situation? I asked myself, figuring if my body wasn't able to escape, at least my mind could.

Everything with Dub and me had just seemed to happen so fast. Less than two months ago I was being introduced to Dub while I sat on the stoop outside of Rochelle's house. The next minute I was in Rochelle's twin bed, deciding whether or not that was where I wanted to lose my virginity. Although I was scared out of my mind, there was a little excitement brewing, as well. I mean, of all the boys to lose my virginity to, who ever imagined it would be Dublen Daniels? Light skin, good hair, white mom, and black dad Dublen Daniels. A pretty mixed boy and me. I thought something like that could happen only in my dreams, yet now my dreams were a reality.

On top of that, I hadn't even chosen Dub. He'd chosen me. He was the one who had told Rochelle he liked me. He was the one who had asked for my phone number. He was the one who called to set up our meetings. He was the one who just a week ago had said to me, "Will you be my girl?" Me . . . I was the one who accepted. I was ecstatic inside that even though I didn't look like an Apolonia or a Vanity, I had still managed to pull me a fellow that looked like Prince—good hair and all!

I'd gotten caught up in the light skin thing too. What other choice did I have? "If you can't beat 'em, join 'em" was still my motto. For me, though, it went even a little deeper. It was almost like a challenge, me getting a boy who looked like Dub to like me, *me,* who was as black as they came. So when I hooked up with Dub, it was like a victory for all chocolate girls. And in this case, not only was Dub light skinned, but he was also mixed! That had to be worth more points, so it was up to me to take one for team dark-skinned and relinquish my virginity.

"See? That wasn't so bad at all," Dub said as he pulled his pants up.

Embarrassed, I got up and ran out of the room and into the hallway bathroom, still giggling. Still giggling to keep from crying. What I had just done hurt. It hurt between my legs. It hurt my heart. It hurt my mind with confusion. I had this eerie feeling that someone had been watching me play big girl in the other room. They were no longer watching me, though, because they had bowed their head with grief and couldn't even stand to look at me. I couldn't even stand to look at myself.

I didn't know then that the word I needed to describe my emotions was *conviction.* Neither did I know at the time that God had been there. He'd come in the form of the Holy Spirit, and He had, in fact, given me an exit route from the situation I was in. It was called free will, yet I'd driven past the exit ramp like a stubborn husband refusing to take directions from his wife.

Regret began to manifest itself as I stood in the bathroom. Fear began to manifest itself as I realized Dub and I hadn't used a condom, no birth control, no nothing . . .

heck, no self-control. We wouldn't have even needed birth control if we'd had self-control.

"This is not how this was supposed to feel," I said to myself as I stood there, trembling. I thought I was going to feel grown up after having sex, sexy even. But there was nothing grown and sexy about a fifteen-year-old girl losing her virginity in her best friend's house, in her best friend's bed. There was no going back in time, no do over, and moving forward wouldn't be a walk in the park, either.

# Stone Number Five

"You're pregnant, aren't you?" Lynn asked me as I lay on the top bunk of our bunk bed set, which we'd had ever since I could remember. Lynn and I shared a room in the small two-bedroom duplex home we lived in with our mother and her boyfriend. She and our dad, Rakeem, had long since been divorced. She'd unfriended her drug habit, denounced stripping, and got a job in housekeeping. Rakeem was still chasing his high, so he wasn't in the picture much. So not only had my biological father chosen another life over me, as far as I knew, but so had his proxy.

"I've been using this same box of maxi pads for two of my cycles in a row," Lynn continued, holding up our shared box of sanitary napkins. "Usually, I would have had to buy more by now if both of us were using them. But obviously both of us are not. This is the only box we have, so either you have been running around bleeding in your panties or you ain't been bleeding at all . . . which means you're pregnant. So which is it?"

Lynn stood there, waiting for my reply.

When I lowered my head, not uttering a word, Lynn got her answer. I was, in fact, pregnant. After having sex with Dub a total of only three times, I was in a state of disbelief. All I had wanted was love, attention, and validation that someone of the male species actually loved me. Feeling that way had led to sex, which ultimately had led to sex that resulted in a now unwanted pregnancy.

"Oh, my God," Lynn whispered. "What are you going to do?" She stood there looking at me through the bunk bed's wooden rails. The rails were there to keep the top bunk recipient from rolling onto the floor. I had to admit that I had had thoughts of removing them in hopes of "accidentally" rolling onto the floor. Losing the baby naturally would be cheaper than the plan I had in mind.

Without even stuttering, I told my sister, "Abortion. I'm going to get an abortion." She could tell by the conviction in my voice that having this baby was not a possibility.

At the time of my pregnancy, it was 1986 and the abortion laws had changed. A girl couldn't get a life sucked out of her without the consent of an adult. Lynn knew this very well, as she'd already preceded me in this dilemma, having turned up pregnant her tenth grade year of high school as well.

"Yeah, but who are you going to get to go with you?" Lynn questioned. "I won't be eighteen for four more months. By then it will be too late."

That part I really didn't have all worked out yet. My first prospect, though, had been Dub's mom. She was cool, one of those moms who let her kids do what they liked and come and go as they pleased. Her kids didn't even have to go to school if they didn't feel like it. But even with that being so, and despite the free spirit that abided in her, abortion was a sticky subject in their family.

When I'd shared my plan with Dub and discussed the possibility of his mother taking me to get the abortion, he informed me that that probably wasn't a good idea. He'd said that Ms. Daniels had already done the abortion thing with his older sister, Kelice. She had forced Kelice to have an abortion when she turned up pregnant at the age of sixteen. Kelice had wanted desperately to give birth to the life that was growing inside her belly, but Ms. Daniels was the boss of her. Under any other circumstances, her children were unrestricted, but in this particular situation, Ms. Daniels put her often concealed authoritative third foot down and forbade her teenage daughter from embarrassing the family with her pregnancy.

Dub said that Kelice had never forgiven Ms. Daniels. He recounted many of arguments that had taken place between the two of them, always ending in Kelice making their mother cry by reminding her how she had made her kill her baby. So the last thing I wanted to do was add another brick to the wall of guilt and regret Ms. Daniels had already built around herself. Asking her to have the blood of not only her daughter's unborn baby on her hands but her son's to boot might have been the brick that brought the wall tumbling down on top of her.

"I don't know who I'm going to ask to go with me," I told Lynn and shrugged.

I didn't really know who else to ask. I had jumped into the ocean of Dub headfirst, leaving everybody who had been remotely close to me back on shore, waving their hands, trying to get my attention. Begging me to come up for air. But it was too late. I had already drowned.

"Even if you do find someone to go with you to get the abortion, how are you going to pay for it? You don't have a job." Lynn was bound and determined to tear my plan to shreds.

I couldn't see where my big sister was being any help at all. She was adding fuel to the fire. But I'd started the fire. Not only had I started it, but then I'd stood there and watched it. So no wonder I'd gotten burned.

"I don't know. I'll think of something." The conviction I'd had in my tone only minutes ago was now gone, replaced by a sense of pure defeat. From the moment I missed my period last month and took that store-bought pregnancy test, I'd known what I wanted to do, which was to get rid of my baby. Now I didn't know exactly how I'd accomplish this. The frustration and defeat built up until they spilled out of my mouth in the form of the following words. "I'll kill myself before I have this baby," I said, more to tell myself than Lynn. But I meant it. I meant it from the depths of my soul. If I couldn't figure out a way to kill the baby, I would kill myself. I'd kill two birds with one stone.

The certitude was back with my last statement. I think it must have scared Lynn, because her tone got even more serious. "Didn't I tell you I'd take you to Planned Parenthood to get on birth control when you first started kickin' it with that boy?" she scolded.

Almost four months ago, when I first told her about my hanging with Dub, Lynn had indeed offered to take me to the clinic.

"You don't want to go through what I went through," Lynn had told me. "It's better to be safe than sorry."

I'd declined. Dub was the first boy who I'd ever simply just liked. I had never imagined I'd be having sex with him. Even if I had, not in my wildest dreams would I have thought I'd get pregnant. After all, my mom had neglected to have "the talk" with me. Lynn had told me that once a girl's period started, she could get pregnant. I somehow had misconstrued that to mean that a girl could get pregnant only if it was actually that time of the month for her.

Just imagining having sex while bleeding made me cringe, so I remember saying to myself, *I'll never get pregnant then, because I will not be having sex while on my period.* If only I'd had a better understanding.

"Look, I don't want to talk about it anymore." I rolled over on my bunk bed, turning my back toward Lynn.

I had a lot of thinking to do. I had to figure out how I was going to get an abortion, and fast, before my mother figured out that I was pregnant. To this day, Lynn had kept her teenage pregnancy from our mother. I needed to be so lucky. I just knew my mom would be pissed to no end if she found out her baby girl was pregnant.

Never mind that my mother had gotten kicked out of high school when she got knocked up at age sixteen with Lynn. And who said there was no such thing as a family curse? This wasn't about my mother and her past mistakes. It was about me. Still, I knew my mother would see her mistakes in me and do what she always did whenever she was mad, upset, and disgusted with herself. She'd take it out on us, Lynn and me, by yelling, fussing, and cussing. It was like because we were the results of some of her bad choices in life, she was going to punish us. The mere sight of us reminded her of her mistakes. At least that was how I felt, anyway.

My mother finding out about my pregnancy ranked last among all the things on the totem pole. My biggest concern was terminating the pregnancy. If I could get rid of the baby, there would be no pregnancy for her to find out about. Believe me when I say I couldn't terminate this pregnancy fast enough. Not just because I had to keep my mother from finding out, but because I was sick as a dog.

Just a couple of months pregnant, I was throwing up every time I moved. I couldn't take it. It was miserable. I couldn't envision that something that was making me feel so bad while inside of me would make my life any better once it was outside of me. It had to go. Heartbeat or no heartbeat. Brain development or no brain development. Fetus, embryo, or baby. I knew one thing for certain and two things for sure: Somebody was going to die. It was going to be either my baby or us both.

# Stone Number Six

"He's so cute. Look at all that hair," my sister said as she stroked Baby D's hair. "He looks just like you, Dub."

"I don't know," my mother countered. "I can see a little of Helen in him too."

In my opinion, my newborn baby didn't look like either one of us. He had my complexion. He had lots of hair. It was coarse like mine, but his facial structure didn't really favor Dub's or mine one way or another. But he was mine. He was ours, and we were loving all over his little chocolate self.

Seven months earlier I had been hell-bent on getting rid of the baby that was growing inside of me. Now, seven months later, I had to grow up because I had the baby.

Dub stood next to my sister's chair, grinning from ear to ear as she held his son, the son I had decided I would not give birth to. But my plan obviously hadn't been God's plan. For someone whose business I managed to stay out of, I couldn't figure out for the life of me why He wouldn't stay out of mine.

Oh, you can best believe that I had gone to the abortion clinic to initiate the procedure. I'd begged, cried, and pleaded with my aunt Lisa until she agreed to go with me. Between Dub and me, we had managed to scrape the abortion money together. Dub had supported my decision either way, so he wasn't tripping on the fact that I wanted to get rid of the baby. By the time the nurse at the abortion clinic had explained and demonstrated the procedure to me, I couldn't bring myself to terminate my pregnancy. I just couldn't do it.

*"This is the needle the doctor will insert to numb your cervix," the nurse said, holding up this huge needle and pressing it against a clay model of a woman's insides. "You will feel a pinch. It will be slightly painful."*

*Sitting there, feeling as if my stomach was making its way up my throat, I had no doubt it would be painful. It looked painful.*

*"And this is what the doctor will insert into your . . ."*

*That was all she wrote for me as I watched the nurse take a tube and place it inside the clay model. I had this vision of my baby being sucked right through the tube, its eyes staring at me before it was completely sucked up.*

*I jumped up out of my seat and ran straight to the bathroom to throw up, and it wasn't because of morning sickness, either. Just the idea of getting an abortion was much different than the visual the clinic was providing. They were showing step by step everything the woman and her unborn would go through in order to complete the procedure so that there would be no surprises causing the patient to lose it right there on the procedure table. I couldn't handle the mock version, let alone the act itself. I couldn't do it.*

I couldn't honestly say that it was more so my conscience than the fear of pain. All I knew was that needless to say, I never returned to that room or the clinic.

Now that the baby was here, Dub and I were proud parents. Way too young to be parents, but proud nonetheless.

"He is handsome, isn't he?" Dub smiled, reaching his hands out, which was Lynn's sign that her time with Baby D was up.

"Dang, I ain't been holding him but five minutes," Lynn spat.

"And that's four minutes too long. Daddy wants to hold his son." Dub's arms were still extended.

"But you got years to hold him. His auntie wants to hold him." Lynn made cooing noises at the baby.

"I hate to break up a good argument," the nurse said, entering the room, "but this little fella has to come back to the nursery with me for a minute." The nurse lifted Baby D from Lynn's arms and placed him in his rolling bed after Lynn kissed him on his little white-, pink- and blue-striped hat.

"Well, I'm coming with you so that as soon as you're done with him, I can have him." Dub looked at Lynn and stuck his tongue out as he began to follow the nurse.

"And I'm going to go have a smoke real quick," my mother said, trailing Dub. She looked just as proud as Dub and I did. I wasn't surprised, considering the day I came home from the clinic after deciding against the abortion and told her I was pregnant, the first thing she did was forbid me from having an abortion. That made me all the more comfortable with my decision not to return to that clinic.

"Just make sure don't nobody be smoking around my son," I heard Dub saying to my mother as they left the room.

"Dub is a mess," I told Lynn and giggled.

"Yeah, but at least he's here." Lynn smacked her lips. "Look at all the chicks at school who be having babies and the daddies won't even speak to them in the hallway at school, let alone want to be there for them in the delivery room. Girl, if you were going to have a baby by any boy, looks like Dub was the one."

I shrugged. "Yeah, I guess you're right," I halfheartedly agreed. I was only sixteen, now in my junior year of high school. While everybody else had been walking through the school halls, talking about the upcoming games and dances, I had been walking through the halls, talking about having a baby shower. At least I could say that nobody acted funny toward me or seemed embarrassed about a pregnant girl hanging around.

As far as what Lynn said about other girls being pregnant and their baby daddy not even speaking to them in the halls, I didn't have to worry about that, because half the time Dub didn't come to school. He figured he was flunking all his classes, anyway, so why bother.

Either way it went, whether Dub was a good guy or a bad guy, I didn't want to be having a baby by any guy. I guess Lynn sensed that in my response as she prepared to ask me a question.

"So are you glad you had the baby? Glad you changed your mind about getting an abortion? I mean, you were so set on having that abortion, I almost wanted to be like Mommy Dearest and get rid of all the wire hangers." Lynn began laughing.

"Shut up," I said to her, rolling my eyes.

"I'm serious. I thought you were going to go old school and use a wire hanger to give yourself an abortion."

"You stupid," I said and chuckled.

"Well, girl, you know I had your back either way. But now that my nephew is here, I'm so happy you changed your mind." Lynn got up from the chair and kissed me on my forehead. "Almost makes me wish that I had kept . . ." Lynn's words trailed off, and I knew what she was thinking.

I grabbed her hand.

She looked down at me with moist eyes. "I'm just glad you kept yours."

I was glad, too, that I hadn't aborted Baby D. Would every baby that God placed in my womb be so lucky?

# Stone Number Seven

Studies showed that most abusive relationships started out with verbal insults and put-downs before they ever got to the level of physical abuse. That was true when it came to Dub's and my relationship.

"You got to be about the sorriest person I've ever met. What good are you? I don't need you. Shut up and go on out of my face. You didn't even finish high school, so how you gon' finish raising a baby? You so stupid!"

This wasn't even half of the insults I flung at Dub whenever I could, even in front of others. I couldn't have cared less about offending his manhood in front of his boys, his family, or mine. My angry words would pierce him with daggers that bore his name.

So much anger had grown inside me. Wounds had formed, wounds that had gone untreated for years, bleeding on everyone who crossed my path. Unfortunately, Dub had crossed my path, and he had Rochelle to thank for the introduction. And on top of that, we now had this colicky baby who did nothing but cry at ungodly hours of the night. This was hard work and a job that stole from me a typical teenager's life.

I loved Baby D and was glad he was here. But would it have been so bad to have just waited until the time was right? But nooo, Dub had to talk me into having sex, so I placed a great deal of blame on him for the predicament I was in. This only added to the anger and resentment I harbored.

"I swear if you talk to me out of the side of your neck one more time . . . ," Dub threatened as we sat on the couch in his bedroom. Three-month-old Baby D lay asleep on Dub's bed, which sat across from the couch.

"What?" I spat. "You gon' what? Nothing. That's what you gon' do. All you know how to do is nothing. You don't go to school, and you don't even have a job."

"I dropped out of school so that I could take care of the baby while you finish school, remember?" Dub reminded me.

"You were flunkin', anyway, dummy, and half going to school as it was, so don't try to act like you were doing me a favor. Besides, so we know why you ain't in school, but why ain't your sorry tail working?"

Dub just sat there, his manhood being chipped away by my sharp words.

I was hurting Dub the same way I had felt hurt when my cousin's words destroyed the life I once knew. I was hurting Dub the same way I hurt when I had to give birth to a baby at the age of sixteen and give up a normal teenage life.

"I don't even know why I had a baby by you in the first place," I muttered, continuing my tirade. "What kind of man—"

I guess Dub had had enough. I guess months of my inexcusable tantrums had finally gotten the best of him. The sting across my face demonstrated that.

"You hit me!" I said in shock, holding my face. "You hit me!"

"I . . . I . . ." Dub stammered. "I'm sorry." His eyes were sincere. "I'll never do it again."

I believed him because he had never done it before. I could tell he had never hit a girl before. I could tell he wasn't used to hurting people much at all. Someone like myself, who was much better trained and knew how to

throw a low blow, didn't have the look on their face that
Dub had on his after they hurt somebody. He had a look
of sadness and remorse, instead of a slight grimace. He
had a look of horror, instead of a look of triumph. He had
a look of regret, instead of a look of honor.

"I'm so sorry," he said, continuing his apology. "I'll
never put my hands on you again. I promise."

I accepted Dub's apology. He kept his promise . . . that
is, until the day he decided to break it, and in the worst
way ever.

I wondered how many parents had teenage daughters
who got up and went to school every day as if living the
normal life of a teenage girl. Sometimes their boyfriends
picked them up and drove them to school. They hung
out at lunch with their boyfriends. They went out on
dates with their boyfriends. Talked to and texted their
boyfriends until the wee hours of the morning. Took
pictures and went to school dances and proms with
their boyfriends. How many of these parents were none
the wiser that their teenage daughter was a victim of
domestic violence?

Everyone was clueless as to what I was enduring at the
hands of Dub, everybody but God. I'd learned in church
that God was an all-knowing God. I could not understand
for the life of me why He knew yet did nothing. Wasn't
that calling the kettle black? I knew and did nothing too.
But I was just little ole me. He was God, this wonderful
and powerful being who had a son who supposedly saved
us from hell. My hell was right there on earth, so why
wasn't He saving me? That was when I began to lose some
of the little bit of faith I had in this almighty creator.

Eventually, I realized that no matter how many times
Dub promised not to ever hit me again, the promise

would be broken. I was so busy trying to come across as this strong, dominant girl, there was no way I could let people know I was being abused, belittled. That was like giving up my powers. I decided it was better that only one person on earth other than myself knew how weak I was, versus the whole world. So I remained silent, sure to cover any bruises with make-up, treat any swelling with ice, and wear turtlenecks or even long sleeves in the summertime to cover bruises on my arms if need be. Or I'd just flat out lie and say that Baby D had accidentally kicked me while I was changing his diaper or something. I equipped myself with excuses. By doing so, I was making a conscious choice to be Dub's punching bag. A part of me, though, honestly thought that I'd brought this on myself, that my verbal abuse of Dub had led him to be physically abusive with me. So maybe if I did better, then he would do better. Then we would be better.

By now, my mom had married her boyfriend and was on her second husband. Lynn had just graduated from high school and had moved in with a roommate. My stepdad was a really good guy. He took great care of us. He was a workaholic, so he was rarely home. My dad had long been out of the picture, dragged away in shackles by drugs and on some occasions by the police.

Only a month after Dub had promised me he would never hit me after that first time, that was all he did. The beatings turned into torture and torment, then escalated to rape. I had once controlled him with my tongue, but now he ruled me with his fists.

At first, the hits here and there didn't really bother me. I mean, growing up, I had witnessed my dad beat my mom. Even our neighbor when we lived in a duplex unit got beaten by her husband on the regular. Lynn and I used to hear the beatings through the wall. With every punch, every blow, we'd jump and our little bodies would tense up.

Sooner than later, this type of behavior no longer seemed abnormal. I grew accustomed to it, so much so that instead of Lynn and I huddling together while we listened to our father beat our mother, eventually we could finish a full game of Monopoly without even twitching when glass shattered or a door got kicked off the hinges. So when I, too, became a victim of abuse, it was more like confirmation that I was normal, after all.

"Run and get me a glass of juice right quick," Dub ordered me, lying back on the bed, kicking up his feet, which were still clad in his boots.

I hated when he put his shoe-covered feet up on the bed, but I'd learned the hard way that voicing this led only to a fight.

"Can you go get it? I'm about to get in the shower." Duh, it wasn't like I wasn't standing there buck naked, with my pajamas in my hand. I headed toward the bedroom door, planning to dash across the hall to the bathroom real quick. Baby D was in his room, asleep in his crib.

Before I could even get my hand on the doorknob to open the door, I felt a hand around my neck and I was yanked backward onto the bed.

"Get off of me!" I yelled as Dub's hands tightly gripped my neck.

"Shut up!" he yelled before releasing me.

At first I thought my plea had worked, but I came to find out that he had taken his hands off my neck only because he needed to use them to slap me and pull my hair.

"Where's all that mouth now?" Dub loved to say. And he'd have this look of victory on his face whenever he said it. It was as if he'd finally figured out a way to shut me up. And he had. I knew better than to get fly at the mouth with him now, because all it meant was me getting busted in the mouth. But it didn't matter anymore whether I talked slick to him or not. Dub had turned into this person I no longer recognized. He'd haul off and hit me for the littlest thing or for no reason at all. I guess this made him feel like the man I had accused him of not being.

"Why are you doing this?" I cried after Dub's final blow to my head before he got off of me.

"Quit all that crying," Dub roared. "You know darn well why. The next time I ask you to go get me something to drink, I bet you won't tell me to go get it myself."

Dub just sat there watching me cry, his eyes lacking any sense of compassion. Where had it all gone? I'd often asked myself. Had the awful things I used to say to him eaten away not only at his manhood, but also at the love and compassion he once had as a person? Eaten away at his soul? Was it possible that I had brought this on myself? Had I taken my hurt, pain, and anger so far that I'd turned Dub into a monster? If I had created this monster, was God punishing me by making me have to live with it?

# Stone Number Eight

"Hey, Ma, I'm ready," I called out to my mom as I lugged both Baby D's and my things to the front door. "Where's your keys? I'll start loading our overnight bags and stuff in the car."

"On the living-room table," my mother called from her bedroom as she finished getting dressed.

Lynn had come over to visit. She and Mom were going to head to the movies after they dropped me and Baby D off at Dub's to spend the night.

I was only seventeen, but because Dub and I shared a one-year-old baby, I was allowed to spend more time and do more things with my boyfriend than the normal teenager would have been permitted to do. It was safe to say my mom treated me a little bit more like an adult now that I was a parent. I didn't have carte blanche freedom, but how we saw it, the damage had already been done. It was obvious Dub and I were having sex. We had a baby to prove it. And there wasn't anything anyone could have done at that point to keep us from having it.

It wasn't unusual for me to spend the night at Dub's house during weekends or on weekdays. Sometimes it was easier if I stayed at Dub's house and went to school from there since he kept the baby during the day, anyway. As far as school was concerned, I was right on schedule to graduate with the rest of my class. The school system had set up homeschooling for me once I was eight months pregnant, so I hadn't missed a beat with grades and assignments. Six weeks after having Baby D, I was right back in school.

I was now a senior in high school and Dub kept Baby D while I went to school and then to work immediately after my classes. I'd been hired by a computer company to do some clerical work as part of a school program. I had earned enough credits and had taken all the required courses to graduate, so I had to go to school only for the first four periods. But today was Friday, and Baby D and I were set to spend the entire weekend at Dub's.

His mom saw things the same way my mom saw them: We already had a baby. How could it hurt more if we spent the night together? At least now I was on birth control, something my doctor hadn't wasted any time prescribing me after I had Baby D.

"They got a nice, decent-looking house," Lynn said to me as we pulled up in front of Dub's house. She had never been to his house before in the two years we had been together. "I'll help you carry your stuff in."

Once my mom put the car in park, Lynn and I got out and began gathering all my things. I bent over and fought with Baby D's car seat for a minute while Lynn gathered our bags from the trunk.

"All right. Thanks, Ma," I said as I removed the car seat from the car with Baby D still in it. I then moseyed toward Dub's house.

Lynn was still removing stuff from the trunk by the time I was halfway up the walkway. I heard the trunk slam, then Lynn's feet connecting with the pavement as she whispered my name.

"Helen. Helen," she called under her breath. "Your teddy is hanging out."

"Huh?" I asked.

"Your teddy. I can see it," she said between clenched teeth, then looked over her shoulder back at our mother.

Just then my eyes grew wide. I realized what she was trying to tell me. The little pink teddy that I had purchased from Schottenstein department store for $6.99 and that was two sizes too small was showing. It was one that snapped between the legs. I hadn't tried it on in the store, but it looked like it would fit. Well, it didn't. Evidently, during my bout with Baby D's car seat, it had unsnapped between my legs, and now the tail part was hanging out. I inconspicuously tucked it away, wishing I could do the same with the embarrassment I felt.

"Thanks," I said to Lynn. "You can just leave the stuff right here on the porch. Dub will get it." I couldn't even stand for her to look at me one minute longer, I was so mortified.

Lynn headed back to the car and rode off with our mom while I knocked on the door.

Dub opened the door. "What took you so long?" He accusingly looked over my shoulder. "How'd you get here? Who dropped you off?"

*Here we go,* I thought. Dub's insecurities were showing themselves. It was no consolation to Dub that he was my first. His main concern had become making sure he was my only.

"Now that you done had a baby, dudes know you give it up," Dub had said to me on more than a solitary occasion. "Now they gonna be sniffing around you like hounds."

Dub's jealousy and possessiveness were oftentimes worse than the whippings I took at his hands. The sting from the slaps would go away. The bruises from the punches would go away. But the mental assaults lodged themselves deep within me and wouldn't betray me with abandonment.

"My mom dropped me off," I assured him nonchalantly. It was no big deal. Of course, my mom had dropped me off. She was the one who usually dropped me off.

He brushed me aside as he stepped out on the porch, looking for any signs of my mother's car. "Where is she, then?" Suspicion laced his tone.

I knew I was in for it. I'd have to have sex with him immediately to prove that I hadn't just had sex with someone else. He'd sniff me, check my panties, and look for any other telltale sign that I'd been with another guy. I'd have to prove him wrong. Usually, proving someone wrong felt good, leaving a sense of victory. But not in this case.

I was only seventeen. I didn't even like sex. I was unlike typical seventeen-year-olds who were sexually active. I hated sex. In all honesty, I was straight on sex after the first time, didn't know what the big hoopla was about it, besides the fact that it made me feel grown up because I was engaging in a so-called grown-up thing. But by having unprotected sex, just feeling grown up was superseded by having to grow up fast.

My mom was working for a cleaning company on the OSU campus, so she was working nonstop, which meant there was no built-in babysitter. While all the other kids at school were going to school functions and sporting events, I was at home, taking care of a baby. Sex before I was ready had changed my life drastically, so in my book, it was definitely the enemy and not an act I was fond of.

Sex was something Dub liked. Something Dub wanted. I hadn't bought that teddy for me; I had bought it for him, in hopes it would turn him on to the point that he'd hurry up and climax so I could get it over with. I guess I was about to find out if my little trick would work.

Once we were in the house and settled, Dub took all our things down to his bedroom, which was in the basement. Baby D stayed upstairs with Ms. Daniels. That was usually how the scenario went. Ms. Daniels loved Baby D. He was her first and only grandchild. The minute I'd walk through the door, she'd rip him from my arms and I wouldn't see him again until it was time for us to go home. So while he was a toddler, he didn't get to witness most of the beatings, all of which took place in Dub's room in the basement, where no one could see, where he thought no one could hear.

"You wearing that because you just got done being with someone else, aren't you?" Dub said as he knocked me upside the head.

We hadn't been in his room a good ten minutes before it all started. Unfortunately, that stupid tail from the teddy had popped out again and Dub had seen it. His jealous rage instantly made him think I had been up to no good, instead of trying to do something good for him.

"You ain't wearing that for me," he spat. "You have never worn anything like that for me. What's his name? Huh? Who is it?" He came charging at me.

"Please, don't!" I cried out. Dub twisted my arm so far behind my back, I thought it would break. Pain tore through my body, and it felt as if every joint connected to the bones in my arm was suffering. My shrill cries were louder than the people's voices on the television. Louder than that rapper's voice blaring from the boom box. These were things he turned on to try to drown out the sound of our fights.

"Shut up!" he warned, balling a fist in my face.

I was afraid, but the pain was just too unbearable. I cried out again as I mustered up the strength to use the weight of my body to try to free myself from him. The next thing I knew, we slammed into his dresser. His lamp fell over with a crash, and his alarm clock hit the floor.

I outweighed Dub by about fifty pounds easily. After having Baby D, I had never got back down to my previous weight. Now I was bigger than I had been before. With the added pounds, when I landed on top of him after our crash into the dresser, the wind was briefly knocked out of him. In that instant, I was able to get away from him, and I immediately hobbled over to his bed and began caressing my arm.

As Dub stood up, he had a look of fury in his eyes I had never seen before. Somehow, when he hit the dresser, he managed to scrape his elbow. He looked down at his bleeding wound and then at me before he touched his elbow with his forefinger, licked the blood that was now on his finger, and then came walking toward me.

His dukes were raised, and I closed my eyes. I didn't want to see it coming. All I wanted to do, all I could do, was brace myself.

"What's going on down here?" Ms. Daniels called from the other side of the door, her voice halting Dub's blow. The knob began to jiggle. She couldn't get in, though, because Dub always closed and locked the door. "Unlock this door," she demanded.

"Ain't nothing going on, Ma," Dub said with a disrespectful tone. "Go on somewhere." Dub's anger relocated from me to his mother.

"Open this door now!" she demanded.

"Hold up!" Dub said as he made an attempt at some minor housekeeping to straighten things up a little.

"Now! Before I come through this door!" She began to push her body against the door as she turned the knob.

Dub knew he'd better unlock the door now. He unlocked it and opened it, but just barely. "What?" he asked through the cracked door.

"Since when do you pay the bills around here?" Ms. Daniels asked as she forced her way inside the room. Her natural blond hair was unkempt. Her blue eyes looked around suspiciously. It was obvious Dub favored his black father more so than his white mother. "What's going on down here?" she asked, repeating her initial query.

When neither one of us responded, she looked from one of us to the other. "Y'all been down here fighting? Why is that clock on the floor?"

"No, Ma, we ain't been fighting. Just go on somewhere." Dub rolled his eyes at his mother.

"Boy, who do you think you are talking to like that?" She snapped her neck.

In frustration, Dub palmed his head with his hands. "Sorry, Mom. But I told you, ain't nothing going on."

"Nothing's going on, huh?" By now she was slowly walking over to him. "Then what's this?" She pointed to his elbow, having noticed the bleeding scratch when he lifted his arms. "Y'all have been down here fighting."

I was surprised that the deep sigh of relief I let out didn't blow the two of them over. Finally, someone had detected that he was beating me, and I hadn't told. Initially, pride alone had kept me from telling others what Dub was doing to me. Now, in the back of my mind, I knew that if I told anyone, chances were that wouldn't make him stop hitting me. It would just make him even angrier, and he'd want to hurt me even more. Maybe even kill me.

Then there had been those thoughts about whether anyone would believe me if I told on him. After all, I did outweigh the guy by fifty pounds. I knew all these excuses and reasons for staying sounded weak, but I looked for any reason possible to explain to my own self why I stayed in the relationship. Why I had made a conscious choice not to walk away. Why I had made a conscious choice to not even tell anyone that Dub was abusing me. But now I didn't have to worry about that. Dub's mother was standing there, right in the midst of the battle. She didn't have a choice but to believe her own eyes. And I was glad that someone was finally coming to my rescue.

My hope was short lived, as Ms. Daniels turned from Dub and came marching toward me. "What did you do to my son? Why is he bleeding?"

My mouth opened, but no words fell out. I couldn't believe it.

"You been down here cat scratching him or something?" Now her finger was wagging in my face. "I'm nice enough to let you come over to my house because of my grandson and everything. But ain't gon' be no fighting and carrying on. You understand?" She looked at Dub. "Y'all understand?"

"Yes, ma'am," he answered.

Now I was surprised that Dub's sigh of relief hadn't blown Ms. Daniels and me over. "It was nothing, though. I'm cool, but could you get me a Band-Aid?" he whined, milking his role as the victim in his mommy's eyes for everything it was worth.

"Sure, baby," she said to him, then walked out of the room and up the stairs to go get a Band-Aid. She returned less than a minute later. He'd walked out of the room and gone to the bathroom across from the way to rinse his elbow, leaving me sitting on the bed, dumbfounded.

"Thanks, Ma," Dub said after his mother went into the bathroom and helped him nurse his wound.

"No problem. By the way, dinner will be ready in a few." She headed back up the steps, but not before cutting her eyes at me as she walked by the bedroom.

I put my head down. I couldn't describe the emotions that were flowing through me, a young teenage girl, at the time. I tried, anyway, and came up with the words *stupidity, alone, left for dead, useless, worthless, pitiful, victim, depressed, miserable.*

The closing of the bedroom door and its locking let me know that Dub was back in the room with me. "That was close." He exhaled. "We almost got busted."

*We?* I thought. *We.* Had I missed something here? Or were Dub and his mother right? Dub had always said that it was my own fault that he put his hands on me, that I made him do it. It wasn't just an excuse anymore. I was truly beginning to believe that in my head. After all, I was only seventeen. I'd met Dub and been under his spell since I was fifteen. This was all I knew. He was all I knew. This was what I was used to.

At the end of the day, some children and teenagers who were abused physically, sexually, and mentally by their parents didn't tell. They never told, not even when they became of age. They still had this love and connection to their abuser that was absolutely unexplainable, to such an extent that they still visited and kept up a relationship with their abuser. The same went with a dog being abused by its master. It was their master. It was all they knew, and they wouldn't dare run out of that unfenced yard when off the chain to take a risk and see if the grass was greener on the other side. We became comfortable with knowing what we were going to get versus the unknown. Something just wouldn't allow us to take the risk of walking away to see if there was better out there. Most of us didn't even believe we deserved better, because we'd been beaten and broken down to nothing.

I'd once heard that no one could do to a person any more than that person allowed them to do. Did that mean I was completely to blame, then?

My thoughts were interrupted when I felt Dub pushing me back on the bed. He was feeling victorious, so now, of course, he wanted to celebrate. Hopefully, the teddy would serve its purpose and this wouldn't take too long.

# Stone Number Nine

"Hey, sweetie," Ms. Daniels said, opening the door to let me and Baby D in.

"Hi, Ms. Daniels." I was all too stunned when she pulled me in for a hug. For the past month, after the whole scene with Dub and me fighting in his room, she'd had a slight attitude with me, hardly speaking whenever I came through the door. I presumed she was over it.

"Dub is downstairs. I'm cooking taco salad." She scooped up Baby D. "I'll call you guys up when it's finished."

"Yes, ma'am," I said. Taco salad was one of my favorite dishes that Ms. Daniels made. I was glad Ms. Daniels and I were back on good terms. I really liked her and didn't blame her for her son's actions at all.

I headed down the steps and went to Dub's room after making a pit stop at the bathroom.

"So who is the dude you been riding around in your car with?" Dub asked before I barely had my foot in the door of his room.

"What?" I was totally confused. His demeanor had all of a sudden changed. Just fifteen minutes ago he'd called my house, talking about, in a voice as sweet as cotton candy, how he missed Baby D and just wanted to see him for a few minutes. Since I was the one with the car, it was a no-brainer that I would pack up Baby D and come to his house.

After saving money from my job, I'd gone out and gotten myself a reliable hooptie. It was a Chevy Chevette. It wasn't much, but it was mine and it was clean, and it sure as heck beat public transportation. Getting to school and work and lugging Baby D around was much easier now. And, unfortunately, so was getting to Dub's house.

"Don't get slick. You know exactly who I'm talking about," Dub said.

"Boy, let me go upstairs and get my son from your mama so we can go home. I ain't come over here for no drama. I thought you wanted to see your son, but I see you on some other stuff." I pushed past him, my heart racing one hundred miles per hour. I knew exactly what and who he was talking about. Only, I knew that even if I dared try to explain it, it would do me no good. But would playing stupid pan out any better?

"Oh, so you trying to play dumb?" Dub said, hurrying to block the door with his body.

"I don't be riding around with no dude in my car, Dub. You're talkin' crazy," I declared, and I would have sworn on a stack of Bibles had there been one nearby.

He marinated my face with the spittle that fluttered out of his mouth with his every word. "Witch, my boy who lives across the street from your school told me how every day when you get out of school, some dude be getting in your car with you. So you trying to say my boy is a liar? Huh? 'Cause we can call him up right now!"

I was so busted it wasn't even funny. I knew playing stupid any longer would only insult Dub's intelligence, so I surrendered the truth and braced myself.

"Oh, you mean then?" I shooed my hand as if a fly was trying to come in between us. Nonchalantly I stated, "Oh, that's just Markus. Our teacher got him and one other guy in our class a job at the computer place I work at. I just give them a ride since we are going to the same place."

I didn't think I could have embedded my foot any further down my throat. Not only had I just confessed to riding around with one guy, but I'd pleaded guilty to there actually being two.

"Oh, so you be riding around with all kinds of dudes in your car? I bet they be runnin' trains on you and everything, you stupid whore. Now you got a baby and everybody know you screwin', you just givin' it up to everybody now, huh?"

I couldn't even describe how deeply Dub's words cut me. I wanted to cuss him out now and worry about the butt kickin' later, but before I could respond, Dub punched me in my head so hard, I literally saw stars. Before that pain could even drive in and park, he slapped me across the face with his open hand.

"Why are you doing this?" I cried, holding my head. "I just gave them a ride. It's nothing," I said, trying to reason with him. It was so innocent, but Dub was so jealous, I knew he would never see it that way, which was why I had never mentioned it to him.

I'd been giving them a ride for only a little over a month. It wasn't even like Markus and the other guy had asked me for a ride. I was the one who had offered. On my way to work I'd drive past them at the bus stop, and knowing we were all going to the same place, it just didn't seem right. I thought I was doing something good. I guess it just showed that no good deed went unpunished. So now it was time for me to take my punishment.

"So you thought it was okay to be riding around with dudes in your car? Is that what you thought? You thought it was cool for my boys to see my girl rolling around town with another dude in her car? You thought it was cool to make me look stupid?" With each question asked, I received a punch in the stomach or the chest.

"Oh God!" I yelped, trying to catch my breath. At that moment I was crying out to God, and not because of instinct. I truly just wanted God to come down from the clouds of heaven and take not me but Dub away.

As awful as it sounded, I wanted nothing more than for him to be ingested by Earth and regurgitated on Mars. But I knew God wouldn't answer my prayers. It wasn't like He and I were close acquaintances or anything. I had never called Him up or stopped by His house to say "What's up?" in quite some time. I made a mental note to do just that for the sole purpose that the next time I did need to call out to Him, He might answer.

"You stupid . . ." Now with each blow Dub landed, he also pitched an obscenity my way. I was every whore, ho, B word, and slut in the book. "Did you actually think . . ."

I tuned him out and just took the licks, pain thrusting through my body. Every now and again I tried to fight him back, but he was just too quick. Too strong. Just like with that little kid on the playground back when I was in fourth grade, I just didn't want to fight. For years my bark had been far worse than my bite. Dub knew I didn't even have teeth.

All of a sudden it was like déjà vu.

"What's going on down here?" Ms. Daniels called from the other side of the door. The knob began to jiggle. She couldn't get in, though, because Dub, of course, had locked the door. "Unlock this door. What did I tell you about locking this door? Open it now!"

Before Dub could even think about honoring his mother's request, the door flew open from the weight of Ms. Daniels slamming her body up against it. Her wild eyes searched the room. I could tell she was just waiting to catch me scratching up her son. But what she saw was a completely different scene than what she'd obviously expected. I could tell by the surprised look in her eyes.

"Honey, what happened?" she said with a concerned tone as she made her way over to me. She touched my swollen jaw and examined the scratches around my neck. I hadn't had time, of course, to reduce the swelling with ice, make myself up with cosmetics, or layer myself in clothing. "What happened to your shirt?"

I looked down, having not even noticed myself that Dub had ripped my shirt. I looked up at her with my telltale eyes. Then I looked at Dub, her son, the boy she'd raised. Her eyes followed my glare.

"You beating on her?" she asked Dub. "You beating on her?" she asked again after not getting a response from him the first time.

I thought Dub would just be filled with guilt and shame after being found out by his mom and would confess and repent. I mean, this time there was no way she couldn't see what was truly going on. But instead he puffed his chest out and got indignant. I guess what he was thinking was, *Forget it. . . . I've been found out now. There's no turning back, so I might as well man up to it.*

He looked at me with such rage and then said, "So what? She deserves to be hit if she's supposed to be my girl and she's cheating on me."

"But I wasn't cheating on you," I cried. "I was just giving them a ride to work." I looked at Ms. Daniels. "I swear I was not cheating on your son." I felt the need to clarify that for her for fear that she might think that since I was cheating on her son, then I deserved to be hit.

Ms. Daniels's words surprised me. "And even if she was cheating on your sorry behind, that don't give you no right to put your hands on her." His mother, to my astonishment, defended me.

Knowing that there was someone on my side who just might listen, I felt something erupt in me and I decided to tell all. "He always hits on me, Ms. Daniels," I blurted.

"And then, afterward, he just likes to get on top of me." I didn't have to spell it out. She knew what I meant.

She looked at her son with disgust. "Just like your father," she told him through gritted teeth.

For some young men, that might have been a good thing to hear, while for others, the most insulting thing a person could ever tell them was that they were just like their father. With Dub it would be the latter.

"He used to do the same thing to me," his mother confessed with moist eyes. "That's why he's paralyzed to this day. All them years of beating on me, when he got into a fight with a real man, he didn't know what to do. Got himself beat so bad, he gon' be in that wheelchair the rest of his life, and if you keep it up, you're going to turn out just like him. I see it now." She glared at her son. "I can see it in your eyes."

A raging heat arose in Dub. He was so angry at his mother's words that I could tell he wanted to beat her down. Instead, he chose to do to me what he wanted to do to her.

"Now, see what you've done!" Dub ran toward me, leaped into the air, and kicked me dead in the stomach with all the strength he could muster in his size ten foot. I never saw it coming. But, man, did I feel it.

"Ugh," I gasped, bending over.

"Dub!" his mother yelled, slinging him back and away from me by his shirt. "What if she was pregnant or something? Did you think about that?" she scolded, still gripping his shirt. Pregnancy wasn't a possibility, since I had been on birth control, but I understood the point she was trying to make.

I was in so much pain, my body felt like electricity was flowing through it. Pain or not, I knew I had to get out of there . . . for good. I began to gather my things as hot tears streamed down my face.

"Where you think you going?" Dub asked me, trying to get past his mother, who was blocking him.

"I'm out of here." Then I got bolder. "I hate you! It's over!" I would have never had the courage to say those things had his mother not been down there.

"Look, I'm sorry," Dub said, apologizing, something he hadn't done since he first started hitting me. "I just love you so much that I lost it for a minute. Me thinking I'm going to lose you over some other guy . . . I don't know what happened." He actually sounded sincere, but it was too late. I saw this as my out. Finally, despite the fact that I gave Him little to nothing, God was giving me a way out. I would finally be free from the clutches of Dublen Daniels.

"Well, now you're losing her over yourself." His mother abducted the words right out of my mouth. "And I don't blame her . . . as long as I still get to see my grandson."

I swear on my mother and father that Ms. Daniels having my back gave me so much courage, it wasn't funny. I guess all I needed was for someone to just know what I was going through, to be there to understand. To support me. To believe me. This time Ms. Daniels had to believe me. She'd seen it with her own eyes. Dub could smell my newfound courage too. He knew I was gone. He knew that I meant every word I'd said. It was over.

"Please don't leave me," Dub said once I had collected all my things and was on my way up the stairs.

I disregarded his pleas and turned to his mother. "Where's Baby D?"

"I had Kelice run to the store to get me a pack of cigarettes. She took him with her," Ms. Daniels said.

I was anxious to get out of there, but not without my baby boy, who'd turned one just three months ago. "Then I'll just wait in my car." I knew better than to sit in the house and wait. Dub would try to sweet-talk me or beat my brains out. I didn't want to subject myself to either.

"I'll get his things together," Ms. Daniels said as she followed me up the steps.

I kept peering over my shoulders to make sure Dub wasn't going to try to do something crazy to stop me. Instead, he just stood there, dumbfounded, watching me walk away.

I stood at the front door while Ms. Daniels gathered Baby D's things. It took her less than five minutes. "Now, remember what I said." Ms. Daniels placed her hand on my shoulder. "Just 'cause you and my son ain't gon' be together no more doesn't mean you can keep my grandbaby from being around me."

I gave a half smile. "I wouldn't do that to you, Ms. Daniels. I know how much you love—"

"Helen, come here," Dub interrupted as he called out to me from the basement.

There was silence as I looked at Ms. Daniels. "Should I go?" my eyes asked her, but my lips said nothing, frozen in fear.

If I went down those basement steps, what fate would be there waiting for me? If I walked out that door, what fate would be waiting for me? Would my disobedience set Dub off to the point where he'd race outside and kill me in front of the neighbors? Would he come after me at my house late at night, taking me out and anybody who got in his way? I couldn't bring that chaos to my doorstep, couldn't compromise my family's welfare. Even worse, what if his sister drove up with Baby D and he killed me right there in front of our son? No, I couldn't have that. I couldn't have my son witness his father murder his mother.

"Helen, come here," Dub called again, shaking me out of my thoughts.

I knew what I had to do. I had to go ahead and get it over with. With my arms loaded with both Baby D's and my things, I took a deep breath and headed down the steps, my life a slide show before my eyes.

Once I got to the bottom landing, I walked straight across into Dub's room. I walked in slowly, but he was nowhere in sight. It was quiet, and I could hear my heart drumming.

"I'm back here!" I heard him call out, his voice darn near making me jump out of my skin.

I exited his bedroom and tailed his voice to the back part of the basement, where the laundry room was. With each tread and with each breath, I came to grips with the fact that they could very well be my last. Right before entering the laundry room, I closed my eyes and took one last deep breath and then advanced . I kept my eyes closed, having decided that I didn't want to see it coming. It wasn't until I stepped on a pile of clothes that I opened my eyes. And what I saw would be embedded in my eternal memory.

"Helen," Dub said, "I can't live without you." And then he jumped.

My heart dropped as I watched eighteen-year-old Dub dangle from the ceiling rafter, his bedroom sheet tied around his neck.

He was gagging and kicking and choking and dying. He was the one dying, not me. My heart began to pound so loudly, it sounded like the background of the song "The Little Drummer Boy."

With that short walk, I had prepared myself to die. But I had not prepared myself to witness another human being die. But Dub wasn't a human being, was he? He was a monster. Didn't monsters deserve to die?

Even with those thoughts scuttling through my head, I just couldn't let him remain suspended there. I just couldn't. I dropped everything in my hands on the floor and ran over to him. As I pulled at his legs, I would look up and see the sheet begin to loosen instead of tighten. It wasn't loosening fast enough, though. I thought about calling out for his mother to come help me, but I was afraid she would think I'd hung him up there myself or would just flat out blame me for his act. So instead, I just kept pulling. With my pulling and all the pressure of Dub kicking, the sheet continued to loosen. But would it loosen quickly enough, or would it be too late?

"Oh, God, please help me!" I called out as my arms began to weaken. The irony of the situation was that just moments ago I wanted God to help me get away from Dub, even if somebody had to die. Now here I was, asking God to help me keep Dub, the cradle of my misery, from dying.

With my arms cramping and aching, I didn't know if I'd be able to hold them up any longer. When I wasn't pulling at Dub, I was trying to lift him to release some of the tension around his neck, but nothing seemed to work. I felt defeated and ready to give up. I was able to muster up enough strength to pull one last time, hard enough so that both Dub and I went crashing to the floor.

It was a surreal moment as I just sat there, crying. Dub sat next to me, crying too. I'd never seen him cry before. I'd never seen a grown man cry, period. His shoulders heaved up and down, and he even made little wailing sounds as tears flowed from his eyes. The image beside me began to tug at my heartstrings. He might have been a monster, but I was a human being with feelings, which I could not define.

Dub threw his arms around me and just embraced me as his chest rose and his shoulders slumped. I just sat there, still stunned. So many thoughts were coursing through my mind, but the main one was, *This man is crazy.* Some people might call it love, but I called it crazy!

"I knew you really loved me," he cried. "If you didn't, you would have just left me hanging there. You would have let me die. I knew you loved me. I'm going to do better this time. This time we'll . . ."

His words trailed off, and all I could hear was my inner voice telling me, What have you done? You were almost free. Not only should you have let him die, but you should also have watched him die, making sure every last ounce of breath was expelled from his body. Why? Why didn't you let him die?

I had no answers to all the inquiries sailing through my head. I couldn't explain why I was here, back in Satan's embrace, when just five minutes ago, I could have been out that door, leaving Dub behind, perhaps to die alone.

But something inside of me just wouldn't stand there and watch that man die. No matter how much he had hurt me, I just couldn't do it.

As I sat there, being held by Dub, I knew I had just waived my only way out. Would I get a second chance at freedom, or would I remain a voluntary prisoner of Dub for the rest of my life?

# Stone Number Ten

"Why didn't I just let him die when I had the chance?" I asked my reflection in the mirror of Dub's basement bathroom. It wasn't but three short months after Dub's suicide attempt, and he was at it again.

"Hurry up!" he yelled from outside the bathroom door. "It don't take you that long to pee."

It was official. Dub had completely lost his mind. It was late Wednesday morning, a morning I should have been at school. But Dub was holding me hostage in his bedroom. He wouldn't let me go to school unless I had sex with him. His jealousy had been over the top ever since the situation with me giving the two guys from my classroom a ride to work. He'd sometimes request that I have sex with him prior to going to school. I guess he figured if I still was sneaking and giving dudes rides to work, at least I wouldn't be having sex with them if he got to me first.

Of course, I was no longer giving them a ride to work. Dub had made sure of that. He had come up to the school, asking for Markus by name. Even though I'd told him I had been giving two of my classmates a ride, he went after only Markus. I suppose because Markus was always the one who hopped in the front seat, something that didn't go unnoticed by whoever Dub's watchdog was. Dub's friends sure did need a life if they didn't have anything better to do than watch my daily routine and then report it back to Dub.

Dub was like some crazy man the day he came up to my school. He stopped anyone who crossed his path and asked, "Are you Markus?" or "Do you know a Markus?" He told everybody he stopped to relay to Markus that once he found him, he was going to give him a beat down for trying to get at his girl, Helen.

"Yo, your man is up here clownin' over you," said this guy I didn't even know as he walked by me when I was exiting the school building.

I was heading for my car so I could go to work. He looked me up and down, shook his head, and chuckled. I felt as if he was silently saying, "And you ain't even hot." Because that was the way he was looking at me.

I felt so mortified. I had no idea how long Dub had been outside harassing all my schoolmates. But by now the word was out, and everybody seemed to know what was going on.

"Girl, Dub is up here, acting like a crazy, deranged lunatic," Synthia said as she came up behind me. Synthia was the prettiest girl at the school and therefore the most popular. Since Rochelle and I weren't that close anymore, Synthia was becoming like my new best bud. The same way I had never imagined dating someone with Dub's looks, I had never imagined that the prettiest and most popular girl at school would ever want to be my friend.

Synthia had exited the building right behind me, so clearly the word had been getting around inside the school but had somehow managed to miss me.

I was completely caught off guard. "I don't know what is going on," I lied to Synthia.

"I hear he's askin' everybody if they know Markus. Something about Markus trying to steal his girl or something. He's probably gone now, though," Synthia said. "The school called the police. I think they tried to come get you out of class, but you were already gone."

I halted my steps. "The cops are here?"

"I think they are gone now."

Dub had gotten wind of the police and had gone on about his business. But even though he and the cops had left, their visit remained the talk of the school.

"Markus don't want her. She ain't all that for no dude to be fighting over," were some of the words spoken that got back to me.

Now, as I stood before that bathroom mirror down in Dub's basement, I agreed. "Look at me. Look how stupid and ugly I am," I mumbled to myself. "Stupid, stupid, stupid." Each time I called myself stupid, I punched myself upside the head. Maybe I did deserve to be hit for being so stupid. So ugly. So dumb. So lost. So confused.

"Don't make me come through this door!" Dub's voice shook me out of my own moment of self-inflicted pain.

I opened the door to find Dub waiting with his arms folded. He pushed me into his bedroom.

"Dub, I need to go to school. I have a test today," I lied, There was no test. I was tired, drained, and ready to go. He'd been trying to have sex with me all morning, and this time I just didn't want to do it. I just didn't want him touching me. My rejecting him enraged him. I was just relieved Baby D wasn't around.

By now I'd learned about a program called Title 20, which was government-funded child care. I only had to pay something like sixteen dollars a week to the child-care provider, and the government supplemented the rest. Believe it or not, I preferred to take my child to a biological stranger's house than have him with his father all day. If Dub could snap off on me at any given moment, he could do the same with my son. I had to protect my son from his father at all costs. And if it meant I had to stay with Dub just to make sure I was always around whenever he was with our son, then so be it. Yep, you guessed it. This was another reason to add to my list of reasons why I stayed with Dub.

After I dropped Baby D off and before I went to school, Dub made me drive to his house, and for the past two hours he'd been hitting me, trying to get me to confess to him that the real reason I didn't want to have sex with him was that I was having sex with someone else. So the fact that I was not giving him sex wasn't really his concern anymore. Getting me to admit my infidelity was.

"You don't have no test today," Dub spat. "You just trying to go get to your little boyfriend. Who is it? That Markus dude? Do I need to come back up to that school and regulate?"

"Dub, please. How many times do I have to—"

"Shut up lying to me, you stupid witch!" he said, giving me a blow upside my head. "Do you think I'm as stupid as you? Huh? Huh?" Two more blows to my head. "Forget this. I'm done playing with you."

He rushed me and pinned me to the bed. "Whoever he is, let him get my sloppy seconds." He tugged my pants off of me.

I just lay there the entire time as he thrust in and out of me. Sex both before and after the baby had always been pretty much one-sided. I always did it more for Dub than for myself, right down to the first time. I was tired. Tired of Dub. Tired of fighting. Tired of fighting Dub.

"Now I know you ain't gon' have sex with nobody," he said upon finishing up with me.

As I lay there, I thought, *Why didn't I just have sex with him in the first place and get it over with? Then none of this would be happening. I'd be at school, like every other able teenager.* I just wanted to be a regular teenage girl. Just regular. But for how many other teenage girls was this type of thing regular?

"Now can I go to school?" I asked Dub. The nonchalance in my tone pissed him off.

"No!" he yelled, smacking me in my mouth. "You think I'm done with you? You still ain't really gave me what I want."

"You wanted sex, and now you got it. What?" I asked, raising my hands in question.

"What? The truth is what. If you hadn't just had sex with me, who was it you would have had sex with?"

I could not freaking believe it. I felt as if there was no way I was going to get out of that room if I didn't tell him exactly what he wanted to hear. Maybe if I lied and told him that there was something going on between Markus and me, he'd leave me alone and go take it out on Markus. I knew that was wrong, but I didn't know how much longer I could take the abuse. Those selfish thoughts went pounding through my head, until there was a pounding on the front door.

Dub looked at me as if I was expecting someone.

"It's your house," I replied, answering his unasked question. "I don't know who it is."

Dub got up from next to me and went to peek through the curtains. After sighing and muttering an expletive, he said, "It's your moms." He then looked at me as if I'd snuck out and called her or something.

"The school must have called her," I immediately thought out loud, once again answering Dub's unasked question. "The school probably called her when I didn't show up and no one called to report my absence." That was a school procedure neither Dub nor I even thought about.

She knocked again. I could tell Dub didn't want to answer the door, but he knew my mom wasn't going anywhere, especially after seeing my bright yellow Chevette parked right outside the house. She knew I was in there.

"Get yourself together," Dub ordered me nervously.

I began to straighten out my clothing, while Dub slowly went to answer the door, asking me intermittently, "You got yourself together yet? You cool?"

I was so afraid. I was afraid that I might have to lie to my mother about why I wasn't in school. I was afraid to tell my mom that for over a year and half now, ever since Baby D was born, Dub had been battering me. I knew she'd be mad at me for being so stupid. For allowing him to do that to me.

Never once had I taken into consideration that because my mom had been through the same thing herself during her first marriage, she just might understand. She just might be on my side.

"Helen, I know you're in there. I see your car," my mom called after knocking a couple more times and getting no answer.

At that point, Dub opened the door. I was now at the bottom of the steps, looking up, as my mom brushed right by Dub and came into the house uninvited.

"Where's Helen?" she asked. Just then she saw me at the bottom of the steps. "The school called me. Why aren't you in school?" she spat.

I couldn't even get a word in edgewise as she continued going off on me.

"You think you just gon' lay up under this fool and not go to school?" My mom pointed at Dub. She couldn't have cared less that she'd just called him a fool to his face—in his own house. "Why didn't you go to school today? I don't care if you do have a baby and think you grown. You ain't quite eighteen just yet. You still live under my roof. Got the school calling me on my job. I got to leave work and come see about you."

There was a brief pause. I just stood there, not knowing if she really wanted an answer from me or if she was going to keep on fussing. That was how my mother was:

fuss, fuss, fussing and cuss, cuss, cussing. This was why as soon as she could after turning eighteen, Lynn had packed up and moved out. She didn't want to endure the wrath of Genie if she didn't have to.

"Well, you heard me. Why ain't you in school?" My mother stood with her hands on her hips, looking back and forth from me to Dub. She resembled a warrior. She was on the warpath. She'd come to see about me. And at that very moment, I felt like any child felt about their parents—that they could protect them.

My mother covered me with a quilt of protection and warmed me. It was something I had never felt before when it came to my mother. After all, when I was home, I had to deal with her madness. When I was at Dub's, I had to deal with his madness. There had never really been a safe haven for me. But at that moment, in spite of how mean I might have thought my mother was, I still felt safeguarded by her.

"Answer me, Helen," my mom shouted. Her loud, piercing voice had the same stinging effect it'd had for years, the one that had put the fear of death in Lynn and me, but right now it didn't faze me in the same way. Right now Genie was ordering me to tell her what was going on. And I felt like I could.

Before I could veto them, tears erupted from my eyes. This wailing sound was discharged from my throat. It was a wail and a cry that only a person who had been through something like this could translate.

"What did he do to you?" she said without me having to say a word. My mom understood. Although it had been years since she and Rakeem had divorced and he'd laid his hands on her, I knew she remembered what it was like. I knew she knew it was wrong. I knew she could translate and understand my cry.

"He wouldn't let me go to school," I whispered, managing to get the words out.

Dub was stupefied. He couldn't believe I'd just blown the whistle on him. I was astounded myself. Perhaps God had answered my prayers a long time ago. Perhaps He'd equipped me all along with just what I needed to free myself from the hell I was living in. I just hadn't used it. A person could have the gun and all the ammunition they needed, but if they didn't know how to fire the gun, what good was it? I didn't know how to ignite the fire in me, the power of the Holy Spirit . . . because I didn't know it was there. So many of us walk around today clueless of the power God granted us. I was waiting on God to help me, clueless to the fact that He'd already given me everything I needed. He was waiting on me to help myself!

"Get your stuff and let's go, Helen," my mom said before turning to Dub and pointing in his face. "And you stay away from my daughter, or I'll kill you."

For the first time, I saw Dub shrink down to the size of an ant. As bad as I wanted to hang around and get a kick out of seeing him lick his pitiful wounds, I knew I'd better get to gettin' before things got ugly. My mom might have been abused herself back in the day, but she wasn't no punk. All those years of getting beat up had given her a courage that enabled her to stand up and challenge any man or woman.

I brushed past Dub at the door, leaving him standing there as I headed to my car and my mom headed to hers. I cried the entire drive home, but this time they were tears of relief. I was free. I was really free this time. My mom was involved now, so there was no turning back . . . was there?

I looked up to the heavens and grimaced, recalling how I had been so sure that I had a way out before—the last time I was going to leave Dub. Only, God got in the midst of things and ruined it for me. God had allowed His spirit to rise up inside of me and beat out my flesh, which would have loved nothing more than to see Dub take his last breath while hanging from that sheet. I'd been so angry at God for that interference, but never again would I let God get in my way. Never again.

# Stone Number Eleven

After pulling off in our cars from Dub's house, my mother and I drove home because most of my classes were already over with. Ten minutes hadn't passed after we walked in the door when Dub came running down the street and began banging on our door.

"Helen! Let me in. Please let me talk to you. Don't leave me! Don't do this!" Dub hollered as he banged on the door. He was practically out of breath. I figured that was because he'd run all the way to our house. He had to have run, considering that his house was a good half hour walk from mine and he'd made it there in ten minutes.

"Call the police!" my mom told me as she scurried into her bedroom.

I picked up the cordless phone to dial 911. I could only half pay attention to the operator because of all the jingling noises coming from my mom's bedroom. This was not the time to be counting money, but that was exactly what it sounded like she was doing as I heard change clinking together. I stood outside her door, which was barely cracked open, on the phone.

"Nine-one-one, what's your emergency?" the operator asked.

"Someone's trying to break into the house."

Dub was knocking, turning the knob, and throwing his body against the door, all the while yelling my name. "Helen!"

"Can you repeat that, ma'am?" the operator asked me.

"Someone is trying to break into the house," I told her.

"Not *someone*. Tell her it's your boyfriend."

It was the way my mother said it that reminded me why I hadn't told anyone what Dub was doing to me. She had said it so accusingly. She might as well have said, "It's your boyfriend, so this is your fault. None of this would be going down if you hadn't picked this nutcase."

It was then that I wished I could recant my earlier statement and tell her instead that I'd been playing hooky from school to lay up under my boyfriend. She would have believed it. That had been her initial notion, anyway. Honesty had invited trouble to our doorstep. Why did I tell?

"My boyfriend is trying to break into our house." I stood corrected.

The 911 operator asked me more questions than a registration nurse at the emergency room. After all was said and done, she told me that because I hadn't seen Dub with a weapon, it wasn't an emergency, so I needed to hang up and call the local police. By that time Dub could be through the door, slitting our throats.

I hung up the phone and searched for the white pages in order to find the number for the Columbus Police Department. That was when my mother came stalking out of her room and past me, heading straight to the front door. I looked down at her hand and realized why I'd heard all that jingling noise.

Before I could even find the number for the police, my mother had flung open the door and taken immediate aim at Dub. With a sweat sock full of coins, she commenced clocking him upside his head. Genie was not playing. With every hit she threw, an expletive was lobbed from her mouth, as well.

After about three swings, Dub found his bearings, and his instinct was to fight back. He balled his fists, and then he looked at me standing in the doorway. Was this man about to hit my mother? That was the question that lingered in my eyes. When Dub saw that look, he halted and backed away. Then, just as quickly as he had come up that street, he headed back down the street.

What his next move was, I had no idea.

"Helen, this is Ms. Daniels," she said through the phone receiver.

Although over the phone I couldn't see the somber expression that probably plagued Dub's mother's face, I could tell by the tone of her voice that something was wrong. Something besides the fact that only hours ago my mother had practically had to do a prison break to get me away from her son.

"Dub tried to kill himself," were the next words that came out of Ms. Daniels's mouth. "When I came home, I found him unconscious. He took every pill in the house, it seems." Her voice cracked as she continued. "I called nine-one-one, and they came and took him to the emergency room, where they pumped his stomach."

*Ain't that a blimp?* When I tried to get 911 to come get his butt, they wouldn't.

"They took him to the Hilltop and admitted him there," she told me, now crying.

The Hilltop was where the crazy hospital was. It was now certified. Dub was a bona fide crazy. It was no longer just my opinion, but a fact!

"He's going crazy, Helen. He said he can't live without you. They can't get him calmed down or anything. They have him restrained. He said as soon as they let him loose, he's just going to try to do it again."

By now I could hardly understand what Ms. Daniels was saying because she was crying so hard. This was his first suicide attempt, to her knowledge, so I could tell she was in complete shock and disbelief. Neither Dub nor I had ever shared with her his hanging attempt. Maybe if we had, she could have gotten him the help he needed before he made this second attempt.

"I don't want to lose my baby." She sniffed and got herself together. "I was thinking, maybe if you could just go see him, you know, to calm him down, that would help."

"Ms. Daniels, I—"

"Who's that on the phone?" I heard my mother call from the dinner table, where we'd been sitting and eating before the phone rang. "Tell them you'll call them back. You're eating dinner. Your food is getting cold. You can gossip later," my mother huffed.

"Look, Ms. Daniels, I have to go," I told her, relieved that my mom had come to the rescue for the second time today.

"Dub told me everything that went on," Ms. Daniels said, beginning her plea, "but I know you wouldn't want him to die, would you?" There was no way I could answer that question candidly. So I said nothing. "If you don't go see him, that's exactly what's going to happen. He's going to kill himself. So please, Helen, just go see him for a minute, will you please? Please, Helen. He's my son."

"Ms. Daniels, I—"

"Please, Helen, you're the only one who can help him."

"Helen, did you hear what your mother said?" my stepfather called out.

"I really have to go," I told Ms. Daniels.

"Fine. I'll let you go," she said, "but just tell me you'll do it."

The pressure was on. My mom started yelling from the kitchen again, while Ms. Daniels cried in my ear.

A decision had to be made.

# Stone Number Twelve

"So you're the one who's causing my baby all this pain," the nurse said to me as I entered Dub's room at the Hilltop. She was standing over his hospital bed, rubbing his forehead in a comforting manner.

I just looked at the chubby little brown woman with gray hair and black-rimmed glasses. Had she really just said that to me, and in front of him?

I looked at Dub, and when his eyes locked with mine, he immediately broke down in tears.

The nurse shook her head and continued rubbing his forehead. "It's going to be all right, baby. Keep your head up. God's gonna keep you," she told him.

God was keeping him, indeed, from the angel of death. He'd made his second attempt at taking his own life, and God had spared him yet again. Why? I just couldn't understand it. Dub was far from a saint. I mean, I wasn't a saint, either, but dang. What was so special about Dub? But then I recalled a scripture, something about God not being a respecter of man. What He did for the saved He'd do for the unsaved. If that was the case, I figured why bother trying to do good if God was going to bless a person, anyway, even in their sin?

"I'll leave you alone with her, because I know that's what you want," the nurse said to Dub, giving me the evil eye. Evidently, it wasn't what she wanted to do, leave him alone with me. She acted like I was going to finish him off or something. I could see it in her eyes as she brushed past me. If she could have things her way, I'd be the one tied down somewhere.

"I'm so glad you came," Dub cried. "I knew you would come. I knew you would." He said it with somewhat of a sinister grin on his lips. As if he had no intentions of actually dying. He just knew that it would have to be practically over his dead body for me to ever be in the same room with him again. He had probably even timed everything just right, waiting to take all those pills at just the right time, when he knew his mother would come home from work. Trick of the enemy, and I had fallen for it.

Since I had already fallen for the hook, just minutes behind came the line and sinker when I promised him I would never leave him. I didn't say it because I loved him. I said it because I was afraid of what he'd do to himself. I didn't want his blood on my hands. Why did I keep sacrificing myself to save him when he kept making the same stupid decisions and getting the same results? Hmm, guess Jesus was probably shaking His head, saying the same thing about me.

Nonetheless, I went back to him. It was now official. I was a bona fide crazy too.

"The house looks good, baby," Dub said as he sat on the couch, which was kitty-corner to the chair I was sitting in. Two-and-a-half-year-old Baby D was sitting on the floor in front of the television, which we were all watching. We sat around like a real family, the makeshift family that we were.

I looked around. The little duplex I'd managed to rent just two weeks after my eighteenth birthday wasn't much, but it was clean, just like my ride. Dub's sister had moved into one a couple houses down. I was most excited when she told me about a place that would charge me rent according to my income. It wasn't Section 8, but a place that received government grants in order to subsidize the rent of low-income families.

It was in the hood, but it was mine. Besides, for twenty-six dollars a month, I couldn't complain. Although Baby D and I were the only ones on the lease who were permitted to claim residence, like lots of boyfriends of women on Section 8 or living in low-income housing, Dub lived there too.

I felt good about myself. Yes, I'd ended up being a teenage mom just like my mother had, but unlike her, I had finished high school. Not only had I finished high school, but I was now going to college at Capital University as well. And on top of that, I had my own car and my own place. I'd achieved what some people never thought I would after I became a statistic.

"Thanks." I had a proud smile on my face. I had to say that was one of the very few times in the three and some years I'd been with Dub that I was almost content. It had been over a month since he'd abused me last. Back then I thought that perhaps all those pleas to God had finally been heard. People say that God can change things in the blink of an eye. Had He finally shown me so much grace and mercy?

I got my answer in the blink of an eye, because it wasn't but a few minutes later when, out of nowhere, I felt a slap across my face. My hand rose to caress my throbbing cheek. I looked over at Dub with a perplexed expression on my face. What had I done to deserve it? I mean, he'd just complimented me on how good the house looked. Maybe it was the laundry I'd done earlier; perhaps I had used too much bleach, and holes had formed in his socks again. Maybe it was the snacks that we were nibbling on, which were spread across the coffee table. Had I put too much salt into the tuna fish salad? Or maybe the Kool-Aid wasn't sweet enough. After all, these had all been reasons why he'd abused me in the past.

It was as if Dub could see the wheels turning in my head and they were making him dizzy. "I hadn't hit you in a while," he stated matter-of-factly, "but I'm sure you've done something that deserved a slap." Then, just like that, he picked up his glass to take a sip of his Kool-Aid and turned his attention back to the television.

I wanted to smack him right back, but I knew better. Just trying to fight him off made things worse. I was afraid to see what would happen if I actually ever inflicted pain on him. Anger filled me so much so that I wanted to cry, but at first I just sucked it in. Then I realized that the best thing for me to do would be to let a tear trickle out of my eye just for show. After all, he'd just slugged me because I'd been sitting there looking way too happy. I wasn't supposed to be sitting around, feeling happy and smiling. I was supposed to remain trembling in fear. So I cried. Not just that day, but I cried a lot of days, always conscious of the fact that I could not get caught being happy ever again.

As I turned to watch television, I noticed that my son was no longer gazing at the TV screen. He was surveying me. I wanted to just crawl under a rock and die, but instead I wiped my tear away, held my head up high, and pretended that nothing had happened. Pretended that my son wasn't watching. But he was. And him watching shrank my soul even more. My son was the only person who had witnessed the torment and abuse firsthand. I hated that he had that knowledge. And his little brown eyes were asking me why I wasn't fighting back. Why hadn't I ever fought back?

I felt like a coward in my son's eyes. Powerless. I wanted so desperately for him to see me as strong and powerful. For now, though, he'd simply sit back with a muted voice while his father made our lives a living hell.

# Stone Number Thirteen

I used to wonder how Dub always seemed to know what was on my mind, how he'd answer a question that might have been lingering in my psyche before I ever voiced it. But then I realized it was because he had control of my mind. He'd watched me and studied me for the past four years now. He knew what I was going to say or do before I ever said or did it. He knew my thoughts before I even thought them, which was yet another reason why I never made a plan to try to leave Dub. If he sensed it, he would kill me for sure. He'd told me a million times that he would kill me if I ever tried to leave him. So eventually I blocked out the possibility of ever leaving Dub from my mind altogether. I'd made up my mind that I'd die being with Dub, even if he was the cause of my death.

"Thank you for driving me to the clinic," Konnie stated as I sat next to her in the waiting room. Konnie was one of Dub's friend's girlfriends. Dub had known Konnie's boyfriend, Boyd, since high school, and Konnie and Boyd had been dating since high school. They were that couple that everyone just knew was going to make it beyond high school sweethearts, and they had thus far.

"Girl, don't worry about it." I waved my hand. "I had to drop Baby D off at Dub's mama's house, anyway, so I was already out. Besides, I'ma go on and get a checkup while I'm here. I can't remember the last time I've been to the doctor."

I must admit, I was never one to take really good care of my body health wise. At nineteen years old, I could count on one hand how many times I'd been to the dentist. The few times I had gone, the dentist always managed to find a spot that needed one of those silver fillings. After I had Baby D, my doctor told me to make sure I got annual Pap smear exams. Tuh! This would probably be my first one since I'd gone back to the doctors for my six-week follow-up appointment after having Baby D.

"Yeah, I don't blame you." Konnie nodded. "Since you probably have to sit in this walk-in clinic all day with me, you might as well see a doctor for something. You got a health card, don't you?"

"Yeah."

"Cool. Then you ain't got nothing to lose."

I really liked Konnie, and not just because she was the only friend Dub would sometimes allow me to hang around. My best friend from high school, Synthia, was way too pretty for Dub to let me hang with her outside of her visits to my place. She was a man magnet. Guys couldn't help but stare at Synthia and boldly approach her as well. That usually meant if the dude that approached Synthia had any of his boys with him, then more than likely they would try to holler at me. Dub wasn't having it, so the only friends I was allowed to roll with had to be average or unattractive in Dub's eyes.

Konnie wasn't ugly at all, but she was plus size. Mo'Nique hadn't shown the world yet just how sexy big women were, so Dub felt it was cool for me to be in the company of Konnie. Plus, she was the girlfriend of the guy he said he was "going into business with."

Dub and Boyd had witnessed many of their old high school friends turn into hustlers, making quick come ups out of the hood. This was all thanks to the fairly new monkey, crack cocaine. So those two monkeys thought it would be a good idea to make a come up too. The two started spending a lot of time together on the grind, which left me and Konnie to keep each other company. I couldn't have been happier to have Dub busy out in the streets rather than in my face, raising hell.

"You think it's true what people be saying about those crackheads out there? That they'll do anything for a hit?" Konnie asked out of nowhere as we waited at the clinic.

"Everybody can't be making up the same lie," was my reply. "Girl, I done looked out the window in my hood and seen some stuff going down in my back alley."

"For real?" Konnie snapped her head toward me like she couldn't believe it.

I guess because Konnie lived in an apartment on what some coined the "good side" of Cleveland Avenue, she didn't have the opportunity that I did, living on the "bad side" of Cleveland Avenue, of course, to see how the drug game was really affecting people.

"Girl, yeah," I confirmed. "I see it every time I look out the window. Baby D won't even go outside and ride his bike. He's just a little kid, and his instincts tell him it ain't safe."

Konnie was silent for a brief moment before she spoke. "You think our men be out there trickin' with them crackhead girls? You know some of 'em are cute. Don't even be looking like crackheads." To make her point, Konnie said, "You remember Alexis from high school? She on that stuff. And you know how cute she is. She was the captain of the cheerleading team and beautiful. You know guys will be trying to hit that, crackhead and all."

"Is that what you're worried about?" I asked. "You worried about your dude out there cheating on you with some crackheads?" I chuckled and then busied myself with a magazine that was lying on the table in front of me.

"Well, ain't you?"

"Not at all," I said with confidence. Besides, as much as Dub hounded me, fought me, and stole sex from me, I knew he wasn't getting it elsewhere. Otherwise, he would leave me alone. "Do you see the look in our men's eyes before they go hit them streets? Nothing but dollar signs. They just trying to make some money. So if I were you, I wouldn't even trip on that."

"You think?" A bit of doubt laced her voice.

I wanted to reassure her once again, but before I could, the nurse called her name and mine, as well as the names of two other people waiting to be seen by one of the doctors on staff.

"Ms. Lannden, you can go to room five," the nurse instructed me. "I or another nurse will be in shortly to ask you a few questions."

I followed the nurse's instructions, and about ten minutes later a different nurse came into the room to ask me some general questions.

"Ms. Lannden, what are we seeing you for today?" the petite blonde asked.

"Just a checkup. I'm not really having any problems," I said with certainty.

The nurse flipped through my chart. "Do you have a primary family doctor, or do you just come here?"

"Just here."

She scanned a page of my chart. "I see we have past records for you, but we haven't seen you in about two years."

"I only go to the doctor when something is wrong," I fretfully acknowledged. "So the last time I was at the doctor was about two years ago."

"Oh, then you definitely need your annual Pap smear," she concluded. She flipped through a couple more pages of my chart before she jotted down some things. She then took my blood pressure and weighed me before setting up all the things the doctor would need to examine me. "I need you to take off all your clothes." She handed me a paper gown.

"From the waist down?" I questioned.

"No, all your clothes. The doctor needs to do a breast examination as well."

"Okay. Thank you."

Once the nurse left the room, closing the door behind her, I traded my jogging suit for the paper gown and hopped onto the examination table. "Dang, I forgot to put lotion on." I shook my head at how ashy my skin was.

"Knock, knock," I heard a voice say, along with some tapping on the door. "Is it okay to come in?"

"Yes," I replied to the doctor, who peeked his head in as if he didn't want to catch me naked. It wasn't like he wasn't about to dang near have his entire face in my crotch and fondle my breasts.

After entering the room and closing the door behind him, the doctor made small talk and then proceeded to give me my checkup. I was slightly embarrassed by the odor that seemed to be coming from between my legs. But if I'd said it once, I'd say it twice, and now I was gonna say it one mo' 'gain; I had never been one to stay on top of my hygiene. My mother had never taught me about douches and all that stuff, and how important it was to keep my feminine parts clean.

Lynn used to have a fit and talk about me like I was a dog when it came to my personal hygiene.

"Did you take a shower today? Because your rag is still dry and is hanging in the same spot it was in yesterday, and you didn't even shower then," Lynn would bark before spouting out the word *trifling* under her breath.

Now that I thought about it, I was always so depressed and miserable that I couldn't have cared less about whether I looked good or smelled good. Besides, the odor didn't seem to be affecting the doctor. I was sure he'd smelled worse.

"You can put your clothes back on, and I'll be back in shortly," the doctor said as he removed the rubber gloves from his hands, pitched them in the trash, and then washed his hands.

After he exited the room, I got up and got dressed. I then sat and waited patiently for his return. Once again, he knocked before entering while he peeked his head in. With my chart in his hand, he entered the room and then closed the door behind him. He sat down on the stool and examined the chart, his eyes never once making contact with me. That was my first sign that everything wasn't kosher.

"Well, Ms. Lannden," he began, still reading his notes, "it appears as though you have chlamydia."

When those words fell out of the doctor's mouth, they had no effect on me at all. I had no idea what chlamydia was. Had the doctor looked up from his notes at my face, he would have determined that by my expression. But, no, he just kept his face buried in his notes, as if he was the one I had contracted chlamydia from.

"So what I'm going to do is give you a prescription that will take care of it," the doctor continued. When he received no reaction from me whatsoever, he finally slightly raised his head and peered at me. After examining the blank look on my face the same way he had just examined my womanhood, he said, "You don't know what chlamydia is, do you?"

I shook my head.

My ignorance seemed to relax the doctor to the point where he laid the chart down, let out a deep sigh, and then looked directly at me. "Chlamydia is an STD, a sexually transmitted disease. It's like gonorrhea, only the physical symptoms aren't always as prevalent as those of gonorrhea. You might not be having the itching and burning and all that stuff."

He was right, because I had none of those symptoms. No abnormal discharge or anything.

"But one of the signs can be a strong odor coming from your private area." He cleared his throat, as if to say, "Hence that odor coming from you." "It's only transmitted sexually, which means . . ."

The doctor's words, one by one, fell off the face of the earth, plummeting to their death. He was still speaking; I just wasn't hearing him. I couldn't get past the part about chlamydia being a sexually transmitted disease. I had had sex with only one person in my life. So there was only one source from which I could have caught the disease, Dub.

Before realizing how ignorant I was sure I sounded to the doctor, I cut him off and said, "But I've only been with one person in my entire life."

The look on his face said, "Then that should make it easy to pinpoint who the dirty birdie is."

"Are you sure there is no other way to catch this disease?" I asked, desperate. I even wished he would lie to me and make something up. I needed for him to see how determined I was to know that Dub hadn't brought home this mess to me. After everything Dub had put me through, now he wanted me to have to deal with a sexually transmitted disease as well?

"Chlamydia is a sexually transmitted disease. The only way to catch it is through sexual contact, be it intercourse or oral."

"You mean like kissing?" I was getting excited now. There might be a chance that all Dub had done was kiss another girl. That I could live with.

"No, not kissing. Sex, which includes oral sex," the doctor explained. "This means he's going to have to go get himself checked out too. Unlike gonorrhea, chlamydia doesn't reveal itself three days after contracting it with dripping and puss and stinging during urinating. He probably doesn't even know he has it, or else I hope he would have told you. So no telling how long you've had it. But guessing from the odor . . ." This time the doctor's words really did trail off, and he didn't say another word. He'd already stuck in the knife, so why rotate it and amplify the pain?

Intruding upon the silence of my mental self-loathing, the doctor stood and said, "I'm going to write you a prescription and leave it at the front desk with the receptionist. I'll need you to come back for a follow-up in a few weeks to make sure we've got this taken care of." He smiled and was gone.

I was disgusted as I dragged myself out of the examination room and to the front desk to pick up my prescription and schedule a follow-up appointment. As I walked toward the door of the clinic, heading to the car, I felt as though all eyes were on me, the girl with the venereal disease. I knew it was all in my head, though. Still, I felt so dirty and disgusting. And I felt pissed off and couldn't wait to confront Dub.

"So were you just going to leave me?" I heard a voice ask.

I turned around to see Konnie walking up behind me.

"You walked right by me in the waiting room. I been done. I was just waiting on you."

"Oh, my bad," I told her as I proceeded to head on out the door.

"You okay?" Konnie asked as she walked beside me, sensing something was wrong.

"Yeah," I lied.

She wasn't buying it. "You sure?"

We approached my car, and Konnie stood there and waited while I got inside and unlocked her door for her.

All sounds were muffled after she got in given the roar of the engine. I'd stomped the gas pedal so hard, as if I was stomping on Dub's face.

"What's wrong? I can tell something is wrong," she said, persisting.

I sighed and then paused for a moment. "You know what we were talking about inside? Before the nurse called our names?"

Konnie thought for a minute. "Oh, you mean about Dub and Boyd sleeping with other chicks?"

"Yeah," I confirmed.

"Well, what about it?"

"I think you may be right, at least about Dub, anyway." With that said, I pulled off, with every intention of dropping Konnie off and then heading back to my place to pack some bags. I wasn't leaving Dub. I was putting him out!

# Stone Number Fourteen

"Girl, I ain't been cheating on you! I caught chlamydia from all the weed I smoke."

Believe it or not, that was what Dub told me in regards to how he'd caught chlamydia and transmitted it to me. What was even more preposterous was that a fragment of me credited his defense. I wanted to call the doctor and ask if it was at all possible, but I didn't want the doctor thinking I was the budhead myself. I didn't know if he had some type of professional obligation to send the police to search my house for drugs or something. I was young, dumb, and wanted to believe I hadn't withstood all that I had with Dub for naught.

My inner voice was on a rampage my outer voice would never have had the courage to go on. "How dare you? How dare you put me through all this hell and not even have the decency to be loyal? How dare you act jealous and deranged when, all the while, you are the one out there cheating?" Some things were starting to make sense now. Dub was so worried that I was out cheating on him because that was exactly what he was out doing.

"Baby, I swear to God I didn't cheat on you," Dub vowed. "You know weed does more than just get people high. My boy Duane, you know he can't even get a girl pregnant because he smoked so much weed."

I'd once watched one of those "Who is the baby daddy?" shows, and that was the same excuse one of the prospective fathers gave the host when asked why he didn't think he was the father of the child in question. I didn't know if this had been scientifically proven or not, but this was now my second time hearing this. Maybe there was something to marijuana use besides getting high.

At the end of the day, I was foolish enough to believe his personally written and choreographed stanzas and waltz. Dub had honestly convinced me that he'd caught chlamydia from smoking weed in excess. Back then I had had no idea what weed was truly capable of. Heck, now they said marijuana even cured some ailments. Bud had come a long way since Cheech and Chong's simple recreational use.

After that incident, the two cases of crabs I caught from Dub were easily explained by him. "I used the bathroom at such and such's house. I know that's where I got it." This was the second time I'd heard this excuse from Dub.

"So you mean to tell me the crab hopped all the way from the toilet seat up to your stuff?"

"No, my stomach had been hurting real bad, so I was sitting down on the toilet, doing number two." He thought for a moment and then continued. "Besides, how do you know that you ain't the one who caught it?" He turned the tables on me. I was not about to set myself up for that fall. I knew if I dared challenge him, by the end of the argument he'd be convinced, and have me convinced, too, that I had cheated on him and had caught the crabs and given them to him.

I was drained. It had been at least forty-five minutes that we had been standing there over a bottle of Nix, arguing back and forth. A bottle of Nix that, to add to the embarrassment of having crabs, Dub had to borrow money from his mother to purchase. Not only had he borrowed the money to get the bottle of medicated shampoo, but too embarrassed himself to go inside the pharmacy to get it, he had even had her go in and purchase it. Great!

My boyfriend's mother knew we were walking around with a Red Lobster entrée in our pants.

Any other chick would have been long gone, but not me. Nope. I'd invested all of myself in this life with Dub. You didn't start a marathon and then quit halfway through it. Through all the cramps and pain, you just kept running. Quitting now, right in the middle of the race, made that first half all in vain. I was in it not necessarily to win it, but to at least finish what I had started. I knew no other life, no other way. This was it. I could imagine there was something different, something better out there. But at the same time, what if there was something worse in store for me instead? Fear wouldn't allow me to take that chance, the same fear that kept me confined to my relationship with Dub.


It wasn't even nine o'clock in the morning yet as I stood at our back door, fumbling for the house key. I had spent the night over at Nana's house because we'd planned on getting up early that next morning, heading to Bob Evans, and then going to yard sales. Dub allowed me to spend time with Nana on a regular basis without ever getting upset, angry, or jealous. Of course, ever since my mom had clocked him with that sock full of change that one time, he hadn't cared too much for her, but Nana was still all right in his book.

When I got up that morning, I realized that I'd never taken my cash out of its hiding place and put it back in my purse. Even though Dub said he was out there hustling in the streets, he was still always asking me for money. One time I lied and told him that I didn't have any. I guess it must have been his bum intuition that told him otherwise, because when I went to use the bathroom, he raided my purse. I came down the stairs and saw him standing there, holding all my money in his hands. Not only did he knock me upside my head a few times, but he also took the twenty dollars he'd asked to borrow in the first place.

"That'll teach you to lie to me," he said before he threw the rest of the money on the coffee table and headed out the door.

I stood frozen for a few seconds before I moved. Trying to find the blessing in the matter, I told myself that at least he didn't take it all, and then I went to gather the money and put it back in my purse. No sooner had I moved a muscle than he made his way back into the house.

With the front door still open, he walked over to the table and grabbed the money before I could. "It's gonna cost you extra for lying to me." And with that, he walked back out the door, leaving me broke financially and in spirit.

Now I made it a point to keep my money in hiding, and if I wanted to go yard saling, I needed to retrieve it.

When I opened the door, there was a loud screech, caused by a chair planted in front of the door. "Who the heck left a chair here?" I said to myself, followed by a curse word or two. "Now, this fool know if I came through the door, this chair was going to screech and make all kinds of—"

My words came to a halting screech just like the chair had. It was at that moment that women's intuition kicked in. I swear, I couldn't make it up those steps fast enough. Something wasn't right, and when I reached the top of the steps, only to find my bedroom door closed, I knew something was very wrong. It only got worse when I went to open the door and the sucker was locked.

With hands on hips, I mumbled, "Ain't this 'bout a . . ." I immediately began banging on the door. "Dub, open the door. Why you got the door locked? Open the door." It took him about thirty seconds to finally unlock and open the door.

"Hey," he said, feigning sleepiness, stretching and giving out a morning yawn like he was Slick Rick.

I gave no greeting in return. I brushed past him and began to look around the room. Nothing seemed out of place, but still, my gut feeling said otherwise. "Why was the door locked?"

He looked at me like I was crazy before he replied, "I always lock the door. You want somebody just running up in the house? You know we live in the hood."

He was right. We did live in the hood. I could look out my window and see crackheads copping or a group of corner boys trailing behind a crackhead female as she went into a dope house so she could barter her body for a rock. One time it was the talk of the neighborhood when one of them got a crackhead to have sex with their pit bull and took pictures and showed them off. Thank God for that woman there weren't social networking sites back then.

"I'm not talking about the door to the house," I spat. "I'm talking about why the bedroom door was locked."

"Oh, uh, that." He swallowed. "I had the guys over, you know, and I didn't want any of them coming in the room or anything while I was asleep."

"Well, then, you shouldn't have people in the house who you don't trust. And on top of that, why would you leave anybody in our house and then go to sleep?"

"Yeah, you right." He sat on the bed and put his head down. "I was crazy high and drunk and wasn't thinking. My bad," he said, apologizing.

*Okay, that was way too easy, and he's being way too nice,* I thought. Dub never did anything nice and easy. He was like Ike with Tina Turner. He always did things rough.

After giving the room one last once-over, though, I didn't see anything suspicious. I felt like a cop who'd just interrogated a suspect who she knew had committed a crime, only she didn't have enough evidence to make an arrest.

Reluctantly, I decided to head back to Nana's, but not before I walked over to the nightstand and discretely pulled my cash stash from between the pages of the Bible that was located inside the drawer. I knew the Bible would be the last place Dub ever looked. Heck, I never even opened it myself unless it was to hide my money. I owned a Bible only because it was passed down to me from my great-great-grandmother on my grandfather's side, who, if my grandmother told it, was the devil herself. But even the devil knows God's word.

"Have fun with your grandmother," Dub said as I exited the room. "And tell her I said hi."

He was way too excited about me leaving. And did he say for me to have fun? He hated for me to have fun. I was supposed to suffer a miserable existence under his watch.

"Yeah . . . thanks," I said suspiciously. "I'll tell her."

As I headed down the steps, I observed every corner of the house. Yeah, the fellas had definitely been over. There were ash-filled ashtrays, fast-food containers and empty forty-ounce bottles here and there. Feeling a little less suspicious, I went on and headed back out to my car. As I turned on the engine and started to drive off, that was when I saw it.

There, in the bathroom window, was Dub, peeking out. As soon as he caught me looking at him, he began to wave cheerfully, as if he was simply seeing me off.

"Negro, puh-lease," I said as I threw that car in park, turned off the engine, and jumped back out.

When he saw me heading back into the house, he jumped from out of that window just as quickly as I had jumped out of that car.

I unlocked the door and made my way straight up to the top of the steps, where Dub was waiting for me.

"What did you forget?" he asked quickly.

Without saying a word, I bumped past him and headed straight toward our bedroom.

"What are you doing?" Dub asked as he stood in the doorway, watching me turn the room upside down.

I was checking the closet, behind doors, in corners of the room. I kicked at the pile of dirty laundry to see if what I was looking for was buried underneath that. I pulled the covers back off the bed. Nothing. I thought for a minute before kneeling down to check the one place I hadn't yet searched, underneath the bed.

"Dang it," I mumbled under my breath. What I was looking for wasn't under there, either. But just as I was about to get up, my eyes caught something. I reached my hand farther under the bed, and when I pulled my hand out, in it was a shoe. A shoe that I did not recognize. "What's this?" I stood up with the shoe in hand, giving Dub one of those Jennifer Hudson looks, my tongue rolling inside my mouth, my neck popping, and my hand on my hip.

"A shoe." He said it as if I was an idiot for not knowing what a shoe looked like.

"Don't play with me, Dub. I know it's a shoe, but whose shoe is it?"

Once again, he gave me that "You idiot" look and said, "Yours . . . of course."

"Boy, you don't think I know my own shoes?"

"Baby, that shoe been up under there since we moved here. It's been so long that you probably forgot you even had those shoes."

I paused for a minute. I swear on everything that this boy really had me thinking about whether or not this was my shoe. I knelt back down and found the other one.

Holding both shoes in my hands, I tried to recall when I'd purchased them, where I'd purchased them, and how much they'd cost. I mean, that was just how in control Dub was of my mind. I swear, if that man had told me that the sky was green and the grass was blue, I'd have thought it was true.

"These are not my shoes, Dub." He could hear the uncertainty in my voice.

"Are you sure those are not your shoes?" He said it the same way Satan had spoken to Eve right before she bit into the forbidden fruit.

I thought for a moment longer and examined the shoes. After finding SIZE NINE printed on the bottom, and knowing I wore a size ten, I adamantly and confidently said, "I'm sure." And on that note, I exited the bedroom in search of the owner.

My blood was boiling like water in a teapot someone had forgotten was on the stove because they were too caught up watching their favorite reality show. Oh, a reality show was about to go down all right—an unscripted one!

I immediately marched into the bathroom across the hall and pulled the shower curtain back. That music from the movie *Psycho* was playing in my head, because I had a feeling things were about to get crazy. To my surprise, there was nothing there but the window and Dub's forehead print from just moments ago, when he'd pressed his head against the windowpane, praying, I was sure, that I'd pull off and go on about my way.

"Baby, what are you l-looking for? There is n-nobody in this house," he asserted with a stutter. "Isn't Nana waiting on you? You better go."

I was filled with so much anger at this point that my fear had been superseded. I was like that pit bull that eventually turned on its master. The tables were turned, because now it was Dub who was acting all scared and nervous. He was more concerned with getting caught than getting mad, and my concern was, of course, catching him.

"What do you sound so nervous about, Dub? And since when do you care if I keep anybody else waiting as long as it's not you?" I said as calmly as I could, looking in the linen closet and then having the nerve to look in the cabinet up under the sink. Still nothing.

"It's just that, you know, my boys and I kicked it here, playing cards, last night. The house is a mess, and I just want you to go ahead and go so I can get it all nice and cleaned up for when you and Baby D come home."

I stopped in my tracks and threw my hands on my hips. "You, clean? Yeah, right!" In the five years that Dub and I had been together, he'd never cleaned. "Since when do you worry about a dirty house? You must be smoking weed again." I laughed, brushing by him.

The fact that Dub stayed on my heels let me know that there was something to find. Had he not been concerned, he would have just been chilling in that bedroom, minding his own business. Or maybe he would have been so pissed and offended that he would have been trying to fight me. But no, he was nervously dogging my every step.

After exiting the bathroom, I went into Baby D's room, heading straight for the closet. Bingo!

Tucked in between Baby D's OshKosh B'gosh outfits was the person who I knew was the owner of the mystery shoes. This chick, even though she'd surely heard me swing open that closet door, stood there shaking, with her hands covering her eyes. She should have been covering up her completely nude body, but instead she was covering her eyes. Even as I stood there, breathing down on her, she kept her eyes covered. It was like she was operating under the childish theory "Since I can't see you, maybe you can't see me, either." She might have looked like a fool, but I was the one who had been played for one.

"Who's this, Dub?" I asked, staring him down, waiting for my answer.

"That was some girl so-and-so had over. I didn't even know she was still here," he replied, sucking his teeth.

I couldn't even recall the name he'd said. All I knew was that if that was so-and-so's girl, then she would have been with so-and-so instead of in my son's closet.

"Negro, please," I said, mugging Dub in the forehead. After realizing what I'd just done, that I'd just put my hands on him, I braced myself for the worst. What had I been thinking, putting my hands on him? Now I knew I was going to get it for sure. But I was wrong. All Dub did was put his head down like a sad puppy dog.

I'd never seen him like this, so weak looking and vulnerable. I took advantage of it and mugged him again. Then I slapped him. I knew God's word said to be angry but sin not, but I couldn't help it. For years he'd been kicking my butt, and now it was payback time. I slapped him yet again. On the other cheek. After all, the Bible said to turn the other cheek, so that was what I did. I turned and slapped Dub's other cheek.

"In my bed?" I said to Dub, shaking my head. "You did her in our bed?" Actually, it was my bed. My bed and my government-subsidized duplex.

I looked at the girl, who was standing there, buck naked, still covering her eyes. I could see her, though . . . very much so. I could see how tall she was. How much lighter her skin was than mine. How much skinnier she was than me. Way skinnier.

But it was my own fault I was fat. After having Baby D, I had lost some of my weight. I hadn't gotten back down to the size I was before I gave birth, but I hadn't been out of control. But lately I had noticed that I had been heading out of control. The weird part about it, though, was that I was heading toward out of control with my weight on purpose. If I was big, fat, and sloppy, Dub wouldn't want me anymore, so he'd go away and find someone much more attractive. If he had to move my stomach out of the way just to have sex with me, then he wouldn't want sex from me anymore. So I ate and I ate and I ate and I became obsessed with food. The fat was there, but the bad thing about it, though, was so was Dub. My plan had backfired.

No matter what I did, Dub was a nightmare that I just couldn't wake up from. I couldn't even recall any good times or romantic times we'd shared. I guess if there were any, they all got obliterated by the bad stuff.

I'd had several situations arise that seemed like sure outs out of the relationship, but they never were. I'd always been too afraid to just pick up and leave on my own. Dub was the type of person who wouldn't rest until he had hunted me down and either dragged me back to my prison of a relationship or killed me. That was truly what I believed. I also believed that he'd take out anybody who tried to get in his way. I wouldn't have been able to live with myself if someone else got hurt in the process. On another note, I knew he was unstable, but was he so unstable that he'd be willing to hurt Baby D just to hurt me?

I couldn't take any chances by just up and walking away. But now, with proof positive, thanks to the naked girl playing peekaboo in the closet and her worn loafers in my hands, this had to be my sure out. What more did I have to go through? Women left men who cheated on them, right? This was a normal reaction, so Dub would have to let me leave. It was weird how I hadn't come to the same conclusion about women who got beaten. They should leave too, right?

I noticed the girl was still trembling. I wanted to be mad at her. I wanted to fight her, beat her up right there in front of Dub to show him that I meant business. But his sick, twisted mind would have taken it all the wrong way. I could hear him now. *You must really love me and still want me if you're willing to fight for me.* I wasn't about to give that fool the pleasure.

Instead, I removed the girl's hands from her eyes. I recognized her as a girl from high school. She was probably about three or four years younger than I was, her perky nipples, which had been looking at me instead of her eyes, confirming her youth.

"Do these belong to you?" I said to the girl, holding up the shoes.

She gave me a fearful nod.

Now I knew how the prince in *Cinderella* felt when he found the girl whose foot fit into the glass slipper. Victory! When God said we were a victorious people, I was sure this wasn't exactly what He meant, but at the time, it was good enough for me.

Finally, I had proof. I had found those shoes in my room, under my bed. That meant she'd been in my room. There was no way Dub could get out of this one, which meant now I could get out of this relationship. For good! Forever! What woman stayed with a man who slept with another woman in her own bed? What man expected a woman to stay with him after he slept with another woman in her bed *and* after she found the woman still in the house . . . still naked, no less? Dub couldn't expect me to stay with him now. He just couldn't.

What might have felt like the worst day of any other woman's life felt like the best day of mine. God just kept opening those doors for me, just waitin' for me to get the courage to finally walk out of my situation. Well, baby, I'd gone to visit the Wiz for my courage that day. 'Cause I was out!

"Here, honey. Take your shoes." I handed the girl the shoes. "Now, get yourself dressed and get out of my house."

At first she didn't move. Finally, having uncovered her eyes, she just stood there in shock, like maybe this was a trick. She acted like maybe as soon as she went to walk away, I was going to jump on her.

"Go on," I told the girl. "Get dressed and go. I ain't gon' do nothing to you. It ain't you I'm mad at." I cut Dub with my eyes.

Figuring she'd already been told twice, the girl didn't say a word. She quickly squeezed by Dub and me and did what she was told.

I then turned to Dub. "Let me guess. You gon' blame a naked girl being in my closet on weed too," I said sarcastically, realizing I'd been a complete fool by not thinking that Dub had caught a sexually transmitted disease and had passed it on to me because he had been having sex with someone else! It might not have crossed my mind at the time, but I just thanked God that the fool hadn't given me HIV. That was just another way God had been looking out for me while I remained blind, with my own hands covering my eyes.

"I'm going yard saling with my grandmother. By the time I get back, I want you out of here. Pack everything you own. If you are here when I get back . . . If you thought having to tell your mother you had crabs and was too broke to even buy the antidote was embarrassing, wait until I broadcast this mess."

As I walked away, Dub didn't even try to stop me. He had no pleas, no logical explanations this time. For once, he felt defeated. For once, I had the victory.

Hallelujah!

# Stone Number Fifteen

"Can you believe he had the nerve to cheat on me in my own bed?" I said to Synthia.

Yep, it had been official for only one day that Dub and I were breaking up, but I felt so free, free enough to hang out with my best friend from high school. There was no Dub around to frown on her and my hanging out together. No Dub to accuse the guys who tried to holler at her of trying to holler at me too. No more getting beat up for having a beautiful best friend.

"How do you feel about that?" Synthia asked with a serious tone as we sat in BW-3, eating chicken wings. "Doesn't it hurt just a little bit?"

That question hit me out of nowhere. For so long I'd been trying to find a way out, a safe way out, of my relationship with Dub, and I felt that this was it. I had never stopped to truly dissect the truth of the matter, which was that my boyfriend, my baby's daddy, had cheated on me!

I was upset, but not at the fact that he'd been sharing himself with another woman. I was upset at the fact that he was getting sex from willing and able bodies somewhere else and at the same time taking it from me. Why in the heck did he take it from me?

"I'm not hurt. I'm pissed!" I admitted to Synthia. "I mean, you know how Dub is, how he acts."

"Now that I think about it, you probably ain't hurtin' none," Synthia said before biting into a buffalo chip. "You're probably happy as a lark to break free from that fool. I don't even know how you manage life with him in the first place. You're working, taking care of Baby D, going to college, maintaining your own place, car and all that." She shook her head. "Then throw a jealous, overbearing, crazy baby daddy on top of that . . ." Synthia laughed, and I added a little chuckle of my own. "But seriously . . ." Synthia took a moment to swallow her food. "You think he'll really let you go?"

"It's not about *him* letting *me* go," I said confidently. "He's the one who packed all his stuff in plastic trash bags and went and moved in with his mama. So how I look at it is, he's the one who left. And yes, I can let him go." I bit into a buffalo chip of my own, giving Synthia a smug look. She could have all the doubts she wanted, but I had made up my mind that it was a wrap with Dub and me.

A week later, at around one o'clock in the morning, the phone woke me out of my sleep.

"Hello," I answered, clearing my throat.

"Helen, this is Ms. Daniels."

Although over the phone I couldn't see the somber expression that probably plagued Dub's mother's face, I could tell by the tone of her voice that something was very wrong. It felt like déjà vu.

"Dub's been shot," were the next words to come out of Ms. Daniels' mouth. Her voice cracked, and she began to sniffle. "He's at Doctors Hospital North, on Dennison."

I just sat on the phone, quiet. I didn't know what I was supposed to say. Inside I was saying, *So what? Sounds like that's your problem or the problem of the chick he's sleeping with. Not mine.* But I knew those words would be hurtful to a woman whose son had just been shot.

"How's he doing?" That seemed more like the proper thing to say, even though I didn't give a darn.

"I don't know yet, but it's not looking good."

"Well, okay, thanks for calling." What else was I sup-posed to say? Obviously, Ms. Daniels thought there was plenty more to say, as she waited in silence, anticipating something more than just that coming from me.

Although Dub had been living with her for the past week, ever since I'd put him out, I was almost certain he hadn't told her the full truth about what had gone down between us. She probably assumed we'd gotten into a fight and I had finally put him out or something. My suspicions were confirmed when she filled the silence on the line with her words.

"I don't know what exactly is going on between you two, but you might want to get up here. It's not looking good."

I sighed. This was definitely déjà vu again. I sat up in bed, contemplating what my next move should be. Should I go to the hospital? If I did, Dub would think I cared, when in all actuality I didn't. If I didn't go, and the police hadn't caught the shooter, they might say that my actions appeared suspicious. Then maybe they'd think I had something to do with it. Maybe they'd think I hired somebody to kill him the same way he'd killed my spirit. Just my luck, they'd label me the woman scorned who tried to kill her cheating baby daddy.

Think it sounds crazy, huh? Well, I'd watched enough crime shows to know that it could happen. That was the last thing I needed in my life, especially since I was in col-lege, studying to be a paralegal. Something like that could hurt the career that I hadn't even started yet. Decisions, decisions.

"Look, Ms. Daniels, it's late. Baby D is sleep—"

"Oh, God! Baby D!" She broke down crying. "I can't imagine him having to live without his daddy."

I could.

As cold-blooded as it might sound, I honestly didn't care that Dub was lying up in the hospital, perhaps fighting for his life. Now he knew what it felt like to feel as though he was on the verge of death. No quality of life whatsoever. If I dug even a little deeper, I'd find a part of me that hoped he lost the fight. There had been so many times that I'd wished I had just let Dub die that day he hung himself. That would have eliminated so many days and nights of pure mental and physical torture. Now a piece of me was hoping that I got the chance yet again to let him die. I knew Dub and I had broken up, but his death would engrave my freedom in stone. I knew it sounded selfish, but the truth shamed the devil. And that was the truth.

I guess it was true when they said that good prevails over evil, because the good in me got off the phone with Ms. Daniels, packed up Baby D, and went to see about Dub. I didn't think I would be able to live with myself if Dub died and I hadn't taken his son up there. My good deed would not go unpunished.

"The surgery went fine," I heard the doctor saying to Ms. Daniels as I walked toward them down the hallway. He went on to explain to her the exact procedure that had been performed on Dub. I couldn't understand all the terminology. All I knew was that once we were finally able to go into the hospital room to see Dub, all his intestines were hanging in a plastic bag outside of his body.

"What in the world?" I said, covering my mouth with one hand while holding Baby D's hand with the other. Dub was in the ICU, where children weren't allowed, but the doctor had said I could go in with Baby D for a couple of minutes. That was fine with me, as it was an excuse to get out of a place where I didn't even want to be in the first place.

"It's called a colostomy," Ms. Daniels said, clarifying the matter. "One of the bullets hit his intestines or something like that. All I know is that the doctor said he has to be like this for several months, until he heals completely."

"One of the bullets?" I questioned.

"Yeah. He got shot twice . . . in the back."

"Do the police know what happened? Who did it? Why?" All of a sudden, I did care to know the answers to these questions. I'd heard of people getting shot before. One day I even listened at my bedroom window while an argument ensued a couple houses down. Moments into the argument I heard a gunshot, I heard the man yelping, and then I heard the ambulance come take him away. But now, for the first time ever, I was seeing a real live gunshot victim, and I wanted to know what type of animal could so easily do this to another animal . . . I mean person.

"They don't know too much of anything yet, since they haven't been able to talk to Dub. He went right into surgery." A tear fell from her eye. "I just thank God he's alive."

"Yeah, thank God." I hoped she couldn't sense my sarcasm. "Where's Kelice?" I looked around, as if Dub's sister was perhaps hiding under the bed or something.

"At home." And she left it at that.

*At home?* I thought. Heck, his own sister didn't care whether or not he was dead or alive. I should have kept my tail at home. They certainly wouldn't have been able to talk smack about my presence or lack thereof.

The doctor walked into the room, followed by what looked like the Verizon Wireless network team. "We need to draw blood and run a couple tests. I'm going to have to ask you all to step out of the room," the doctor announced.

"I'm his mother, and this is his wife," Ms. Daniels said as something of a protest.

"That's fine," the doctor said, "but we'll still need you to step outside." He immediately turned his attention away from Ms. Daniels to let her know that the conversation was over.

I headed out of the room first, still cringing from the fact that Ms. Daniels had just referred to me as Dub's wife.

She must have seen the perplexed look on my face, because she asked, "Are you okay?"

I sat down on a chair in the hall, and she sat next to me. Baby D jumped from tiled square to tiled square.

"Yeah, I'm fine," I began. "But you know that Dub and I broke up, broke up." I said it in a tone that let her know that this breakup was for real. This was not one of those "we argue, we fight, he goes out, and he comes back in the middle of the night" breakups. No, this was a "for real, for real, it's over" breakup. I mean, why did she think he'd shown up at her doorstep with two Hefty trash bags full of his clothes? "He was cheating on me."

Since Dub had failed to tell her, I needed to. She needed to know that her son had hurt me in more ways than one.

"Dub wouldn't cheat on you. In all these years, he ain't never brought another girl around me. He ain't never even spoke of another girl. He knows I wouldn't have that. I love you like a daughter, so you know I'd tell you if he did."

*Yeah, right.* Mother's did not rat out their sons. No way, no how. It was just an unspoken rule between mothers and sons.

"I caught him, Ms. Daniels," I blurted. "I caught the girl naked in my bed," I said, exaggerating. Well, she was naked, and they had been in my bed. Close enough to the truth.

She threw her arms around me and let the floodgates open. "Oh, Helen," she cried. Whether she was taking my side or just being sympathetic, I needed that hug. I was going through a lot in life, and I honestly couldn't recall the last time someone had just put their arms around me. It felt good.

Baby D stopped jumping to look at his grandma wail on his mother's shoulders.

I just sat there, not really knowing what to do. She appeared to be more hurt about Dub cheating on me than I had been. I hesitantly patted her back until she finally pulled herself away from me.

In my heart I felt she must have known that it was really over between Dub and me, and that even though she might have loved me like a daughter, I never would be her daughter in any shape or form.

She sniffled and then wiped her eyes with her arm before saying, "I'm so glad Dub has you as a girlfriend."

Now even more confused than ever, I couldn't help but wonder what part of "Dub and I aren't together" she had missed.

"Ms. Daniels—," I began, but she cut me off.

"When you heard that your baby was shot, you put all that behind you and came to see about your man. Now, that's real love. Thank God for you. I know your and Dub's relationship isn't always the best, but I know deep down inside you love him and don't want to see him hurt, right?"

I was in between a rock and a hard place and a cement slab and a brick wall and you name it. I was stiff, but not so stiff that my head didn't move up and down to tell that silent lie. I was afraid that if I didn't tell Ms. Daniels what she wanted to hear, she would break into tears again.

"And it's very evident that Dub loves you too." She shook her head, dumbfounded. "I had no idea you two had even broken up. He acted like he was bringing all them clothes over to wash. Said something was wrong with y'all's washer. I guess he knew it wouldn't be long before y'all got back together. It's a shame it had to take something like this for you to take him back, but all that matters is that the two of you are back together again."

I was confused beyond measure by Ms. Daniels. One minute I thought she understood that her son had cheated on me and it was over. The next minute she was saying how she was happy that I'd put all of that aside after he was shot. Where was she getting all of this? Surely not from me, because I wasn't saying a thing. . . . Perhaps I should have.

Ms. Daniels pulled me into a hug once again. But I couldn't take it anymore. I was not at the hospital as Dub's girlfriend. I was there as the mother of his child, seeing about my child's father and nothing more. I needed to convey this to Ms. Daniels before things went any further.

"He's semiconscious now," the doctor called from Dub's room as he and the team exited. "You can see him, but only for a minute." He looked down at Baby D. "Only a minute, please," he repeated sternly.

"Thank you, Doctor." Ms. Daniels grabbed my hand and dang near dragged me into Dub's hospital room, with Baby D on our heels.

"Look who's here." Ms. Daniels pointed.

Thinking she was pointing at Baby D, I looked and realized that she was pointing dead at me.

"Helen's here. I called her up and told her what had happened, and she came running to see about her man. All that mess that went on between you two before is water under the bridge. She's back, and now you have to get strong so you can do right by her."

Dub couldn't really talk, so he just looked at me with teary eyes. His eyes were thanking me so much for being there. His eyes were thanking me so much for taking him back in his time of need. For being there by his side, for being his girlfriend.

I gave a half smile. How could I do it now? How could I leave him now? Dub and his mother sat there as if it was me, not God or the doctors, but me who had his fate in my hands. How could I walk away now? Walking away from my son's father right now would make me the cold-blooded monster. Looked like the door God had once again opened for me just got slammed in my face before I could even walk through it.

# Stone Number Sixteen

Somehow, one and a half weeks after being shot, Dub was released from the hospital and allowed to go home under my care. Not under his mother's care. But under my care. After all, I was his girlfriend. He was my man. I'd put everything behind us and came running to him the night he got shot, or at least that was how it all went down if I let Ms. Daniels tell it.

Speaking of Dub getting shot, to this day I didn't know the real reason why Dub was shot. I did know the guy who did it was arrested and put in jail. At first I assumed Dub was out there doing his little hustle thing and someone probably tried to rob him. He told his mom and me, though, that he was just walking down the street. He claimed the shooter shot him when he refused to give him the leather Troop jacket he was trying to rob him of.

When the cops came to Dub's hospital room to interview him, he made me and Ms. Daniels leave, so we never really got to hear exactly what he told the police. I had a strong feeling that whatever it was he'd told the police was a far cry from the song and dance he had serenaded his mother and me with. All I knew was that wearing his guts outside of his body and having a near-death experience didn't change Dub one bit. He was still as mean and as cruel as ever.

Because he couldn't physically hurt me the way he wanted to, Dub made sure he assassinated me with his put-downs and insults. There were so many times when

I just visualized snatching that colostomy bag right off of him and watching him die a slow, agonizing death. I could get him right where I wanted him if I was just that cruel. If only I had the same caliber of cruelty as the girl in *Diary of a Mad Black Woman*. But I didn't. Any dignity I had and any chance I had at being a strong black woman had been crushed by Dub. And there was something else that having the colostomy bag hanging from him didn't change about Dub . . . his sex drive.

"Dub, I really don't want to. What if I hurt you?" I said squeamishly as I lay next to him in bed.

"I ain't in the mood to play with you, girl," Dub said firmly as he slowly removed his pajamas.

I could hear the contents of the bag squishing. I gagged just thinking about it. I mean, it was disgusting. Every time he had a bowel movement, it would just begin to fill the bag up. That was all I could think about as he tugged on me, and his request soon became an order.

*At least someone even wants to have sex with me,* I told myself as I pleased Dub sexually. My mind traveled back to that insecure, ugly little black girl whose own father didn't want her. The little girl who thought no one would ever want her. Well, someone wanted her now. I simply closed my eyes and pretended that it wasn't Dub.

# Stone Number Seventeen

"Quit being a crybaby!" I scolded Baby D, who wasn't that much of a baby anymore. He was now four years old and was in preschool.

"Oh, don't fuss at the baby," Nana said as she walked over to Baby D and hugged him.

"You wouldn't let us cry and whine when we were little," my mother reminded Nana as she sat next to me on Nana's flowery patterned couch.

Three generations of women were in Nana's living room as we prepared to go yard saling. Lynn didn't come around much these days. She worked and went on trips with her girlfriends. Baby D was having a fit that I was trying to make him go to the bathroom before we left after he'd made several declarations that he didn't have to go.

"I did the best I knew how with what I knew then," Nana told my mother with a hint of regret in her tone. "If I could go back and do things differently, I would."

I could see the sadness Nana was trying to hide behind her eyes. And I knew why too. I remembered growing up in Nana's house while she was a single mother, trying to raise six kids. Even though Nana was as sweet as cotton candy now, back in those days, she was a mean mama jama.

It was my aunt Angel, the baby girl, who had always seemed to get the brunt of Nana's wrath. I remember one time Nana was beating Aunt Angel so bad with a broom that she cracked the broom right in half over Aunt Angel's back. Then there was that time Nana beat Aunt Angel with a Pepsi bottle, back when Pepsi came in tall, sixteen-ounce glass bottles. Aunt Angel was getting beat so bad, she couldn't catch her breath in between licks. It got to the point where her face turned beet red as she gasped for air. In between her gasping, I remember her yelling, "I can't breathe. Please stop!" But Nana kept on swinging.

And now here Nana was, all compassionate to Baby D, who wasn't getting anything more than a fussing out.

"Well, ain't nothing wrong with that boy," I told Nana. "He cries over every little thing. All he does is cry."

Out of nowhere Baby D stopped his fake sniffling and said, "You cry too. You cry when Daddy slaps you." He said it with such malice. As little as he was, he knew his words would embarrass me. He knew he was telling a secret. My secret. I'd sworn to my mother that Dub treated me well, that Dub hadn't put his hands on me again. And now Baby D had gone and opened his mouth. I couldn't describe the anger that rose up in me. I wanted to go over and yank Baby D up, take him in the bathroom, and beat him down good for running his mouth.

It was a comment that I was certain did not go unnoticed. It was a comment that I knew my mother and grandmother would want me to respond to. How was I going to explain myself now?

There was literally five seconds of dead silence in the room after Baby D's comment. Then, all of a sudden, his words became the large pink elephant in the room that everyone walked around and walked right by on their way out the door to go yard saling.

Neither my mother nor Nana ever questioned me about what Baby D had said. Maybe they wanted to spare me the embarrassment and humiliation that they could see was covering my face. Maybe they just didn't want to discuss it in front of Baby D. Whatever their reasons, neither chose to speak about Baby D's comment. I was almost certain, though, that once they got Baby D alone, they would pick his little four-year-old brain. Perhaps they did, but I never knew about it. But what I did know was that Baby D would pay for the humiliation he'd just forced me to endure.

"Bastard!" I yelled at him. "Stupid idiot!"

We couldn't have gotten back home from those yard sales fast enough. As soon as we did, I lit into Baby D. Aside from the few and far between spankings Baby D might have gotten through his diapers, I'd never hit him. But today all the anger inside of me, all the rage, all the hurt and pain—no matter who had been the original source of it—just released itself. Unfortunately, Baby D was the only one around to receive it. The only person around who I could lash out at and know that they couldn't do anything to hurt me back.

When my hand slapped Baby D right across his little brown face, he didn't know what had hit him. He looked at me with such shock, sort of the same way I had looked at Dub the first time he hit me. I hit him again, this time with a closed fist. A cry came out of Baby D's mouth like I'd never heard before. It was this piercing cry from deep within. I realized that he was crying out in excruciating pain. It wasn't from the pain that I had inflicted on his flesh. It was a pain I had inflicted on his soul. A pain that, as his mother, I knew I could never assuage. Healing a soul was something only God could do.

So as it turned out, I'd found a new source to direct my hurt and anger at. The only person around that I could be angry at and have control over. Baby D, the product of the monster. The product of the monster that I felt I had created. The product of the monster who had now created the monster in me.

Poor Baby D. He had had four and a half years with only one monster for a parent, but now he had two. He'd need God's hand on him to help him survive all the demons he was locked up with in that duplex.

# Stone Number Eighteen

Dub, Baby D, and I were sitting in the living room. Dub and Baby D were watching television, while I was reading an assigned book from one of my college courses. Dub had gotten the colostomy bag removed by this time and was back to his mean, horrible self again.

There was a knock on our back door that sounded like the po-po.

"Dang, who is knocking on the door all crazy?" Dub said as he got up and went to answer the door.

"What's up, man?" Dub greeted the visitor, his boy Boyd, all cool, calm, and collected. He even held his hand out to give Boyd some dap. Boyd dapped him, all right. Right upside his head.

Dub turned around and said to me with a look of embarrassment on his face, "Helen, let me holler at Boyd for a minute." His expression couldn't have matched the look of shock on my face.

Dub hadn't hit Boyd back. All those years he'd been beating my tail, I thought this man was a true fighter. But he hadn't even attempted to return the blow.

I took Baby D up to my bedroom, where I stood in the doorway and listened intently to the brewing explosion. Baby D was almost five years out of the womb and was already listening to drama go down. He wasn't the least bit fazed by the commotion going on in our downstairs living room as he sat in front of the television. After all, he'd witnessed fights firsthand. Hearing one had no effect on him.

"Where's my money?" It was Boyd's voice. Then there was a thump.

"Man, I . . . I . . . I . . ." Dub stuttered. Then there was a smack. "Come on, man. I got you."

Dub was whining like a baby. I couldn't believe it. His pleas were falling on deaf ears, though. The next thing I heard was what sounded like a chair being thrown. I heard tussling and Dub pleading, which meant he was getting the bad end of the fight.

"Man, come on! Please stop!"

*Crack.*

"Boyd, man, please!"

*Pow!*

There was so much commotion going on down there, a part of me honestly thought that if somebody didn't get Boyd off of Dub, he would kill him. I was not going to be that somebody. Needless to say, I was not that down chick willing to ride or die for her man . . . not for Dub, anyway. Not the man who ran a close second to Ike Turner. I didn't care if he was weaker than another man; he was still stronger than me.

I closed the door and went and sat down next to Baby D, and we enjoyed the show on the television. The fight going on beneath us started to get louder and louder, so loud that I had to turn up the television.

As I sat there next to my son, a smile stretched across my face that was a mile wide. Vengeance was God's. I'd never clobbered Dub upside his head, no matter how many times I'd thought about it. God had sent someone else to do it for me. Maybe God wasn't so bad, after all.


Lately, Dub hadn't been around much. Once he'd gotten that colostomy bag removed, he'd been back on the streets. He was what I called a tennis shoe hustler.

He made just enough money every night to buy a pair of shoes. For all the hours he stayed on the streets, he still never seemed to be able to pay a bill. At first I'd argued with him about spending all that time in the streets but never having money to contribute toward our home. Heck, even when he got shot, I had to buy all those stupid colostomy bags and stuff to cover his guts up. Talk about not having a pot to piss in. That tired negro couldn't even afford a plastic bag, let alone a pot. One time he ran out of bags and I didn't get paid until the next day, so he had to wear a plastic grocery bag. Disgusting. It was just as bad as a baby running out of diapers and having to wear a paper towel instead.

My arguing and complaining about Dub's absence from the home and meager contributions to the home quickly ceased once I realized that as long as he was out there on the streets, then he wasn't at home, making my life hell on earth. Eventually, Dub got to the point where he wouldn't even come home for a couple of days at a time. I thought he was probably out there living a double life with some other girl. But soon enough Konnie, who had always managed to have her ear to the street, would let me know the new love of Dub's life.

"Crack," Konnie said through the phone receiver. "Boyd told me that's why he had to go upside Dub's head a couple days ago, 'cause Dub was spending all the money on crack for his own personal use, instead of giving my man his share."

"What?" I'd heard her, but had I really heard her correctly? Was she sitting on my phone, trying to tell me that Dub was using crack?

"Dub spent all the money. Boyd is riding on E," Konnie spat. I could tell Konnie had an attitude about it. To her, Dub not only played her dude, but at the same time took food from the mouth of the baby Konnie and Boyd had just had.

I could understand her bitterness, if that was in fact the truth. I mean, yeah, I could see Dub not giving Boyd what was owed to him, but what I couldn't see was him spending the money to buy crack for himself.

"Yep. He supposed to be taking their cut to re-up," Konnie explained, as if she was the middle man, "but Dub be spending it right back on drugs for himself . . . little by little. Or he just uses the product he's supposed to be out there selling."

Dub on crack. My mind couldn't consume that. Dub was a lot of things, but a crackhead? It was the early nineties, and I personally didn't know a whole lot about the drug that was dominating the drug game at the time, but I knew it was the worst and most addictive drug of them all.

"That's just talk," I told Konnie.

"Girl, what I'm doing is talking. What Dub is doing is smoking crack!" Konnie continued her mission of being the bearer of bad news. I couldn't help but hear a hint of delight in her voice, though. "He called himself testing out his product one day. Now he's hooked."

I was silent, still trying to pick up everything Konnie was putting down.

With a newfound tone of sympathy, Konnie said, "Girl, I'm not telling you in order to try to start no mess. I'm only telling you so that you can start watching your stuff. Go to the hardware store and buy you some chains and locks or something. Start chaining your stuff down. 'Cause I hear it only gets worse."

Konnie was right. Things only did get worse. It started with a so-called break-in at our place, during which all my jewelry was stolen. I had collected some sterling silver jewelry over the years and kept it in a special velvet box I'd picked up at a yard sale. The thieves took only the contents of that box and a fancy corvette-shaped VHS tape rewinder that I'd purchased brand-new at a yard sale. This was easy stuff, a couple days of high. But then other stuff started to come up missing, and Dub, who'd recently been staying out on the streets, now seemed to be hiding from the streets. He'd stay cooped up in our place, acting weird.

We'd fight over money, bill money. Not about him not giving me any, but about him forcing me to give him the bill money.

"The gas bill is already overdue," I said to Dub as he ransacked our bedroom, looking for my hidden purse. "If I give you the money, they are going to shut it off. Then what are we going to do?"

"Boil water to take baths," Dub spat back. He literally spat out those words, as spittle flew about my face.

There was this desperate look of rage in his eyes. Now, I'd seen Dub angry before, but this was different. It was intense life-or-death desperation.

"Dub, no. I can't," I said, shaking my head, trying to brace myself as I noticed him ball his fist.

"Mom, I want to color this," I heard Baby D say as he entered our bedroom. He was holding a work sheet he'd gotten from preschool and a box of crayons.

"Baby D, get out of here!" Dub said, keeping his eyes on me.

"But I got some coloring homework. I have to stay in the lines," Baby D said.

"Baby D, go!" Dub pointed to the door. "Mommy and Daddy are talking."

"I just need help staying in the lines." Baby D was being as relentless with his homework inquiry as Dub was being with his money inquiry.

Baby D walked up on Dub and tugged his shirt. "Daddy, please. I just want—"

The next thing I saw was Dub's open hand slamming against Baby D's face and then blood pouring out of Baby D's nose. Baby D was in shock, and so was I. I moved to go comfort him, but Dub blocked me, giving me a threatening look, letting me know that I needed to stay there and finish our business at hand.

Baby D ran out of the room, crying. It had happened again; someone whom Baby D loved and trusted, someone who was supposed to take care of him and protect him had hurt him. Now everybody in the house was hurting, and like the saying went, hurt people hurt people. *Let the pain begin.* . . .

# Stone Number Nineteen

"What do you mean, we gotta move out?" Dub spat.

"They found out you were staying here, so we have to move out," I explained to Dub. It said in the lease that, as with any type of subsidized living, if someone other than the persons on the lease was found to be residing in the dwelling, then it was grounds for eviction.

"Where am I supposed to go?" Dub asked, as if I were his keeper.

"Where are *you* supposed to go? The first thing you should have asked is where I and your son are supposed to go." I got even more sarcastic. I mean, after all, he was a twenty-one year-old man. By now he should be able to take care of himself. "But since you asked, Nana said that Baby D and I can stay with her until we figure something out. You're just gonna have to stay with your mom."

"In that little ole place?" he spat.

Dub's mom no longer lived in the house she lived in when I first met him. I had thought they owned the house, and all the while they'd been renting it. For some reason, this last go-round, the landlord didn't renew the lease. I think it was because of all the fighting and arguing that had taken place there. Not just between Dub and me, but between his mother and her boyfriend of the last year, who was only three years older than Dub. Dub's sister and her boyfriend had had their share of fights there as well. With so many complaints from the neighbors, not to mention all the holes in the walls, thanks to fists and bodies being slammed into them, the landlord had cut his losses.

By then, of course, his sister had moved out and into her own place a couple houses down from us. Ms. Daniels had ended up renting a small two-bedroom apartment in the hood. As luck would have it, that second bedroom was available.

One month later, we were all packed up and moved out. Baby D and I were living with Nana, and Dub was living with his mother. I'd finally figured a way out, and this time I knew it would work. I'd lied about the entire eviction thing. My landlord hadn't really put us out. Ever since Dub had bloodied Baby D's nose, I'd been determined to get away from him.

One night I was just lying in bed and the idea to fake an eviction in order to move away from Dub just popped into my head. Or perhaps it was what Oprah Winfrey referred to as a God whisper, which saved, sanctified, and baptized folks would refer to as the Holy Spirit. Either way, the idea to finally get away from Dub came to mind: *Lie and tell him that you've been evicted.*

I wasted no time executing it, either. If I didn't get away from Dub, it would only be a matter of time before I killed myself just to be away from him. I'd tried to kill myself twice before. The first time was prior to finding out Dub was a crackhead.

The night before I tried to kill myself, I made creamed corn for dinner. We ate in our bedroom and put our remains on the round night table next to the bed. After refusing to have sex with Dub so many times, I found myself not only beaten up but also wearing the leftover creamed corn on my head, not to mention the grape Kool-Aid and melted ice that had sat on the night table next to the bed.

Dub had found a new way to humiliate me. And even after all of that, he still managed to take what I wouldn't give him. Afterward, I stood in the shower, crying, as the water soaked my body and my hair. It had to be the most humiliating episode I'd ever endured at the hands of Dub. I needed it to be the last. The next day I took at least twenty sleeping pills. At that moment, I didn't even think about trying to stay around to protect Baby D. He was better off without me. I just wanted to be dead.

When I woke up five hours later, puking my guts out, I cursed God.

"Why? Why are you doing this to me? Isn't it bad enough that you let me be born? And now you won't let me just die already?"

It was a year after that first attempt when I hung myself from the downstairs living-room closet bar. My bare feet were just barely able to touch the floor. I remembered kicking fiercely until the coward in me couldn't take the thought of death anymore and I stood to my feet. I remembered looking down at the blood on the beige carpet beneath me, wondering where it had come from. Then I looked down at my feet and noticed the raw, bleeding wounds where my skin had been rug burned from all the kicking.

Baby D had been with Ms. Daniels during both failed attempts. Those two suicide attempts had failed, but the third time I swore to God I'd get it right if He didn't help me. Lucky Him, my lie to Dub about getting evicted worked, or else I'd be dead right now.

With all that aside now, my vendetta against God and my past suicide attempts, everything had worked out as planned. I now enjoyed peaceful nights, a peaceful sleep, and energetic mornings without the likes of Dub around. But sometimes fear would creep up on me. I worried he would somehow do some type of investigation and find out the truth.

"For all I know you're probably lying to me," Dub had once growled at me through his teeth. "There probably never was an eviction in the first place. This was probably just a way for you to get away from me."

*You think?* I thought to myself, but I never dared allow the words to escape my lips. Still, every now and again I'd tremble inside just thinking about the consequences I'd face if Dub ever did find out the truth. I'd even lied to Nana, telling her we'd been evicted, in order to get her to let Baby D and me come stay there. The only reason I fed the lie to Nana, as well, was that I never wanted her to be around Dub and have the truth accidentally slip out.

"*Zephyr* is not a word!" I declared to Nana, who was sitting across from me at the Scrabble board. We played Scrabble almost every night. Living with Nana was a breath of fresh air. I'd almost forgotten all about the suffering I'd endured for almost five years.

Baby D was a lot happier now too. He had finished his last year of preschool and was ready to go into kindergarten. We'd been staying with Nana for about four months, and the only time we had to see Dub was when he picked me up and dropped me off at work and school.

"I thought you had your own car," one of the temps at my job said one day, when she saw me waiting in the parking lot for Dub, who was already about twenty minutes late.

"I do," was all I said to her, not that it was any of her business, anyway.

Dub had always driven my car more than I did. Even before I moved in with Nana, he had often taken me back and forth to work and school. While I was trying to make money to support us, he was off lollygagging all day. Then he'd come pick me up, and sometimes he'd keep the car afterward too. I didn't mind. It kept the peace between us. If he didn't have transportation to rip and run the streets, then I knew he'd be up under me, bothering me, trying to see what I was doing. I'd be playing Scrabble with him instead of Nana. I was willing to be stuck at home all day and night if it meant Dub was out of my hair. Besides, playing Scrabble with Nana all night wasn't bad at all.

"*Zephyr* is too a word," Nana argued as she got up and went to the living-room side table drawer.

*Oh, Lord, she's getting the dictionary,* I thought.

She slipped on her reading glasses and flipped through the little red Webster's dictionary she'd retrieved. "A gentle wind," she read. "Light woolen or worsted yarn." She pointed and showed me.

There it was in black and white. And there it was. I'd just lost the second game in a row to wise old Nana.

She celebrated her victory as the loser, me, began to clean up the board. That was when we heard repeated hard knocks on the front door. Nana gazed at me curiously after looking at the clock, which read 10:00 p.m. No one came to Nana's house unannounced that late, not even her own children.

We both silently crept to the door, Nana in the lead. She looked through the peephole, then turned to me and said, "It's Dub."

I wasn't expecting to see Dub until the next morning, when he showed up to take me to work. Dub showing up at ten o'clock at night, unannounced, was not a good sign. Nana unlocked the door. Before she could even say hello to him or ask him what he was doing there, Dub barged in.

"Help!" he exclaimed. "Help!"

Just as soon as he entered and I got a good look at his arm, I could feel the vomit clumping in my throat. There were at least seven deep slashes in his left arm. The wounds were so deep that when he moved his arm, it looked as though his arm had lips that were trying to speak. No words poured out, though, only blood.

"Oh, my God! What happened?" I asked.

"They cut me!" he yelled. "They cut me."

By this time, Nana had disappeared from the room. I was fixated on the bloody sight before me, so I had no idea where she had gone. At first I thought she might have gone to call 911, but when she returned to the room, ripping a towel she had retrieved from the hall closet into shreds, I knew better.

"Here. Let's tie this around your arm," Nana said as she began tying the strips of towel around Dub's wounds. I was so glad that Baby D had fallen asleep and was not awake to witness this scene. I was a grown woman and I could barely stand it. I couldn't imagine how a child would react.

"That will stop the bleeding for now," Nana assured Dub and then looked at me. "But he needs to get to the hospital."

Selfish, mean, and nasty thoughts entered my head. Why did I have to take him to the hospital? Why couldn't we just let him bleed to death? The last time I saved this man's life, I lived to regret it.

As if my nana could see the hesitation in my actions, she looked at me strangely. "Did you hear me? If you don't get this boy to the hospital, he's going to die."

I'd heard her, all right, and her last comment had sounded pretty darn tempting, but not wanting to disappoint Nana, but still not wanting to save Dub's life, I felt like I had no choice in the matter. "Come on. Let's go," I said, sucking my teeth quietly.

Dub handed me my car keys; then he and I headed to my car. I started the engine, but before taking off, I looked over at Dub, who appeared to be getting weak and entering a state of shock.

"Lord, don't let me regret this," I mumbled as I once again headed to Doctors Hospital North.

# Stone Number Twenty

That night at the hospital had been like déjà vu. For the second time Dub had been injured, and for the second time when the police arrived to talk to him about it, he asked me to leave the room so that he could talk in private.

I, of course, excused myself and stood outside the door, blowing off steam. "I'm the one who brought your sorry tail here, and now you want to give me the boot?" I seethed to myself. "Ain't this about a . . ." I went on and on, talking to myself, while Dub talked to the cops on the other side of the door.

Dub knew it bothered me too, because every time I asked, "How's the arm?" I had such disdain in my tone. He knew I had my suspicions about the entire incident, which he seemed to be keeping hushed. I had to admit that it surprised me one night, about a month after the incident, when out of the blue Dub decided to speak about it.

"You know that night last month," Dub said to me as he sat next to me on the couch at Nana's. He'd decided to hang out for a minute after dropping me off after work one day.

"What night?"

"No one cut me. I really did that myself. I didn't want to live anymore. But then I thought about you and Baby D and how much I love y'all, and I knew I had to live for y'all. I couldn't bear the thought of you living without me."

There was something about Dub's last line that didn't sit well in my spirit. How I understood it was that this man was at a point in his life when he really wanted to die, but he couldn't handle the thought of me still walking the earth without him overseeing my every step. His next words confirmed my interpretation.

"I couldn't leave this earth knowing someone else could possibly have you." He shook his head, looking as if just the thought pained him. "No, I couldn't leave this earth without you coming with me."

That chilling thought was a centipede through my veins.

"I just didn't want to live, though," Dub reiterated.

My concern shifted to Dub's self-imposed injury. What could be so bad that he would inflict on himself seven wounds that would surely be life threatening had he not gotten to the hospital and gotten stitched up?

"Why'd you do it?" I asked. "What was going on that was so bad that you inflicted such pain on yourself?" I cringed at the thought of self-inflicted stab wounds to the arm.

Dub looked at me, his eyes such a dark brown that they looked black. He opened his mouth but then decided against saying whatever it was he had initially intended to say. "I can't tell you. If you knew what I was going through, you wouldn't care. You wouldn't try to help me. You'd just leave me, and I can't live without you. You are my life. It's the thought of not having you and Baby D that made me change my mind that night and want to live. And since it was you and Baby D that were on my mind so heavily, that's what led me to you that night. I needed to see you and him, y'all's faces, just in case I didn't make it."

I began to feel sorry for Dub. I didn't want to. After all he'd done to me, how could I? But there those feelings sat, doggy paddling in my heart. But I'd never seen him this hurt and vulnerable in my life. If pain could be seen and not just felt, it would look like Dub looked at that very moment.

"What is it, Dub?" Not only did I feel sorry for him, but my curiosity was piqued as well. It was clear that something heavy was on Dub's mind. He wasn't the dominating warrior I'd grown to fear over the years. He was now a man who couldn't even look me in the eyes as he sat there with his leg doing a nervous bounce. It was apparent he was holding so much inside that he wanted to explode. Every time he opened his mouth, on the verge of telling me his truth, he would slam it shut and would then shake his head.

"I can't," he said as his eyes became moist.

This was deep. It was driving me crazy. I needed to know what was going on inside that head of his. "You can tell me," I said patronizingly.

"No, I can't!" he was quick to say, standing to his feet. "You won't understand." He paced. "I got a serious problem going on, and I can't tell you about it. It's a problem that's making me do stuff I never imagined me doing."

It was at that very moment that I knew exactly what he wanted to tell me. It was something that deep down inside I already knew, but still, I wanted him to confirm it. I wanted him to confirm what Konnie had already told me months ago. That was why I'd never mentioned the rumors to him. I just wanted to hear him say it. I wanted it to be from the horse's mouth, so I pressed, trying to sound more convincing.

"What's the problem, Dub? What's so bad that you cut yourself up?"

I ended up hearing what I wanted to hear, not from Dub's mouth, but from his body language. I watched him agonize over whether or not to tell me he was addicted to crack cocaine.

Without him saying a word, I came to my own conclusion that the night he showed up at Nana's house, he'd just done something so humiliating for a crack rock that he could no longer live with himself. I knew that if I sat there and pressed long enough, I could probably get to the bottom of everything. I could probably even get him to confess exactly what it was that he had done that night that made him not want to live. I didn't, though. And I was glad I didn't.

Some things only God needed to know. Some things were just too much for a person to be able to handle. I knew picking at Dub that night would have been like picking fruit from the tree of knowledge. I wouldn't have been able to handle knowing what Dub kept submerged within. Deep down inside, I knew that I didn't want to know. To this day I still had no idea what it was. I could only imagine.

"Is Dub there?" I asked Ms. Daniels through the phone receiver.

"He's still not here," she replied.

I had been calling him all night long, and now it was early morning. I hadn't heard from him since he picked me up from work in my car the day before. His possessiveness still had him checking in on me often, even though he had my car and knew I couldn't get around town. But when he hadn't checked in, something told me that when it came time for me to go to work in the morning, I'd have to hunt him down.

"Did he happen to say where he was going when he left yesterday?" I asked.

"He borrowed twenty dollars from me before he left. Said he was going to lunch with TJ."

Two things about what she'd just said didn't sit well with me. One, he'd asked to borrow twenty dollars. We had enough drug addicts on both sides of the family to know that when a person constantly borrowed twenty dollars, it wasn't a good sign. Secondly, I recalled Dub mentioning when he and Boyd first started their hustle, that TJ, an old classmate of ours, was on crack. He'd learned that from being on the streets. As a matter of fact, he'd even stooped so low as to sell his friend crack to support his growing habit. So why would he all of a sudden want to start hanging out with a crackhead?

"Thanks, Ms. Daniels," I said, defeated. "If you hear from him . . ." My words trailed off, because just then there was a knock at the door. With phone in hand, I looked out to see who it was. Lo and behold, it was Dub. "Never mind, Ms. Daniels. He just got here."

I let out a sigh of relief and ended the call.

"Dude, I'm going to be late," I said as I opened the door. "Where have you . . ." Once again, my words trailed off. Something was wrong with this picture. Something was missing. I looked over Dub's shoulders in an attempt to find what I was looking for. Dub was standing on the porch in front of me, but my car was nowhere in sight. "Dude, where's my car?"

"They stole it. They stole it." Dub charged past me and into the house. He began pacing nervously.

That was not what I was trying to hear. Tell me it got a flat or that it ran out of gas or something. But not that it had been stolen.

"What do you mean, they stole it?" I panicked. "Who stole it? What's going on?"

"Man, they stole it," was all he kept repeating, and the more he repeated it, the angrier I got. That wasn't telling me anything. I wanted to know who, when, where, how, and why.

"Well, we need to call the police." The phone was still in my hand, so I raised it to my ear.

"No, wait!" he shouted, snatching the phone from my hand. "Let me think."

"Think about what? What is there to think about? My car has been stolen, and we need to call the police." I snatched the phone back from him, and then the next thing I knew, we are both tussling over the phone.

I couldn't believe this guy. It was as if he wanted to protect this criminal who was rolling around in my wheels, making me late for work.

"Just hold up," Dub finally said, causing me to cease hyperactively jumping to my own conclusions about the situation at hand. "Let me go check into something." And with that, Dub was gone, leaving me standing there, dressed for work, but with no ride.

"What's going on, Mommy?" Baby D asked as he came down the stairs, rubbing his eyes. "What's wrong?"

I usually allowed him to sleep right up until we were about to walk out the door. All I'd have to do was wash his face and make him brush his teeth. Nana had taught me a trick that had saved me, a single mother, lots of time. I'd bathe Baby D the night before and dress him for the next day, usually in something cotton and comfy so that it wouldn't wrinkle, like a fleece sweat suit or something. Not have to fuss around with dressing Baby D really helped me save time in the mornings. He ate breakfast at school, so I didn't have to worry about that task, either. But who knew that this morning I'd have to deal with explaining to him that Mommy's car had been stolen?

"Nothing, baby," I told Baby D, even though it clearly showed on my face that something was wrong. "You go on back to bed."

"But what about school?"

Every time I dropped him off at school, he would whine and sometimes cry his eyes out. He hated school. Now, all of a sudden, when we had no transportation, he was worried about going.

"It's not time yet, Baby D. Go on back to bed." I ushered him up the steps.

After getting Baby D nice and settled back in bed, I went and called my job. "My car has been stolen," was what I should have told them when citing my reason for not being able to make it in that day. But something inside of me knew that wasn't the full truth. I might not have known exactly where it was at the moment, but something told me my car hadn't been stolen—not in the ordinary sense, anyway. I could just feel it. Dub wasn't telling me the whole story. There was a missing link, otherwise known as the truth. So until Dub told me the truth, all I could relay to my job was a lie. "My son is sick."

After hanging up the phone, I just flopped on the couch and cried my eyes out. Nana had gone walking around Northland Mall with a girlfriend of hers. It was something the senior citizens did. Mall security opened the doors to the mall two hours early just for them. The Northland Walkers was what they were called. After walking, they'd usually go to breakfast too, so I knew having her take me to work would be out of the question.

I couldn't understand why things in my life just kept going from bad to worse. Even though I was no longer living with Dub, he still seemed to cause havoc in my life.

After I sat on the couch for an hour, crying not just about the loss of my car, but also about the loss of my soul, my life, my identity, there was another knock on the door. It was Dub, with car keys in hand. This time when I looked over his shoulder, I saw my car parked in the driveway.

I looked Dub dead in his eyes, not even asking a single question while snatching my keys from him. "Never again," was all I said. He knew exactly what it meant; never again would he drive my car. "I don't have time to take you home. I'm running late," was all I said before leaving him standing on the doorstep while I went to get Baby D.

I rehearsed in my head what I would tell my job once I showed up at work in spite of having called in. *He threw up and is feeling better,* I thought. *My grandmother is staying home with him.* One of those two lies would work for sure.

Dub must have walked home, because when I came back downstairs with Baby D, ready to go, he was nowhere in sight. Surprisingly, he hadn't even put up a fight. How could he? He knew and I knew he'd done what was becoming very popular for crackheads: they'd rent their car out for a hit of crack. Only, he'd rented my car out. Lord only knows what he had to do to get it back. But he got it back. For that I was relieved, but still, this was only a sign that even though I thought moving away from Dub would make things better, they were bad. I thought maybe me being out of his sight would mean that eventually I'd be out of his mind, ultimately leading him to find another girlfriend to live with and terrorize. Dub had found someone else, all right. Her name was crack. I knew that sooner or later he'd be so caught up in his new chick that he wouldn't even remember my name. But could I wait it out that long?

# Stone Number Twenty-one

Now that I finally had my car back, I was so happy. Dub didn't even think twice about asking to use it. Whatever mess he was getting into, he was getting into it on foot. For almost six years, nothing had been able to keep him away from me. He'd be hounding me constantly to see what I was up to. And now it would be days before I would even hear from him. I was the last thing on his mind. Most girlfriends would have had a problem with that, but not me. Free at last! Free at last! Thank God almighty, I was free at last.

Four days straight had passed since I'd last heard from Dub. During those four days I thought that any minute he'd show up, demanding the car, threatening me with bodily harm or something. But that never happened.

On day five, after still not hearing from Dub, I felt confident that my car was mine again. It was a Saturday afternoon in May, about one week before the swimming pools would officially open. I pulled out the water hose and put Baby D in his swimming trunks and a T-shirt, and we washed down my car while the radio played inside it.

I felt like I'd just gotten a new car for my sixteenth birthday and I was proud to be shining it up. Baby D splished and splashed in the water puddles in the driveway. He looked so cute. He was getting so big that he made regular trips to the barber shop now. His little fade was perfect for his little chocolate self.

I pulled out Nana's old orange vac, which everyone had used over the years to clean the inside of their car out. I wore a smile as I sang along to what I called a happy song on the radio, one of those songs that just made a person smile when it came on. Like Janet Jackson's "When I Think of You."

After unraveling the cord from around the sweeper and plugging it in inside the house with an extension cord, I started with the backseat, but not before stepping back and taking a minute to admire my shiny car.

There was so much trash and dirt under and down in between those seats, it was disgusting. In the past four days I hadn't gotten all up under and in between the seats, so I hadn't noticed. There had been a couple of fast-food bags and soda bottles I'd had to pitch, but what I was now finding growing in between my seats was stomach turning. Dub must have had everybody under the sun back there in my car.

"Baby D, go inside the house and get Mommy a brown paper bag from the basement stairwell so I can put all this trash in it," I ordered my only son.

While Baby D went inside to get me a trash bag, I let a string of expletives fly from my mouth regarding how I felt about Dub's treatment of my vehicle.

"Hurry up, Baby D," I shouted in frustration as I threw all the stuff out onto the driveway. Baby D was taking so long that I decided to just go ahead and start vacuuming off and down in between the seats. I turned on the vacuum and started moving the vac head up and down the seats. Burn holes decorated the entire backseat. There were some burns where cigarette ashes had fallen and burned a hole through the seat, but the majority of the burns were from hot seeds spit out of a joint that had settled onto my seats.

"Son of a . . ." I spat. I was so disgusted. That feeling of delight I'd had less than five minutes ago was gone. I didn't feel like I had a new car anymore. I felt like I had something old, abused, and broken down. Something that nobody wanted, something like me. Looking at that car was almost like looking at a reflection of myself. I'd let Dub do the same thing to me that he'd done to my car. Had I really expected him to treat my vehicle any better than he had treated me?

So much anger boiled up inside of me that by the time Baby D made it back outside with the trash bag, I was on fire.

"Here's the bag, Mommy. I—"

"What took you so long?" I screamed as I snatched the bag from him. "How long does it take somebody to go in the house and get a bag, stupid? You blind or something?"

I could tell by the look on Baby D's face, in his dark brown eyes, that he thought he'd just entered the twilight zone. A minute ago he'd left a sweet, kind mommy outside who looked like she was enjoying life more than ever before. He'd returned to find some unrecognizable beast. But he just kept that innocent, loving smile on his face.

"I can't stand you sometimes," I shouted.

Still he just smiled.

No matter what I did to Baby D, he loved me. No matter what I said to Baby D, he still loved me. He would cling to me as if I was the only person he had in this world, me, the person who was hurting him. The person who was calling him names and words that he didn't even know the meaning of. The person who was hurting so much inside that she wanted to make sure everyone around her hurt. It just so happened that Baby D was pretty much the only one around. Would I take that young, sweet, loving, and innocent boy and turn him into a monster too? Would he become me? Would he become his father? The answers to those questions were something I would fear the most.

# Stone Number Twenty-two

"You have a collect call from—" the operator began after I answered the ringing phone.

"Dub," I heard a male voice interrupt.

After that I received instructions from the operator about which prompt would accept the call and which prompt would refuse it.

"Dub, what's going on?" I asked after accepting the call. I had talked to Dub only a couple of times in the last two weeks. I had had the pleasure of not seeing him at all during those two weeks.

"I'm locked up," he answered.

"That I know, but why? What for? What did you do?" I shot off question after question, giving the impression that I was genuinely concerned about the fact that my man was locked up, when, in all actuality, what I really was feeling was excitement.

"Me and TJ got into it. He called the police on me, and they arrested me."

"You beat up TJ?" I questioned. "But why . . ." My words seemed to trail off. This was the first time Dub had beaten anybody up besides a girl. For the first time he'd manned up enough to fight another man. Thing was, though, the man he'd beaten up was wheelchair bound.

Just some months prior, TJ had been shot. The bullet hit him in the spine, and unfortunately, he was now paralyzed from the waist down. God had showed him enough favor in his upper body so that he could still use his hands to grip the crack pipe and his arms to lift the crack pipe to his lips.

"Anyway . . . ," Dub said, changing the subject so that I wouldn't dwell on the fact that he was incarcerated for beating up a paralyzed man, an offense that surely wasn't gaining him any street cred behind the jailhouse walls. "I need you to get with my mom so y'all can figure out how to get me out of here."

"Excuse me?" I was quick to say, all the while thinking, *Me and your mom didn't figure out how to get you in there, so why we gotta figure out how to get you out?*

"I told her I was going to have you call her. So y'all call the courts and all and see what's what. I gotta get outta here."

"I'll call her," I said in a tone that let him know that I was calling her only because he had asked me to, not because I planned on playing any part in getting him out of there. I knew if I didn't call her, he would blow Nana's phone up, trying to get at me.

After ending the call with Dub, I kept my promise and phoned Ms. Daniels. "Hi, Ms. Daniels. It's Helen. I just got a call from Dub."

"Yeah, me too," she informed me. "His arraignment is tomorrow, at nine o'clock. I figure you can come pick me up and we can go see what his bail is set at."

"Sure," I agreed. I didn't even put up a fight about going. I didn't have but two dollars and fifty cents in my back account. Ms. Daniels lived paycheck to paycheck. I knew this because she borrowed money from me on occasion. I was certain she didn't have any extra money lying around to bail Dub out of jail. Couldn't get blood from a turnip. So I was actually eager to go to court the next morning. I wouldn't have missed going to that courthouse and watching with my own two eyes someone finally take Dub's freedom from him.

The next morning, after calling the job to let them know I'd be in late, I got Baby D off to school and headed over to Ms. Daniels's apartment. We arrived at the courthouse at about 9:15 that morning, but Dub's case wasn't even called until about 10:00 a.m.

When the deputies led Dub into the courtroom, I gasped. I didn't even recognize him. Even though it had been only a couple of weeks since the last time I laid eyes on him, it looked like he'd been living on the streets since then. He had had a nice slim build before, but now he looked like a skeleton, like he hadn't eaten since God knows when. He looked like he hadn't shaved or gotten a haircut. He looked like he probably hadn't even bathed. He looked like . . . he looked like . . . Who was I kidding? That wasn't what my baby's daddy, my boyfriend, looked like. He looked like what he was . . . a crackhead.

I looked over at Ms. Daniels, who didn't even seem fazed by her son's appearance. She had a look of expectancy in her eyes, like that was what she figured he was supposed to look like. That was her baby, and she was looking at him with as much pride as she probably had the day he was born. There was no shame on her face whatsoever. I guess that was what a mother's love was all about.

I, on the other hand, was appalled, embarrassed, humiliated, as if he'd come out of my own womb. As if I was responsible for raising him into the man who stood before us in the courtroom.

"Hey," Dub turned around and mouthed, his eyes going to me first, then to his mother. He then turned his attention to the judge, who within seconds set a bail of fifty thousand dollars and a future court date. "See what you can do," was the next thing Dub turned around and mouthed to us as he was escorted out of the courtroom.

"How much you got?" his mother asked me as we exited the courtroom while the next case was called.

"I don't have a dime," I said, trying not to sound so excited about being broke.

"I don't know what we're going to do." Ms. Daniels sounded so exasperated. "I bet his bond would have been set lower if you hadn't called the police on him that one time."

I felt like I'd been hit with a bolt of lightning. For one, I'd forgotten all about that one time, out of hundreds, Dub had beaten me up and I'd actually gotten up the courage to go downtown and press charges against his butt. Secondly, he deserved to go to jail. He could have blinded me that night. How dare Ms. Daniels try to put the blame for her son's violent temper on me?

Chills ran through my body as I thought back to that night. Dub himself had had to rush me to the emergency room. I'd had to lie to the doctors about how I'd come about my injuries so that Dub wouldn't go to jail right there on the spot. I'd lied only because Dub had stayed by my side the entire time, his presence intimidating me.

Dub's uncle's girlfriend, Nique, had moved next door to us before I moved into Nana's. One evening she and I had sat out on the stoop, watching our two boys play together while she gave me a piece of her mind about what she thought about Dub's uncle and his family.

"They all ain't really nothing but white trash," Nique had said, with her chubby brown cheeks and pouty lips. Her skin was so clear and smooth. She was going to be an example of black don't crack. "Or should I say some white and some gray," Nique added, taking a shot at the fact that all the women in Dub's family had babies with black men or biracial men. "My man too. And all the men don't do nothing but beat on the women." She let out a harrumph. "But that don't include my man. He knows better than to try that mess with me."

Nique reminded me of Sofia from *The Color Purple*. I imagined her boyfriend would have the same hard time trying to beat on her as Harpo had trying to beat on Sofia.

"And even though all the women don't date nothing but black men," Nique continued, "I still think they lightweight prejudiced. I even heard Dub and Kelice's mom talking about you one time. Called you a black witch, or something like that. I was saying to myself, 'Why she got to be a black witch? Why can't she just be a plain witch?' That's how I know they prejudiced."

I had to admit, I was hurt when I found out that Ms. Daniels had been talking smack about me. All this time I had thought that she and I were back on good terms. She never came across as racist or prejudiced. How could she when she, a white woman, had married a black man and had had two children with him, two children that were, according to their birth certificates, black?

"Black witch?" I said, mocking the name Nique had said Ms. Daniels had called me, still in disbelief.

About two weeks after Nique's and my little chat on the stoop, I confronted Ms. Daniels with a couple things that were mentioned in our conversation. It didn't take her long to figure out where I'd gotten the information. A couple days after that, Nique came charging over to me like Miss Sofia, accusing me of lying about her. Well, I came to find out that Ms. Daniels had added some yeast to the things I'd said. She had put words in my mouth about Nique that Nique had never really said, or maybe she did say them. I didn't know. I guess I had no business revealing what somebody had told me in confidence in the first place.

Nonetheless, I was so mad that I took on the role of Miss Sofia and stormed over to Ms. Daniels's apartment, where I let her know that I didn't appreciate one bit the fact that she'd put my name in her mouth. I kindly asked her to keep my name out of her mouth in the future before I retreated to my place. I thought that was the end of all the confusion until Dub came storming into the house a few hours later.

"Tramp, don't you ever go over my mama's house acting like you ain't got no sense," he said as he punched me upside the head. "Disrespect her again, you hear?" A slap across the face followed.

Baby D just sat there, engaged in whatever it was he was watching on television. "Ah, ha-ha." He even laughed at something one of the characters was doing, as if it was the funniest thing in the world. Baby D pointed at the television screen, laughing, as if his dad and I weren't even in the room, raising hell.

I supposed it was safe to say that the beatings, the yelling, and the fighting were nothing new to him. He had stopped paying attention. It had become normal . . . for all of us.

I was way caught off guard by Dub's attitude. Since when did he care about his mother being disrespected? This was the same Dub who, I found out through the grapevine, had stolen the television out of the room he was staying in at his mother's house. I'd also been told that he'd stolen the stereo system too. And one day he left her apartment with some other appliances tucked in his jacket while someone waited for him in a car parked outside. His mother noticed the bulge and went after him.

I didn't witness the incident personally, but as I listened in sheer astonishment, I felt as if I was there. From what I was told, Dub managed to jump in the backseat of the waiting car and told the driver to hurry up and leave. The driver hurriedly backed up but couldn't pull out of the parking lot, because he had to pull onto a main street and traffic was coming both ways. Ms. Daniels managed to get the back door open while Dub tried to shield whatever it was he had taken from the house.

As Ms. Daniels reached into the backseat to retrieve what she knew was her property, Dub, who was wearing black leather hiking boots, kicked Ms. Daniels right out of the car and onto the pavement. He kicked her the same way he'd kicked me in the stomach that day, knocking the wind out of me, only he kicked her dead smack in her face . . . his own mother. She lay in the parking lot with a busted-up face as the car, its wheels screeching, drove away. Her boyfriend was coming up the street and caught the tail end of the altercation. He was the one who had shared the incident with me. It was something I never, ever mentioned to either Ms. Daniels or Dub.

Dub kicking his mother dead in the face while wearing a pair of boots was the ultimate in disrespect, and yet there he stood, having the nerve to be mad at me for getting lippy with her. Not only that, but he demanded I go apologize to her. "Now, take your tail right on back over there the same way you marched over there earlier and tell her you are sorry."

Now I was really Miss Sofia. "Heck, naw," I was quick to say. Seconds later I saw stars after Dub clobbered me upside my head.

Holding back all my tears, I calmly said, "Baby D, come on. Let's go to the car."

"But I'm watching—"

"Baby D, now!" I scolded. And with that, he was by my side. I grabbed my purse, and we were on our way out the door.

"And fix me something to eat when you get back!" Dub said before slamming the door behind Baby D and me.

I buckled Baby D into the back of the car, and then I climbed into the front seat. I started the car and pulled off. I had no intention of going over to Ms. Daniels's to apologize. Where exactly I planned on going, I didn't know, but it was going to be far away from Dub.

I thought about driving to Nana's, but after Dub figured out I hadn't gone to his mother's and probably wasn't coming back home, that would be the first place he'd go to look for me. I could have gone to my mom's, I supposed, but she would have shot and killed him if he brought drama to her house, and then I'd have a mother in jail and it would be all my fault. I couldn't do that. I thought about going to Lynn's, but she now had a two-year-old child of her own and was staying with her fiancé, the baby's father. Visions of Dub finding me there and killing us all played in my head. It wasn't just about me anymore. I couldn't risk endangering the lives of the people I loved.

I'd finally mustered up the courage to leave Dub, and now there I was, with nowhere to go, nowhere I felt safe. So after driving around, passing everyone's house that I considered taking refuge at, I ended up just driving to this shopping mall strip, Northern Lights, where I sat for hours. How many hours, I can't recall. But when I finally looked in the backseat and saw Baby D sound asleep, I knew I couldn't stay there. I knew I couldn't let my child sleep on the backseat of a car in a parking lot in the middle of the night. That didn't feel safe, either. So if we weren't going to be safe, then I reasoned that it might as well be in the discomfort of our own home.

When I drove up to the rocky driveway, I could tell Dub wasn't home. The house was pitch black, still, and silent. I knew he was out hunting me down, getting angrier each minute he couldn't find me. The entire drive there I'd envisioned him coming out of nowhere in the darkness of the night, snatching me up, and beating me to death right there in front of my son.

"God help us," I said out loud with my hand on the car handle, prepared to get out of the car. I had already sat there for at least fifteen minutes with the car running before I finally decided that it was time to pull the handle and open the door. I turned off the ignition, prepared to make a quick exit, snatch Baby D up from the backseat, and make a run for the door. I pulled the door handle, but before I could even push the car door open, I saw him. Dub was heading down the street on foot, at full speed, as if he couldn't wait to get ahold of me. He was huffing and puffing, almost salivating, like a rabid dog on its way to devouring a pile of raw roast beef.

I immediately released the handle and pulled the car door closed tight. I locked my door and made sure all the other doors were locked as well. Dub approached the car so quickly that I thought he was going to jump right through the window. The first thing he did was go for the car door and try to yank it open so that he could snatch me out of the car.

"Get out of the car, Helen!" Dub screamed. "Get out of the car."

"No, Dub. Go on somewhere." I tried to sound unmoved by his tirade.

"Open the door." He pounded on the roof of the car, startling Baby D, but not waking him. Baby D was a very hard sleeper. Dub peered down into the darkness at me through the window. "I swear to God, if you don't get out of this car right now." He balled his fists so tight, I swore I saw blood dripping from the palms of his hands, where his nails were digging into his own flesh.

I knew that if I got out of that car, I would endure so much pain that I probably wouldn't even survive. That was when I did it; I put the key back into the ignition and started the car, determining that the strip mall parking lot was safer, after all.

Before putting the car in reverse to back out, I looked up at Dub to make sure that he wasn't in the way, that I wouldn't run over him. Imagine that. Something in me cared whether or not his life ended at the hands of my two-ton vehicle. And when I looked up at him, from the look he gave me, I knew what was coming next.

My mind instructed me to close my eyes and to put my arms up to shield my face, but everything happened so fast . . . too fast. The next thing I saw was Dub's foot coming through the window and smashing me in the face, pressing in all the flying glass right along with the sole of his shoe.

"Arrrggh! Ugghhh!" I yelped. My eyes were now closed, but inside them were shattered glass particles.

Dub immediately began to apologize. "Oh God! Baby, I'm sorry! I'm so sorry!"

Hard sleeper or not, there was no way Baby D could sleep through that. He woke up, and I could hear him yelling for me.

I placed my hands over my closed eyes and just cried out in fear. "I can't see! Help me! Help me!" I just knew the last thing I'd ever see was Dub's face, his foot coming toward me. I knew there was no way I'd ever see again, especially since it meant I had to open my eyes. I couldn't open them. They hurt too badly.

"Let me see. Move your hands," Dub ordered. I could feel him trying to remove my hands from over my eyes.

I pulled back from him. I didn't want him touching me. I didn't want anyone touching my eyes. I could hear the car door open. "We gotta get you to the hospital. Get out."

He pulled me out by my elbow, and I could hear all the glass that was in my lap fall to the ground.

Dub led me around to the passenger side. I hated having to trust him to lead me anywhere, but I felt helpless. I heard him open the car door, and he gave me a slight shove so I'd get in. He closed the door and then ran around to the other side. I could feel the car backing out and then, a few minutes later, going full speed down the road.

I was crying the entire time. My eyes were so painful, and I was so afraid. So many things flashed across my mind. Things like, would I ever get to see my son's face again? If not, with time would I forget what his face even looked like? Perhaps that was exactly what I deserved. Perhaps I didn't deserve to see his little face again. Maybe I was being punished for how badly I'd treated him in the past.

*God, if you just let my eyes be okay, if you just let me see my son again, I promise I'll never be mean to my baby boy for as long as I live,* I prayed silently as Dub drove me to the hospital. I could feel the chilly night air traveling through the car from the driver's side. I didn't need anything else to send chills running through my body, but it wasn't like we could roll the window up.

What felt like only five minutes went by before Dub said, "We're here." He put the car in park and then got out. "Come on, Baby D," he said before walking around to let me out of the car.

I had no idea what hospital we were at. I couldn't recall one that was such a short distance away, but then again, Dub had probably gone way over the speed limit. He had probably even run a few red lights, for all I knew.

"She's got glass in her eyes!" Dub shouted the minute I heard the automatic sliding doors of the emergency room open up. There was complete darkness, but I could feel people staring. "She needs help fast!"

"What happened? How did she get glass in her eyes?" I heard a voice ask. I presumed it belonged to the desk nurse. "Uh, we were, uh . . ." Dub stammered.

All the while I was thinking, *Is he going to tell them? Is he going to tell them that he's the one who did this to me?* I waited in anticipation to see what Dub would say. I knew that if he told the hospital the truth, they would have to call the police. They would arrest Dub and take him away forever. Everything might just work out for my good, after all. I might have to go blind in the process, but my choice wasn't that difficult: a life of blindness or a life with Dub? I instantly chose blindness.

"We were driving," Dub continued. I could hear what sounded like him shifting Baby D from one of his hips to the other. "And . . . and . . . the next thing we knew, someone threw a brick or something at the window, and *bam,* the glass shattered everywhere, right in her eyes."

"Oh, God!" the woman exclaimed. Next, I felt a set of soft, cold hands grab hold of my elbow, the one Dub hadn't been holding, and begin leading me.

There was no registration desk where one had to sit down and be asked a million and one questions. I was immediately led to an examination room. I could hear scurrying around me after I was seated in a chair. I could hear others entering the room and the nurse relaying my situation to them.

"Mommy, are you okay?" Baby D asked, but before I could answer him, I heard a male voice.

"Hi, Helen. I'm Dr. Rosenthawl. What we are going to do right now is flush your eyes out. Now you're going to feel fluid, lots of fluid, but it's only water. Can you open your eyes at all?" he asked me.

I shook my head.

"Can you try?"

My tears and murmurs increased at just the thought of attempting to open my eyes.

"Okay, then, calm down. I'm going to have the nurse hold your eyes open one at a time while I flush."

After that I heard something being rolled in front of me, and then soft, cold hands found their way to each side of my face. The hands slowly tilted my head until it was resting comfortably on some type of cushion. The next thing I heard was running water, and then, all of a sudden, it was like I was a swimmer floating peacefully in the ocean with my eyes closed, only to open them and see a large wave coming at me. That was exactly what it felt like when my eyelids were pulled open and an endless gush of water poured into my eye. Then the other was done.

I started gasping, as if I was underwater. It was all psychological, though. My eyes saw gushes of water rushing toward me, immediately signaling my brain to fight to breathe. It was one of the scariest moments of my life. One I'd never forget.

Once the doctor, with the nurse's assistance, flushed both my eyes, he examined them and assured me that everything would be okay. One of the particles of glass had bruised my eyeball, causing a permanent brown mark on my eye. But the doctor said that my vision would not be affected.

"Now, how did you say this happened?" the doctor said once he'd done his duty. Now it was time for him to investigate the situation, to see if he was obligated to act in any other manner; like reporting the incident to the police.

"Uh, I, uh . . . ," I stammered. I looked up at the doctor, and then I looked over at Dub.

Dub's eyes were pleading with me. He was pleading with me not to tell that doctor the truth. "I promise that if you don't report this, I'll never hit you again. I'll never hurt you again. If you tell them the truth, I'll go to jail. Don't put me in jail." Although he spoke not a single word, his eyes said it all.

The look on Dub's face was so serious, so sincere. But I'd heard it all before. So many similar promises made by Dub had gone unkept. So many times he had promised not to ever put his hands on me again, promises that might have lasted a month or two at the most.

I looked away, thought for a moment, and then turned to Dub one last time. This time I was able to read between the lines of the expression on his face. "And if you don't lie, I promise you that I will hunt you down one day and kill you!"

Now, that promise I believed.

I allowed my attention to go back to the doctor. I took a deep breath and told him exactly what Dub had told the nurse when we had arrived at the hospital. "We were driving, and the next thing we knew, someone threw a brick or something at the window, and *bam,* the glass shattered everywhere, right into my eyes," I lied.

There was a gust of wind as Dub exhaled. His shoulders fell as he relaxed.

His actions were so obvious, though, that even the doctor took notice, which prompted him to continue to drill me. "So what street were you driving down?"

I paused. I was prepared to tell only one lie.

Realizing that I was unequipped to make this charade believable, Dub answered for me. "Cleveland Avenue," he said confidently. "We were driving down Cleveland Avenue."

The doctor looked at me for confirmation. I said nothing. It had been hard enough telling the one lie. I couldn't part my lips to tell another, so I just gave the doctor a look, as if to say, "Yeah, what he said."

"Did you get a look at the person who threw the brick?" The doctor was still looking at me.

I simply shook my head.

"It was too dark," Dub added for effect.

"Well, where is the brick?" The doctor was now looking at Dub, since he seemed to be the voice for me.

Now Dub was stuck. Looked like he hadn't been prepared to take the lie that far, either. I guess he never figured this white, upper-class doctor would give a darn about a girl from the hood. But he was wrong.

"It must have just fallen onto the ground." Dub shrugged.

"Hmmm." The doctor's tone was laced with disbelief, but based on the information we were telling him, his hands were tied. I could tell he didn't believe my story. I could tell he could see right through Dub. I could tell that he could tell I was scared, as he leaned in close to me and, with a very serious expression, asked, "Are you sure if I report this to the police, you couldn't identify the person who did this to you?"

So there it was. Another door of escape was opening, which I just refused to walk through. I was so paralyzed with thoughts of what Dub would do to me if I told the truth. I pictured him locating a scalpel and cutting my throat while we waited for the police to arrive. I pictured him doing the same to the doctor for interfering. I looked down at the doctor's hand while I bit my bottom lip out of nervousness, noticing his wedding band. Why should his wife have to live without a husband or, if he had children, his children without a father all because of me? I couldn't have his blood on my hands. I just couldn't.

"I'm sure," I told the doctor, fighting off the tears in my eyes. Tears of anger. I was angry at myself. If only I'd known then the scripture Psalms 27:1. "The Lord is my light and my salvation; whom shall I fear? The Lord is the strength of my life; of whom shall I be afraid?" If only I'd known then that God had not given His children the spirit of fear, I would have stood up and declared my freedom. Instead, I chose to walk out of the hospital that night still a scared prisoner.

About four days later, while I was standing in the mirror, looking at my bruised pupil, the entire incident played back in my mind. I saw Dub's foot coming at me, the glass shattering, the glass in my eyes. I felt the pain all over again. The next thing I knew, I was downtown, on the seventh floor of the courthouse, in the prosecutor's office, pressing charges against Dub.

There was just something about staring at myself in the mirror that day that angered me to the point where I wanted Dub to pay for what he'd done—this time and all the other times.

Dub was picked up that very same day I reported the incident, due to my story being corroborated by the hospital. He called me collect and let me know all the gruesome and horrible things he'd do to me if I didn't get him out of there. The things he said he'd do to me if I didn't bail him out of jail and then drop the charges, I'd never seen done in horror movies.

Scared to death that he would see all his threats through, shortly after that call, I made it my mission to get Dub out of jail. I withdrew from the bank all the money I had left from my student financial aid after paying my tuition. I hadn't purchased my books and school supplies yet, but I couldn't worry about that. I flipped through the pages of the phone book until I found a bail bondsman to get Dub out of jail.

Needless to say, after getting Dub out of jail, I didn't show up in court, either.

"As long as you don't show up in court," Dub had said to me the day I got him out of jail, "this whole thing should just go away and everything will be good."

I was not about to be forced to be a witness against Dub and have him make good on his threats, so I did as he instructed and didn't appear as the state's witness. The arrest still showed up on Dub's record, though. And that was why now, as Ms. Daniels and I rode in the courthouse elevator, she let me know that the fact that Dub had a previous record, thanks to me, might keep him in jail for quite a while.

I was not the one who put Dub in jail this time, and I sure wasn't going to be the one who helped him get out, either. *God,* I said in my head, *if you are giving me yet another chance to break free from that monster, I swear on everything, I won't let you down. I will not pass up this opportunity. Not this time.*

It was at that moment that I just felt consumed by a shield of protection. It made me feel so safe that no monster, no devil in hell, could touch me. No devil on earth, either, for that matter, not even Dub.

# Stone Number Twenty-three

*Helen,*

*My boy's been seeing you out at da clubs and stuff. The last time Baby D was at my mom's, he told me 'bout some dude named Dino you been goin' out wit'. You're dead. I promise you when I get outta here, you dead, b\*t#! I'm going to kill you and your entire family.*

*Wait until you see what I do to your nana. I'm going to take a hot curling iron and shove it up her you know what. And it's all going to be your fault. Your whole family has to die and be tortured because of you. I want you to have their deaths on your conscience, so I'm going to kill you last.*

*Trust and believe that you are going to pay for playin' me like this while I'm locked up. You're dead!*

*Dub*

I had been receiving hateful, threatening letters from Dub at Nana's house for three months now. That was how long it had been since Dub got locked up without bail for beating up TJ. The judge thought Dub was extremely violent and heinous for abusing a disabled person, and therefore decided to revoke his bond. As I looked back, I realized that perhaps that was God using His strength and power to dominate my weakness, which probably would have led me to get cash for tin cans so I could pay Dub's bail and get him out of jail.

E.N. Joy

So Dub got locked up, and the key was thrown away . . . for eight months, anyway. He had been sentenced to a year but would have to serve only eight months or something like that. I couldn't recall the exact details. All I knew was that it was plenty of time for me to break all ties with Dub. It was plenty of time for Dub to get over me, to get over the fact that I was a free woman and was moving on in life without him. Evidently, three months hadn't been enough time, as the letters came nonstop.

I had never known until he started sending me letters from jail how horrible his literary skills were. Only about four out of ten words were spelled correctly, and he'd often use the wrong form of a word. But in between it all, I understood clearly the point that he was trying to get across, which was, enjoy life while you can, live it to the fullest, because when I get out of here, you're dead.

The day the judge sentenced Dub to jail time for beating up TJ was the day I knew for sure no man could close the door God had now opened for me to walk through and escape from Dub. From day one I refused Dub's phone calls. My mind was made up. It was over. Dub was now under lock and key. There was absolutely no way he could get to me, not for eight months, anyway. Surely without having contact with me for that long, he'd just let things go between us once and for all. But once the letters started coming, the next even more threatening than the last, I started to doubt my newfound freedom.

Those letters were so tormenting that they gave me nightmares. I wasn't sleeping or eating, and I lost twenty-five pounds in only three months to prove it. Maybe I needed to face the fact that perhaps my freedom would only be temporary. That was when I decided that just in case these next few months were the last months I'd ever breathe, I was going to live them to the fullest. I was going to do all the things I'd never gotten to do before, things most twenty-two-year-olds took for granted, like listening to rap music, for example.

Dub had never allowed me to listen to rap music. Even though he was permitted to hang out with his friends and listen to rap music and smoke weed, I had to keep my ears closed to it. He said the rappers didn't rap about anything but sex, and he didn't want me to get any ideas or start fantasizing about a rap artist.

He didn't allow me to listen to the local R & B radio station for fear I'd hear rap music there. So for years I listened to the most popular contemporary pop music station, which played artists like Duran Duran, Madonna, Tears for Fears, and U2. Every now and then they would throw in a Whitney Houston or an En Vogue song.

I should have seen the signs then. That should have been my very first sign that Dub was off balance. But since I was a young teenager, it actually made me feel good that he even cared that much. So even though the writing was on the wall from the beginning, I simply chose to paint over it with my favorite color.

Now that Dub wasn't around to control what I listened to, I turned my dial to the radio stations that kept rap music and R&B music flowing. In addition to just listening to rap music, I decided that one of the things I wanted to experience before Dub got out of jail was going to a club and actually getting down on the dance floor to some rap music. So as I set out to do all these things I'd been barred from, things that I thought would make me feel like I was on top of the world and in heaven, I began my descent into hell.


"This is a nice little spot Uncle got going on here," Lynn said as she looked around my uncle Pookie's, my father's brother's, new house.

My uncle had purchased a nice little bachelor pad and was celebrating by having a set-style housewarming. Lynn had talked me into riding there with her. I had never, ever been to a set, otherwise known as a house party, in my life, although I'd heard about them when I was in high school.

Some of the kids at school would have lunchtime sets while their parents were at work. This meant that during the lunch hour a group of kids would gather over at the hosting classmate's house to drink and smoke and listen to music. The liquor usually came from the hosts' parents' liquor stash, which, they figured, their parents would never miss, anyway.

Synthia had gone to a few and would tell me about them. I'd been invited because I was friends with her. I'd been way too much of a nerd to go. Besides, if Dub had found out, it would have been the end of my high school days for sure. I no longer had to live vicariously through Synthia; I was now at a set of my own.

My uncle was into old-school music, so those were the mellow tunes that blared through the speakers. The ambiance was nice and dim, and there was plenty to drink and smoke, although I wasn't a smoker or a drinker. While everybody else got their drink and smoke on, I just looked around in awe. I mean, this was big business to me to be out and about in a social setting with the opposite sex. Crazy coolest!

Lynn had always been a partygoer. Very popular in high school, she went to all the school activities and got invited to all the parties. She was on the school drill team and dated dudes from other schools. So it was safe to say she was popular in the streets. That explained why almost everybody who walked into my uncle's set knew who she was. I, on the other hand, didn't know a soul. But that was fine with me. Since Dub hadn't allowed me around people too much, I wouldn't have known how to act, anyway, and it showed.

No one was more perfect to school me than my older sister, who was now twenty-four.

"Girl, why don't you get something to drink and chill and relax?" Lynn finally said after getting sick and tired of me acting like a social struck nerd. "Here. Try some of this." She handed me the red plastic cup she was drinking out of.

Without even thinking, I put the drink to my lips and swallowed a gulp. The smell alone should have been a warning. "Yuck! What is this?" I exclaimed as the burning sensation the liquid had left warmed my throat.

"Rum and coke, baby," Lynn said, taking her cup back.

"How in the world do you drink that stuff?" I said as I pretended to spit out any trace of the junk I'd just drunk that might be left on my palate.

"Oh, yeah, I forgot you a rookie. You can't mess with the hard stuff." She got up and walked over to a cooler. "Here. Try this." She pulled out a mini bottle that had something that looked like cherry Kool-Aid in it.

"What's this?" I accepted the ice-cold bottle.

"It's a Bartles and Jaymes wine cooler. That's more up your alley. It tastes like juice."

I examined the bottle.

"No, it's not no rum and coke, but eventually, once you get immune to those, you can graduate to big girl stuff," Lynn said, then winked at me.

Lynn was right. It tasted just like Kool-Aid. Way better than that yucky rum concoction. After popping that thing open, I had it halfway drunk in less than five minutes.

"Slow down, chick. Those things can sneak up on you. They ain't called wine coolers for nothing. They got wine in them, you know. And wine is alcohol."

I took heed of my big sister's advice, and within an hour I was finishing up my second wine cooler. I was feeling so good. I was relaxed and was socializing like I had been hanging out like this for years. The alcohol had me feeling like I was someone else, like for now, as long as I was buzzing, I was an entirely different person. The perk was that when the buzz was gone, I could go back to being the old me with no regrets.

"What time is it?" Lynn asked the guy sitting next to her, with whom she had been yapping it up for the past hour. He was one of my uncle's friends and was about ten years my uncle's junior. I could tell he had an eye for Lynn, and she was feeling him too.

"It's eleven o'clock," he replied.

"Wow," I said, interrupting. "We been here that long? We got here at about seven." By now, most of the guests had come and gone, and there was just a handful of us left. My uncle had even passed out on the couch, which was a sign that the party was over, but it was obvious the night was still young for Lynn.

"Shoot, I just broke up with my man, and I got my babysitter for the night. I ain't had a babysitter to have a night out in a grip," Lynn said, "I ain't ready to go home yet."

"Well, what y'all trying to get into?" the dude asked her.

Lynn thought for a minute. "Let's hit Poppa Jack's. It's usually jumping up in there on Saturday nights."

"Well, I can tell you ain't been to that spot in a while." The guy chuckled. "It ain't even called Poppa Jack's no more. It's called Alexander's."

"Poppa Jack's, Alexander's, whoever. Let's just go," Lynn said, standing up from the love seat she had been sitting on.

*Club? Club?* I wasn't allowed in clubs, but Lynn was driving, so how could I tell her that I couldn't go, that

Dub . . . *Wait a minute*. Dub was on lockdown, and I was supposed to be living it up. Dub couldn't get to me. It was pure irony that Dub's imprisonment was the key to my freedom.

"You game?" I heard Lynn ask.

Although I had been pumping myself up that Dub was in jail and I could do what I wanted, a little part of me still feared going out. Not because of Dub, but because I had never been to a club in my life and I had no idea how to act. And I guess Lynn could see it written all over my face.

"Girl, come on." She grabbed me by the arm and led me out the door, and her male friend followed. "You'll have fun. You know big sis will look out for you."

And with that, we were all out the door and headed to the club. For the entire drive my stomach ached with anxiety pains. I knew nothing about club etiquette. Was I supposed to ask a guy to dance, or was he supposed to ask me? Did people even really dance at clubs or just stand around, trying to see and/or be seen? It was safe to say that I feared the unknown.

We arrived at Alexander's after 11:30 p.m., and there was a line a mile long. It wasn't a case of any one of us knowing the owner of the club or someone working the door, so we had to stand in line with the rest of the common, non-VIP folks.

The entire time I stood in line, Lynn and the dude chatted while my belly grumbled. If there had been a Porta-Potty outside, I would have gone inside of it to get rid of whatever the heap of crap was that was clogging my stomach. Instead, I just let the butterflies that were also inside my belly gnaw at it.

We stood in line for about twenty minutes before we made it through the door of the club. But once inside, we still had a line to stand in. Lynn complained, but I was too shell-shocked to even care.

The club was very dark, with ceiling lights of red, yellow, and blue. I could see the DJ booth situated up high at the back of the club. The DJ sat in a Plexiglas booth with nothing but red lights lighting the inside. He was spinning a fairly new artist named Snoop Dogg, accompanied by veteran Dr. Dre. The name of the song was "Gin and Juice." I'd heard the song being played on the radio, but the words I was now listening to I had never heard before on the radio.

"Oh, my God!" I exclaimed, tapping Lynn on her shoulder while she was in midsentence, talking with dude. "Did you hear that? They are cursing."

Lynn looked at me like I was crazy. "Who is cursing?"

"The song. They are cursing up a storm in that song."

After telling me, "Girl, that's the uncut, real version. Your nerdy butt ain't heard nothing but the radio version," Lynn shooed me like a fly with her hand and then continued her conversation.

I almost wanted to cover my ears as the song played on. I had had no idea until that point that some songs had two different versions: the radio version and the uncut grown folk version. Someone should have warned me that rap music had all that cursing in it, I mean, big curse words—the F-bomb and all. That was just how out of touch Dub had kept me.

Lynn's gentleman friend, who had paid our way into the club, found us all a table. I almost lost them as we headed to the table because I was too engrossed in my surroundings. Everybody had a drink in their hand, and if they didn't, it was only because they were on the dance floor, dancing, and the DJ had made it clear that no drinks were allowed on the dance floor.

The couples on the dance floor were dancing as if they were longtime dance partners, some even longtime lovers, the way they were grinding and rubbing all up on each other. But once a song would end and the couples would part and go their separate ways—the guy with his boys and the chick with her girls—I realized quickly that most were complete strangers.

"What you drinking on?" Lynn's gentleman friend asked. I looked up from the dance floor to see that he was talking to me and that a waitress was staring down my throat, waiting on my reply. "What you drinkin', little mama?" he repeated. "Lynn and I already ordered."

"Ummm," I said. I had to admit I was parched. A Coke would have done me just fine, but I was not about to look like lame by ordering a Coke. However, the only other drink I knew of was the wine coolers. "A Bartles and Jaymes wine cooler please," I told the waitress. "Red, cherry, or whatever." I didn't even know the flavor I'd been drinking earlier.

The waitress scribbled on her tablet and was about to walk away when Lynn stopped her. "Hold up. Bring her a fuzzy navel instead." The waitress nodded and then walked off.

"Fuzzy navel?" I had a puzzled look on my face.

"Yeah, it's a drink. But it's a cutesy drink, so you'll like it." Lynn sucked her teeth. "I'm not about to let you be babysitting wine coolers all night your first time out clubbin' it. You done had your taste of Bartles and Jaymes at the house party. You out in the club like a big girl now. It's time to graduate up a notch."

I just shook my head, wondering if I should continue to put all my trust in Lynn. But once again, after the waitress brought back our drinks, Lynn proved to be right. The concoction of peach schnapps and orange juice with a hint of gin, a drink affectionately called a fuzzy navel, was delicious. I was drinking grown-up drinks, and I was feeling all grown up.

"Ooooh, that's my song," Lynn said as she closed her eyes and snapped her fingers while grooving in her seat.

"Then what you sittin' here for?" her male friend said. "Let's go do something out there on the dance floor."

"Let's do it, then," Lynn said as she got up. "Helen, watch our drinks."

I watched the drinks, all right. For the next hour it seemed I watched the drinks while Lynn got busy on the dance floor, dancing to song after song after song.

I sat in my chair, bobbing my head and grooving, hoping somebody would notice how enticed I was by the beat and would choose me to go out on the dance floor with them. I looked around, even made eye contact with a guy or two. Just when I thought I'd spoken to a dude clearly with my eyes, dang near begging him to come ask me to dance, I would be let down.

At first I thought maybe the guys were just too shy to ask a girl to dance, but then, five minutes later, I'd see them out on the dance floor with some hoochie, stroking her up and down while getting their groove on hard. I had lost several more pounds and had gone down a couple sizes in clothing, so I was looking pretty decent in my size fourteen black jeans and crisp white blouse. So why didn't any of the guys choose me? That was when it dawned on me that I didn't fit the scene. I didn't look like the type of chick who could really get out there on the dance floor and have fun.

I looked down at myself; then I looked around at most of the chicks in the club. The outfits some of those girls were wearing were scandalous. I mean, these chicks were all woman, and they were letting it be known with some of the skimpy outfits they were wearing. Boobs and butt cheeks were the name of the game. The guys were catcalling and checking for them.

There were girls who were dressed conservatively like Lynn and me, wearing a nice pair of jeans and a cute blouse. But those weren't the chicks getting all the attention. The more skin the women showed, the more attention the men showed. I made a mental note of that, because the next time I decided to venture out to the club, I was bound and determined to be one of those girls who got the attention.

# Stone Number Twenty-four

"I can't believe you are actually out with me," Synthia said. "I thought I'd never see the day Helen Lannden hit the club scene. But I guess the fact that now you ain't on lockdown no more makes all the difference." Synthia couldn't help but tease me as she and I stood in Alexander's, sipping on our drinks.

"I'll drink to that," I said as I raised my fuzzy navel to her rum and Coke. I didn't know how she and Lynn drank that hard stuff. It made me want to puke. There was nothing flavorful about rum, if you asked me.

"Dang, I don't know which one to ask to dance," I heard a voice say behind Synthia and me.

When I turned around, there was this dude standing behind me. His eyes were traveling from me to Synthia and then back to me again. I could not believe this guy was even having a conflict after seeing Synthia. I mean, how hard was the choice? Synthia looked like the typical video girl. Due to her mixed heritage, she had that exotic look. That "good" jet-black hair raced down her back. Her size eight clothing fit her like a glove. She exuded beauty.

On top of that, Synthia stayed in the tanning salon, so she always had a perfect, glowing, golden complexion. And did I forget to mention her gorgeous dimples were the icing on the cake?

I, on the other hand, was aw'ight. I had dark skin, but thanks to Wesley Snipes and Denzel Washington, it wasn't such a bad thing anymore. But at the end of the day, it still wasn't light skin. I had shoulder-length hair that I wore in a nice roller set. Fourteen was an average size, but it wasn't skinny. So was this dude blind or something? But then again, this second time at the club, I had dressed for the occasion. Perhaps that had made all the difference.

I was wearing as little as I could without being arrested for indecent exposure. I was bound and determined to get the attention this time that I had failed to get the last time I was at the club. And it appeared as though my plan was working well.

The little black miniskirt I had on just barely covered my butt cheeks. And I made sure it fell down my hips in such a way that the little strings of my thong showed. It was an idea I'd gotten from the late hip-hop princess Aaliyah, from one of her videos, only she had been wearing a long skirt. The little black tube top just barely stayed over my 36 Cs. I had purchased the black sandals with the three-inch heels that I was wearing three days ago, after which I had called Synthia and had told her that I wanted to hit the club this weekend.

She had agreed, of course, but had told me that she wouldn't believe it until she actually saw me up in the club. Well, now she could believe it. Because there I was, in the club, in the flesh . . . literally. And I was workin' them pumps like a pro.

"So you trying to get your groove on?" Synthia responded to the dude. She'd been hitting the clubs since before she was even old enough to get into them. Light skin and dimples could get you into places and provide you with opportunities that black and ugly couldn't. So she wasn't shy about conversing with anybody who stepped to her. I decided to let her do all the talking while I just took notes.

"Yeah, but I don't even know which one of you fine ladies I want to hit the floor with," the dude said, still allowing his eyes to go back and forth from Synthia to me. But now he started licking his lips as well.

"Well, you look like a strong, growing boy." Synthia gave him the once-over and then licked her lips. "So why is it you can't handle the both of us out there?" She nodded toward the dance floor.

"Oh, Miss Lady, you ain't said nothing but a thang." He raised each of his hands to both Synthia and me in order to lead us onto the dance floor.

My heart was beating ninety miles per hour. I'd never, ever danced in front of a lot of people like this before. Dub and I had never even danced at the prom. It was mainly because we arrived late and I had an attitude. Baby D had gotten real sick the day of the prom, and I had had to tend to him and take him to the doctors. I'd been unable to go to my hair appointment and get my makeup done, like I had planned on doing with Synthia, so I had had to wing everything myself. I didn't feel the least bit pretty, to say the least, so I declined getting on that dance floor, where all eyes could see me.

Synthia sat her glass down on the square wood railing we had been standing against and took his hand.

I shot Synthia a look that asked, "What in the world have you gotten me into?"

"Come on," the dude urged me. "You ain't scared, are you?"

"She's scared of how bad she 'bout to hurt you out there on that dance floor," Synthia said, coming to my defense.

"Ooh, then you must be heaven-sent. Because I love pain," he said, looking me dead in my eyes. "Now, put that drink down and let's go do the darn thang."

I drank the last few swallows of my drink down straight, hoping it would give me the courage I needed, like it had done before. I sat the empty glass next to Synthia's and allowed dude to escort me to the dance floor with one hand, while Synthia hung on to his other hand.

Once I got out there on that dance floor, I felt like a star. At first, I barely moved, though, not knowing if I looked crazy or not. So I just wore a smile and slightly mimicked the dances Synthia and the other girls were doing. By the second song the alcohol had kicked in full blast, and I was popping and shaking and bending and grinding. Synthia and I were giving this guy a run for his money. We were doing to him what everybody in the club would call "freakin' him." And it was all in fun, but I guess that was usually what sin started out being . . . all in fun.

Once other guys saw how I got down on the dance floor, I had a dance partner for every song the DJ played and a drink waiting on me when I got finished. Yep, I felt like a superstar, all right. It didn't even matter that the guys didn't see me, but instead saw all my body parts hanging out.

I loved all the attention, negative or not. I never wanted the feeling to end. And since the club was the only place I'd ever experienced this type of acceptance, I knew I had to make it my second home, and that was exactly what I did.

Between calling up Synthia, Lynn, and even Konnie on occasion, I had club partners for Thursday, which was the day of the week the clubs started jumping in Columbus, and I had partners for Friday and Saturday as well. I would dump Baby D off with whoever would keep him: Dub's mom, Nana, or whichever one of my girlfriends I wasn't going out with.

I was having a blast clubbin' it. The more I got used to the club scene, the more relaxed I became. I even upgraded my drinks to sloe gin fizzes and Long Island iced teas. Oh, it was on and poppin'.

At first, Nana was my main babysitter, but she started to travel out of town quite a bit to visit her sister, my aunt Martha, in Florida. After a while it got to the point where it didn't even matter whether I had a sitter or not for Baby D, who was now in first grade. Like I said before, he was a hard sleeper. I'd bathe him, feed him, then tuck him in for the night, and he never even knew Mommy had tiptoed out the door in the wee hours of the night, secretly and selfishly leaving him alone.

After a night of clubbin' on Thursdays, I could barely make it to work the next day, but I always managed to. I remembered one coworker overheard me talking with another coworker about my nights out on the town. Her nights out on the town consisted of evening church service. So whenever I spoke about how I spent my time versus how she spent hers, I always felt guilty. She recited scriptures, while I recited rap lyrics. But any shame I felt would quickly go down the drain the minute I stepped up into a club and was back in my element. I used to say, "Show me in the Bible where it says drinking and going out to the club is a sin." And nobody ever could.

But deep inside, even though nobody could show me anywhere in the Bible where it said that drinking and the kind of dancing I was doing was a sin, I knew it wasn't glorifying God. It was the infant stages of sin. I had a feeling that sooner rather than later, if I didn't stop dancing to the devil's tune, I'd find myself so deep in the pit of hell that not even God could find me.

# Stone Number Twenty-five

Lynn hipped me to this club called Ashley's, where an older, more laid-back crowd hung out. The most popular and most moneymaking night for Ashley's was none other than the day of rest and the day most Christians designated for the Lord. So now I even had a spot to hang out at on Sunday nights.

Just to try to balance my evil with good, I started going to church with Nana on Sundays. She had been going to this predominantly white nondenominational church for the past seven years. I'd tagged along with her on many occasions. The church service lasted only an hour, which was why I loved it. It didn't take up all of my Sunday, and I felt as though I was doing my spiritual deed. It didn't require much work, either, like looking up scriptures, writing down notes from the pastor's teachings, or turning to our neighbors to say this, that, or the other. As a matter of fact, we didn't even really reference the Bible. We just sat there and listened to the pastor, voted in by the church board, give us a moving message. We sang a couple of hymns, listened to the announcements that were read, heard the message, took up the collection, and that was that. My Christian duties were fulfilled in one hour.

It was funny how I'd go from saint to sinner in a matter of hours, because by ten o'clock Sunday night, Baby D was tucked in his bed, if he wasn't spending the night somewhere else, and I was on my way to pick up one of my girls so that we could hit the club.

On one particular Sunday night, Lynn couldn't get a sitter to watch my nephew, so I talked Synthia into going with me to the club. As soon as Synthia and I walked through the door, I could tell that Ashley's was much more lively than usual. It had a whole bunch of new faces I hadn't seen in the month I had been a regular. There was one face in particular that caught my eye. I couldn't help but notice him as he sat across from me at the bar, conversing with his boys.

What made this guy stand out from all the others was that he was smiling. All the other guys were pinned up, trying to look cool or hard-core. But this guy was smiling. He was smiling so much that I felt my jaw beginning to ache from smiling myself. It was like his smile was a magnet. It pulled with such force a smile from the face of anyone who was looking at him. I never remembered Dub making me smile. Ever.

"Yo, what's up, Dino, man?" I heard a guy say. He had just entered the club and had walked over to where this guy and his boys were.

"Nothin' too much," the guy responded, still smiling as he gave the other guy a handshake.

*A handshake,* I thought. A regular, old-fashioned hand-shake. No dap, no secret handshake with a snap or anything else. Just a regular ole handshake. So perhaps he was just a regular ole guy. I hoped he had a regular name, though, because Dino was the name the Flintstones had given their pet dinosaur.

I was sitting there, with my eyes all down this Dino dude's throat, a smile still plastered on my face, but then he busted me. His eyes were dead on me. I had been in such a trance, I didn't even have a clue how long he had been staring back at me.

"What's got you all in a zone?" Synthia asked me. It was her voice that finally made me tear my eyes away from Dino. Even when he busted me, I hadn't looked away.

"Oh, nothing," I lied.

Synthia's eyes followed the trail mine had journeyed just seconds before she'd spoken to me. "Oh, I see. Dude in the button up, huh?"

I looked up, only to see Dino looking over at Synthia and me. First, he'd caught me staring, and now my best friend, so he knew something was up. Just as I expected, a few minutes later Dino made his way over to Synthia and me.

"Hey, smiley," he said, looking dead at me.

"Hey," I replied, my smile even wider now. I couldn't help it. The energy on this dude had just taken over me. "The name is Helen."

"Well, *Helen,* I couldn't help but notice . . ."

I swear on everything, I just knew he was going to say that he couldn't help but notice me staring at him for the past ten minutes.

"Your smile," he said, finishing his thought. "It's refreshing to finally run into a girl in this city who isn't sitting around with an attitude, looking like somebody owes her something or that the world is on her shoulders."

I noticed that he said, "In this city," as if this wasn't his hometown. I decided to fish for some clarity to my suspicions. "I've never seen you around. Are you from here?" I knew that was a corny line, but I didn't know what else to say. The only guy I'd ever been in a relationship with and had to communicate with in this fashion was Dub.

"Naw, I'm from the East Coast," Dino replied to my inquiry.

His smile and the fact that he wasn't from this city were music to my ears. I didn't know why, but there was always something mysterious and exciting about meeting people who weren't from around the way.

"So, how long you been living in Columbus?" I asked him.

"Not even a year," he replied before Synthia cleared her throat to remind me that she was standing there.

"Oh, my bad," I said. "Synthia, this is Dino, Dino, this is my best friend, Synthia."

"Nice to meet you, Dino." Synthia extended her hand, and when I looked up at her, she was smiling too. Like I said, there was just something about this guy.

"Same here." He looked at my almost empty glass and Synthia's empty glass. "Can I buy you two ladies a drink?"

Another point for Team Dino. I hated it when a guy would just walk up to the girl he was trying to holler at and offer to buy only her a drink, leaving her girls feeling all left out. Although Dino had racked up quite a few points when he stood and walked over to me, I knew I had to start deducting them. Because once I was able to take my eyes away from Dino's smile, I discovered the one thing that I didn't think I'd be able to deal with: his weight.

Dino was a little on the chubby side. He wasn't ridiculously obese or anything, but he was pretty thick. Excess weight on a man had just always been a turnoff to me.

"Bartender, can you get these two ladies a glass of whatever it is they are drinking?" Dino told the bartender.

After we gave the bartender our drink order, Synthia, Dino, and I talked and laughed for about the next half hour. Even when Synthia's favorite song came on, she didn't walk off to go dance. That was how interesting it was to be around Dino.

"Look, I'ma go check on my boys over there for a minute." Dino nodded toward the friends he had left to come over and chat it up with us. "I don't want them to think I've forgotten about them or anything."

"I understand," I replied.

"But, hey, do me this one favor," he said as he reached over and picked up the pen the bartender had been using.

He then grabbed a napkin, placed it in front of me, and laid the pen on it. "Have your number ready for me when I get back." He winked and walked away.

"I love him for you," Synthia said with this schoolgirlish purr once Dino was out of earshot. "He was soo sweet. I mean, he is everything Dub never was. Did you see how nice he was? Girl, you better jump on that."

I smiled in agreement, but Synthia could see that something else was lingering in my mind.

"What? What's the matter? You afraid Dub got a couple goons in here watching you or something? I mean, I know you haven't given out your phone number or talked to a guy like that since Dub was locked up, but, girlfriend, move on."

"I know," I whined. "But, girl, don't try to play me and act like you didn't notice."

Synthia looked back over at Dino to see what exactly it was she had missed. "What? Heck, he had all his teeth and both his eyes. What?"

"Girl, he's a big guy. I don't know about dating no big guy."

Synthia looked over and examined Dino again. "Girl, he ain't that big. Besides, his smile is bigger. Ain't nobody gonna pay attention to his big stomach over his big smile."

On that note both Synthia and I couldn't help but burst out laughing.

"See? You just made up my mind for me," I said as I pushed the napkin and pen away without writing my phone number.

"Girl, I was just playing." Synthia playfully hit me on the shoulder. "He is so nice. If you don't give him your phone number, I'm going to give it to him for you, and you'll just have to be mad at me later."

This wasn't supposed to be how this "clubbin' it" thing worked out. I was simply supposed to be out living it up, doing all the things Dub had prevented me from doing. To see what I was missing, to have fun, not to get a boyfriend out of it. I could just look at Dino's fabric and tell he was boyfriend material. Besides, that thing that he had said attracted him to me, my smile, was fake. It was fake because it wasn't mine. It was his, something his smile had incited my own lips to do. What if this thing turned out to be serious and he discovered the real me? The unhappy me? The hurt me that was filled with anger, pain, and bitterness? But then again, what if he was just the antidote to eat away all those poisons?

"Well, here he comes," Synthia said, nodding toward Dino, who had gotten off of his seat and was coming our way. "I'm going to the ladies' room, but if by the time I get back you haven't given him your phone number, I will."

Just as Synthia picked up her purse and headed to the ladies' room, Dino approached me. The first thing he did was look down at the blank napkin. He looked at me, then at the blank napkin again. Next, he pulled the napkin and pen over to himself and began writing.

"Here's my number," he said, handing the napkin to me. "I have no doubts about whether I want to give you mine. Hopefully, you'll have no doubts about using it."

I looked down at the napkin, which had only his phone number on it. "You didn't write your name down."

"Well, I figured since you introduced me to your girl before I even told you my name, you already knew it." Once again, he winked. "But by the way, my name . . . .my real name . . . is Tarino Morton. I got the name Dino because when I introduced myself to the guys at work"—he nodded over at his friends—"one thought I said Dino and he started calling me that. So everybody else did as well. It's kind of stuck with me now." He shrugged. "Nice to meet you, Helen." He shook my hand and then walked away, this time leaving the club.

I couldn't help but smile. He'd busted me. He knew I'd paid enough attention to him that there was a slight chance I'd be calling the number that was in my hand.

# Stone Number Twenty-six

I ended up calling Dino the very next day. I didn't think the same bugaboo rule applied to women that applied to men. The one about not calling a woman the same day, or even the day after, she gives a guy her number.

Just like it was when Dub and I first started dating, Dino and I talked on the phone for hours. I was even reminded of one of Dub's and my early times together; one I had completely forgotten about. Dub had come and tapped on my bedroom window in the middle of the night because he missed me and wanted to say hey and it was too late to call my house. I thought that was the sweetest and most romantic thing. I'd almost forgotten about those times, with so many bad times outweighing the good.

I met Dino on a Sunday, I called him Monday afternoon, and we talked for hours. I was abusing my phone privileges at work, while Dino said he was off work from the Honda plant. All I remember was thinking, *Yes! He's got a job . . . and a good one.* I knew dudes who would have killed to land a position at the Honda plant. It was like working for GM. They made good money. So in turn, any girl would love to have a dude who worked at the Honda plant. That meant that when they went out to dinner, he could afford to pay for the meal.

While I was on the phone, getting to know Dino, one of the office secretaries kept coming over to my desk, asking me stupid stuff just to be nosy. She would smack her lips about me still being on the phone. I knew then that I better end my phone sessions with Dino for the day . . . at least while I was at work. That particular call started at noon, the beginning of my hour-long lunch period, and ended after two. But before hanging up, Dino asked me out to the movies that night. I eagerly accepted. I couldn't remember the last time Dub had taken me to the movies or if we'd even gone. And I was sure if we had gone to the movies, I was the one who had flipped the tab.

"Nana, is it okay if I leave Baby D here asleep tonight while I go catch a movie?" I asked her once I got home from work. Baby D was seven and in second grade now, and was not nearly as much of a handful as he had been when he was a toddler. Nana could handle him even if he woke up during the night.

"Movie? On a Monday night? Who in the world goes to the movies on a Monday night?" Nana replied.

"I met this really, really nice guy last night, while I was out, and he invited me."

Nana frowned. "Go on. Baby D can stay here and sleep. But I don't get you girls today." Nana shook her head. "I mean, I've gone out in my days and met some really, really nice guys. But I ain't never met one where I wanted to just jump up and go out with him the next night after meeting him." Nana left the room, almost in disgust.

Perhaps she was right. Perhaps I should have at least taken that entire week to get to know Dino. He could be a psycho for all I knew. I mean, after all, looks could be deceiving.

The next two weeks I spent almost every single day with Dino. I started slacking off on my schoolwork. I even got called into my college counselor's office, and he warned me that if I didn't maintain decent grades, I would lose my grants and scholarships. I couldn't believe I was starting to mess up in my senior year. I'd come too far, but my real concern seemed to be how far Dino and I would go.

With Dub, I had used school as an escape—anything to get away from him. With Dino, though, the time I spent at school and on schoolwork I wanted to spend with him instead.

Rather than going out to the club with my girls, I'd go with Dino and we'd dance the night away. It was so fun, because club hoppin' wasn't something Dino was used to. He'd been out the night I met him only because he had agreed to join his friend from work to celebrate his friend's birthday. But me, I was a pro on the club scene.

I'd always thought going to the club with a guy was like taking sand to a beach, but I had never had more fun in my life than I had dancing the night away with Dino. He was everything his smile suggested he was. If he stubbed his toe and needed stitches, he'd still be smiling. Nothing could get him down. He never got upset or raised his voice. Not even when a guy at the club bumped into him and made him spill his drink all over himself.

"That's all right, partna," Dino told the guy. Even when the guy offered to buy both Dino and me another drink for our troubles, Dino refused, replacing his own drink himself. I knew there was nothing I could ever do to make Dino get upset with me and yell at me, degrade me, let alone beat on me, like Dub had done for so many years. I had had no idea a man like this even existed. There was a God, after all, and He'd sent me an angel.

When I was spending time with Dino, I truly felt as though I was in heaven. I introduced Dino to all my family, and everyone loved him. Absolutely everyone, even Baby D. Close to three months into my and Dino's relationship, Baby D and I spent more time at Dino's one-bedroom apartment than we did at Nana's big ole house. We even started spending the night there.

"Helen, Baby D tells me that you all sleep on the couch and the floor at Dino's," my mother said to her dismay as we sat in her living room one day. "I don't like that."

"Mom, you make it sound like Dino and I are *sleeping* sleeping together . . . like we are having sex with Baby D right there or something. That does not go down. Believe me."

"Well, I just don't understand why with all those beds at Nana's, you are staying at this guy's place, on the floor. You haven't even known him that long."

I could understand where my mother was coming from, but that still didn't change my mind about wanting to be up under Dino all the time.

By now, Dino and I had become sexually involved, our first time being just a month after we met. I was so nervous that the first time he actually tried to sleep with me, I just couldn't bring myself to do it.

"I can't," I'd said, pushing a naked Dino off of me before he even had a chance to penetrate me. My body had been trembling, like I was about to be raped instead of made love to. I guessed that was just what I'd been used to.

"I understand," Dino had said, putting his clothes back on. And he really did seem to understand, never trying to initiate sex again. A week after that, it was I who ultimately initiated our intimate encounter, which was something I'd never done with Dub.

I have to admit, with Dino, it was so different. It didn't feel like he was taking me. I felt as though he was giving me a part of him. It was safe to say that I had gotten my mojo back when it came to sex.

Dino was only the second man in my life who I'd been with, and he was nothing like the first. He was twenty-one, two years younger than I was, but he worked it like a vet!

Dino was the glory to outweigh all the suffering I had been through with Dub. I felt like the children of Israel when Pharaoh finally let them go. But then, just like for the children of Israel, the journey toward the promised land was nothing like I thought it was going to be.

# Stone Number Twenty-seven

One day I decided to go visit Dino on my lunch break and surprise him with lunch. I stopped by Roosters and grabbed us some chicken before heading to his apartment. Once I arrived at his door, prepared to knock, I couldn't help but notice the piece of paper that was stuck to Dino's front door.

I sat the food down that was in my hands and tenderly peeled the paper off the door and opened the note. I just knew it was going to be from some other chick. *Yep,* I told myself, *I knew he was too good to be true. He's probably got broads all over town, and now one is throwing salt in his game by calling herself leaving him a love note.*

I began to read the letter and realized that it wasn't a note from some other woman at all. It was an eviction notice. My mouth formed a capital letter *O*. Eviction notice? But he worked at the Honda plant. He made good money. He'd been treating me and Baby D to dinner and movies and skating and everything. He had money. There had to be a mistake. Perhaps the landlord had inadvertently placed it on the wrong door. I double-checked the address printed on the letter, and it matched Dino's.

I placed the note back on the door and picked up the food, even though I'd just lost my appetite. I couldn't eat, let alone think, until I got to the bottom of this.

Dino opened the door, all smiles, after I knocked.

"What are you doing here?" He embraced me with a big smile on his face. "Ooh, and you brought lunch." It wasn't unusual for Dino to be home during the day, because he'd told me he worked the evening shift. There were some occasions when he worked the day shift, and usually it was those times when Baby D and I would spend the night at his place.

"And it looks like someone else brought you a little something too." I nodded toward the door.

Just then Dino looked up at his door, and his face flushed with embarrassment. He didn't have a look of wonderment, but a look that told me he knew exactly what that letter hanging on his door was. He peeled it off as he stepped aside and allowed me to enter. There was complete silence as he debated whether or not to discuss the letter with me.

When he looked at me and saw me standing there, waiting for an explanation, he knew I wasn't going to let him enjoy a good meal until he started talking.

"I had hoped I'd have my settlement before it got to this," he said as he shook his head and sat down on the couch.

He'd mentioned to me early on in the relationship that he'd gotten hurt on the job. He had hired an attorney and had been going to therapy and everything. He was expecting to ultimately receive a big payoff.

"So what's up?" I just came right out and asked. "Why would you be getting an eviction notice, unless you haven't been paying rent?" The look he gave me let me know that he hadn't been. "You haven't been paying rent?" I needed to hear him say it.

He shook his head.

"Why not, Dino? Did you expect them to let you live here for free?"

"I expected to have my settlement by now."

"Why didn't you pay them with the money your job has been paying you?"

"What money? My job hasn't been giving me any money."

Okay, now I was stunned. I didn't know anybody nowadays who went to work at a job but didn't get paid. "Then where have you been getting money?"

He paused, then took a deep breath. "Well, at first, my job was paying me for being off—"

"Being off?" I interrupted. "But you haven't been off." My eyes pleaded with his that it wasn't so. But when his eyes were downcast, I knew my gut feeling was correct. This fool had been faking going to work

"Then, when I went to their doctor," he continued without verbally confirming the fact he'd been lying about going to work, "he said there wasn't nothing wrong with me. But my doctor's report was different, so my doctor wrote me off work. My job told me if I didn't come to work, then they were firing me."

"So you let them fire you?"

"My doctor wrote me off work. So I let them fire me, and then I started getting unemployment. When that ran out, I got extensions, but now the extensions have run out."

"Let me get this straight. You've been living here all of this time and not paying your landlord a dime?" I sighed. "I can't believe they ain't put your black tail out before now."

"My landlord has been really cool. I had explained the situation to him, showed him my paperwork and everything."

"So your landlord has been letting you slide on rent, thinking you were going to get this huge settlement and just pay everything in one lump sum?"

It was as if Dino realized at that moment just how stupid everything sounded, how he'd been living on a hope and a dream that wasn't guaranteed. That adorable, kind, and loving smile that had attracted me to him in the first place now looked like a big, stupid grin. It was probably that same big, stupid grin that he'd used to convince his landlord to let him get away with not paying rent. I had to give it to Dino: that smile of his had gotten him a long way, but now, as far as I was concerned, it was at a dead end.

"Look, I have to get back to work." I headed to the door with so much disgust, I couldn't see straight.

Nana had always told me that if something seemed too good to be true, then it was. Dino was just as broke as Dub had ever been. At least Dub had been real about his destitution. He had never put on a front or pretended he had two nickels to rub together. Dino had been acting like everything was good. He had had me fooled. But at that moment, I knew I wasn't going to be the fool anymore.

It wasn't that I was a gold digger or anything, but I'd spent seven or eight years with a man who was broke. Romance without finance was a nuisance whether you were getting beat on or not. I felt that I'd been through so much in my last relationship that I deserved a man who could do all the things the last one couldn't. I had dreamt of this fairy tale; a fairy tale that consisted of me being wined and dined, taken out on the town, on trips and vacations. You name it. And now Dino had pinched me and woken me from my dream.

Dino didn't even try to stop me when I walked out his door that day. He could see disappointment written all over my face. When I stepped out his door, I had made up my mind that I wasn't coming back.

"Pregnant? You're pregnant?" Dino said with excitement.

I just sat there, looking at him like he was crazy. I'd sworn I'd never set foot in his apartment again, but I had to tell him the news face-to-face. Besides, by now his phone had been turned off.

I did not expect the reaction I got from him. What man in his right mind would be excited about a girl he had picked up at the club and had known for only four months being pregnant? And although usually Dino's smile and excitement elicited the same type of reaction from me, they certainly didn't this time.

"I just don't understand how in the world I let this happen," I said, burying my face in my hands and shaking my head. "What was I thinking? What were *we* thinking?"

I knew darn well I wasn't on the pill. I had stopped taking the pill months ago. I knew I wasn't going to have sex with Dub anymore, and I had never imagined in a million years I'd ever have sex with another man. That was just how much Dub had made me hate the entire act of sex. I'd vowed that I'd never let a man inside my body again. But somehow I had got caught up in the whirlwind romance with Dino and all of that went out the window, and now here I was, paying the piper.

"Why do you look so sad? I mean, this is a life growing inside of you." Dino came and sat down next to me on the couch in his living room. "There is a little me or a little you inside there." He smiled and rubbed my stomach.

For the first time in the four months we had been together, his actions, his happiness, were ticking me off. This was not the time to be happy.

"What's wrong with you?" I pushed his hand off my stomach and stood up. "Do you really think I'm about to have this baby? You are out of your mind."

The look on Dino's face said it all. It was as if he didn't even recognize me. He'd never witnessed me poppin' off like this before. "Baby, I know you're not thinking about doing what I think you are."

"What else is there to do?" I shot back. "Have a baby by a man who is not my husband? No way, Jose. No more babies out of wedlock for me." I shook my head.

He jumped up, as if he'd just had the brightest idea he'd ever had in his life. "Then let's get married."

Was this dude serious? I mean, he couldn't be Mr. Do the Right Thing all the time, especially not now. He couldn't marry me. He had no idea what he'd be getting himself into. But Dino was relentless. He went on and on and on about how we could make this thing work. It was as if I was speaking a foreign language when I reiterated to him that I did not want to keep this baby. The more he pressed, the more I knew I'd have to do something to make him change his mind. I needed him to see the real me. There was no way in the world he'd want to marry the person buried beneath the one I had been pretending to be for the past few months.

"What do I look like marrying, let alone having a baby by, a man who don't even have a job? I mean, look at you. . . ." And that was when it began. It was like history repeating itself. I began to spew the same type of insults I used to chuck at Dub in the beginning, only now they were directed toward Dino.

My insults continued. "You are only a day in court from being put out on the streets. Then what you gonna do? Come live with me at my nana's? Negro, please." I rolled my eyes and sucked my teeth. "What am I going to do with a man who can't provide for me and the child I already have? I wouldn't have even given you the time of day in the club that night had I known you were dang near homeless. Heck, we could have skipped the movies, and you could have put it toward your rent."

Dino just sat there, speechless, as I rambled on, string after string of insulting curse words spilling from my mouth. I was so angry, but truth be told, I wasn't angry at Dino. I was angry at myself. I was angry for allowing myself to even be in this position. But unfortunately for Dino, when I was mad at myself, I was mad at the world. And so the world would pay.

"I can't even believe this is you standing here, saying all this stuff to me." He got up from the couch and walked over to me, as if someone had just punched him in the gut and knocked all the wind out of him. "Helen, baby, it's me."

He was acting as if I had been knocked over the head and had lost my memory and he was trying to get me to come to. But I'd already come to my senses. I'd come to my senses a week before, when I'd left his apartment after finding out he was jobless and would soon be homeless.

"Look, just forget I ever came. I don't know what I was thinking, coming here, anyway. It's not like you have any money to put on the abortion."

I grabbed my purse and headed to the door. Unlike the last time, this time Dino stopped me.

"I just want you to know, I do not want you to do this, but since you are set on doing it, I at least want to be there for you."

"Sure," I replied nonchalantly. "Let me look into it, and I'll give you all the details. I'll let you know the date and time, and you can come pick me up and take me."

"That's cool, but . . ." He looked down.

*Oh, God, there's more bad news?* I thought.

"My car broke down a couple days ago. The guy who lives a couple doors down from me is a mechanic. He said the car is dead. Engine is shot. So . . ."

"So that means not only are you jobless and homeless, but you're carless too?" I snapped, shaking my head. "And you wonder why you're about to be babyless."

I left Dino's apartment and went straight home and pulled out the yellow pages. I was going to call and make an appointment at the same place I'd gone when I aborted Dub's baby, which was an act *nobody* knew of, not even Dub. I had actually pushed it so far to the back of my mind, I'd often forgotten completely about the incident.

About two years after having Baby D, I had gotten a double ear infection and had to take antibiotics. When I turned up pregnant, I was shocked because I'd been on birth control pills. The doctor concluded that all the antibiotics in my system had decreased the effectiveness of the birth control.

I knew if I had that baby, I would be making a horrible mistake. Plus, I thought there was a chance that since it was Dub's seed growing inside me, it might turn out to be a monster too. I couldn't let that happen, so I went to the clinic and got an abortion. I felt so bad as I sat in the waiting room, about to kill my baby. But when I noticed the stomach of the girl next to me, which looked as if it harbored a full-grown baby, one that she was about to abort, I didn't feel so bad anymore.

I was home free until Dub found a paper from the doctor's stating that I was pregnant. By then there was no more baby, so I thought fast and told him I'd miscarried. Thinking his unborn child had died tore him up. I told him I knew he'd be hurt, which was why I kept it from him. I didn't want to hurt him. Lucky for me, he bought it.

Unlucky for me, Dub became hell-bent on trying to get me pregnant again. Whenever my period came, he'd beat me for not being pregnant. So I prepared myself to get a beating at least once a month, because I knew I'd never get pregnant. Unbeknownst to him, I was popping birth control pills left and right. I couldn't take a chance on ever getting pregnant again by him. I couldn't risk giving birth to a monster. I'd gotten lucky the first time with Baby D, but who was to say I'd be so lucky the next?

Dino wasn't a monster, but I couldn't see myself having his baby, either. I was able to get an appointment the very next day after Dino's and my talk, during my lunch hour. The visit went nothing like I'd expected. I wanted to get the abortion over with quick, fast, and in a hurry. I couldn't have been any further than about four weeks along, but I'd been as sick as a dog.

After my appointment, I was so upset, I couldn't even think straight. They'd told me that because I was only four weeks along, they couldn't perform the abortion. They said I had to wait until I was six weeks because there was a risk that if they performed the procedure any earlier, they'd miss the baby entirely and I'd remain pregnant, ultimately perhaps giving birth to a deformed baby.

I didn't care, though; I needed this sickness out of me. One thing they did mention at the clinic was that my insurance might pay for a portion of the abortion bill, so once I got back to work, I called up my insurance company and asked them about it. The insurance company was willing to pay fifty dollars toward the procedure at the clinic I wanted to have it at and $280 toward the procedure if it was done by an in-plan doctor. After doing my research, I learned that the closest in-plan doctor was located all the way in Cincinnati, which was a two-hour drive from Columbus. So a week later, on a Friday afternoon, after I had decided I'd push the date of my missing period back a week so that this place wouldn't make such a big fuss about me not being six weeks, Dino and I were on the road to Cincinnati, where once again, I'd violate Him, who was in me.

# Stone Number Twenty-eight

When Dino and I arrived at the Cincinnati clinic, the protestors were out in full force. Their harmonious chants invaded the stillness that had taken on the role of a backseat passenger for the past two hours. Dino and I succeeded in making our way through the multitude of like-minded individuals who were carrying signs that had gruesome pictures of abortions gone bad. We signed in at the front desk and then waited in the waiting area. Several ladies' names were called, and they were escorted back to the prep room.

"Amy, Susan, Helen, Felicia, and Tabatha, you can come on back," the receptionist called out.

It was like a webisode of a bootleg *The Price Is Right,* where the contestants were told to "Come on down!" Only, there would never be a right price for what was about to take place. And nobody was going to take the grand prize home.

I stood upon hearing my name being called. I was not sure how long it took me to take that first step. I wasn't having doubts about getting an abortion, just thoughts about keeping the baby. Love in my heart was scarce. I felt as if there was barely enough to go around as it was. It wouldn't be fair to bring a child into this world if I was able to nourish it with cow's milk but would starve it of a mother's love. I took that first step.

This was the part where I had to separate from Dino. I wished he could come back there with me to hold my hand, but I was a big girl, making big girl decisions after making big girl mistakes, something I was terribly perfect at.

The nurse led me and some other women into a room that was as cold as an icebox. I didn't mind the numbing cold. In fact, I was grateful for the counterfeit anesthetic, praying it would sedate my soul.

In the prep room, the other women and I changed into hospital gowns and sat in a subdivision of identical chairs. Once again, we waited for our names to be called, this time so that we could go into the room where the procedure was going to be performed. The quiet atmosphere was undisturbed until one of the girls next to me molested it with her voice.

"I can't believe just a few months ago I was one of them," she said to no one in particular.

"One of who?" I decided to ask. I needed voices to drown out the persistent one in my head that was trying to pick apart and invalidate my reasons for being at the clinic. So I wanted to keep the conversation going.

"Them." The girl nodded toward the window that kept us estranged from the protestors. "I actually marched in a pro-life rally. I was chanting the same stuff they are chanting against abortion and carrying some of those same signs. Can you believe it?" She chuckled a nervous chuckle. "Funny how different the shoes look when *you're* wearing them, and not that girl next to you."

A woman across the room chimed in. "My husband used to always speak against abortion too."

All the other ladies wore the same countenance that I did when we looked over at the woman and then down at the wedding ring hugging her finger. For some reason, I just never pictured a married couple choosing to abort their child. I thought it was just mixed-up, unwed chicks like me who subjected their bodies to this act akin to butchering.

"What changed his mind?" I was too curious not to ask.

"The fact that after so many years we are just now able to get our heads above water. I mean, it seems like we had been struggling forever. Just when things are going good, I find out I'm pregnant." She rubbed her belly. "My husband and I both agree that having this baby will only put us back in the poorhouse." She looked down at her belly. "God will give us back this same baby someday, when we are ready to have one."

"You'll never be ready," said a heavyset woman, jumping in. She was so big that she could have already been nine months pregnant, for all we knew. "If God sat around waiting until man was ready, we'd never get anywhere."

No one either concurred or challenged the big girl's claim. The mere fact that God was being mentioned made everyone stir and feel even more conviction than the protestors had already deposited in us.

Silence revisited and plagued the room as we all sat lined up, waiting to be called into the procedure room one by one, as if we were in a meat factory and were cows waiting to be slaughtered. Finally, the turn was mine.

"Helen Lannden," the nurse called out.

"Right here," I replied as I got up. I followed her into a room that was the size of a closet. I looked around the room with my nose turned up. I didn't know what I was expecting, but I guess it just wasn't this. I knew it sounded tasteless and callous to be comparing abortion clinics, but the last one was a nice size room. Everything in it was white and nice and clean. This room was dark and dingy, and instead of lying on a table, which I would climb up on, I would have the procedure done while sitting in the kind of chair you might find at the dentist's.

I nervously mounted the chair, wondering what, if anything, could make this daunting process more comfortable. It wasn't supposed to be comfortable. This wasn't a day at the park, where I was about to fly a kite. This was more like a funeral, a death.

The doctor knocked on the door and then entered the room. After fiddling with some instruments, he said, "I'm going to need you to relax while I inject this into you. It's going to numb your cervix walls."

I cringed as I looked up and saw the colossal needle dribbling fluid from its tip. I became infuriated with this medical professional for having the audacity to command me to relax.

I recalled this part of the procedure—being injected with the needle—from my last abortion. It hurt. I braced myself for the injection, but before the doctor could inject me, there was a thud on the door and a nurse peeked her head in.

Both the doctor and I gave her a look that said, "Couldn't this wait until we've finished up here?"

"Uh, there is a very angry gentleman out here who insists on seeing the patient," she told the doctor and then looked at me. "You don't have to see him."

In other words, she was telling me I could go ahead and get this abortion done so that they could get their money before the jerk outside tried to talk me out of it.

"I'll talk to him," I said, not because I cared that Dino was outside the door, demanding to see me, but because I dreaded having that medical spear pierce me between my legs and I wanted to stall for time.

I got up out of the chair and walked out of the room, wearing nothing but a paper gown. The nurse stayed right there in the doorway, with a look on her face that told Dino that if he tried any mess, she was either going to call 911 or go for the gun she kept under her desk for any pro-life psychos who tried something crazy.

"What's up?" I asked him, as if we were two teenagers posted up in the school hallway.

"I don't want you to do this," he said flat out. "I can't let you kill my baby."

What was going on here? On the drive up, Dino had been fine. I figured that even though he hadn't voiced it, he had finally agreed with me that bringing a child into the world wasn't the best of ideas, considering I was living with Nana and he was about to be living on the streets. I thought I could rightfully assume this since Dino hadn't even once tried to talk me out of my decision on the drive to the clinic.

I looked down at his hands to find him holding a couple of brochures. My question had been answered. It was now clear that the protestors had infected him with their beliefs. They'd wrapped their pro-life doctrines firmly around his conscience, and here he was, trying to contaminate my made-up mind. Just that fast, Dino's emotional weather forecast had gone from a cool summer breeze to Hurricane Sandy. But I was not about to allow him to enforce his evacuation plan on me.

"Look, Dino, I don't know what them crazies out there said to you, but I'm not keeping this baby."

"Look at this!" he screamed at me, holding up one of those brochures in my face. "Look at this dead baby that was sucked out of a woman during an abortion procedure! I'm not going to let you do this to our baby."

I refused to look at the mutilated baby, keeping my eyes locked with Dino's instead. "This is my body. You can't tell me what I am and am not going to do. I am not having a baby by you, or anybody else, for that matter. I'm not about to be some breeding machine for broke men who can't even afford to keep a roof over their own heads, let alone a baby. Where are we going to get money for milk, diapers, baby clothes, and baby food?"

"You can get on WIC or welfare or something," he replied.

"Fool, are you crazy? What woman in her right mind has a deliberate welfare baby? Why would anyone want to have a baby that Uncle Sam has to take care of and not the daddy? That's stupid and selfish, and I'm neither." I turned away to go back into the room.

"So you'd rather kill the baby than have it and be on welfare? And you don't think that's stupid and selfish?" Dino said as he snatched me by my arm and yanked me back to face him.

"Is everything okay?" the nurse asked me, giving me the look. I felt like she had my back like one of the chicks in the movie *Set It Off*.

"Yes, everything is fine," I assured her as I jerked away from Dino and turned back to the door.

"My legacy," he cried. "It's going to be destroyed."

I tried to drown out his exclamations the same way I'd done triumphantly with the protestors who welcomed me in the abortion clinic's parking lot earlier.

"Sorry, Dino, but my mind is made up." I looked around. "I mean, we're here now, for God's sakes. Let me just get this over with already."

I left a heartbroken Dino outside the door while I went back in the room. The jaunt back to the chair was punctuated with weeping, and it wasn't coming from me. Through the door I could hear Dino tipping the scale of devastation, defeat. He was just a plain ole hot mess. One would think he was the one who was about to go through the procedure. Once again, I positioned myself in the chair.

"Ready?" the doctor asked.

I took a long deep breath. "Ready," I replied as I closed my eyes and put a voluntary end to my pregnancy.

# Stone Number Twenty-nine

It had only been a week since the abortion, and prior to it I had been staying with Nana on a more regular basis, after discovering the eviction notice on Dino's door. I'd made up my mind that I was through with Dino, but just like all the times I'd said I was through with Dub, something just kept pulling me back in. I'd felt abandoned and alone so much in my life that maybe I honestly didn't want to be alone . . . with myself. Perhaps being with myself was the worst of two evils, so I opted to be with a man instead, any man willing to keep me company just so I wouldn't have to keep myself company.

Nana knew nothing about the fact that I'd had an abortion. She and I were close, but that was not something I wanted to sit and talk to her about over a game of Scrabble. I honestly couldn't say that I felt a boatload of remorse or shame about the abortion. I hated to admit it, but I truly felt relieved. Men changed. Dub had, and just in case Dino did, I didn't want to have any ties to him, especially not a child.

Even though prior to the trip to Cincinnati I had stayed with Nana, for the past week, ever since returning from the abortion clinic, I'd stayed at Dino's every night. The day we drove back to Columbus from the clinic, I ended up staying the night at Dino's. I had made arrangements for Ms. Daniels to pick up Baby D from school, and since it was Friday, she just agreed to allow him to stay over the entire weekend. I was glad that both I and Baby D had a place to lay our head besides Nana's. For one, I didn't want Nana asking me a whole bunch of questions about why I was so drained and dreary, or catching me taking my meds and then questioning why I was on medication. It was just easier that way.

Another reason why I stayed at Dino's was for his sake. I mean, he was a complete mess on the drive back home. I feared that if I didn't stay by his side and allow him to continue spilling his emotions out on me, he'd get to calling up all his friends and family and putting our business out there. I did not want my name or business in the streets of Columbus.

Even though he was hurt and upset with me, a couple hours after arriving back home, he managed to pull himself together enough to be the gentleman that he was and cater to me. He put himself and his feelings aside and treated me how he would have wanted to be treated had the tables been turned. He treated me as though I'd just given birth to his child instead of aborting it. He never let anyone or any situation alter his character. Not even me . . . not yet, anyway.

*In jus' a few more weeks you're dead. Everybody in your family is dead, you whore. I spoke to Baby D on the phone when he spent the weekend over at my mom's. He told me 'bout that Dino cat you lying up with and got my son around. I can't believe you whorin' in front of my son. I'm going to show you what happens to whores when I get out of here. And let this Dino guy know that as a token of my appreciation for him tearing my family apart, he's a dead man too. I hope when I creep up on y'all, I catch y'all in bed together so I can carve y'all up together. You better let Dino know he better get his*

*last one off with my girl, because when I'm out of
here, it's over for the both of you.*

*Ha, ha, ha. I can see your face now while you're
reading this letter. I bet you forgot all about me,
didn't you? I bet you even thought I forgot all about
you. Well, you may have forgotten about me, but I
didn't forget about you, whore.*

*You thought you could just play me, kick me
when I was down? You once said if I ever went to
jail, you'd leave me. Well, I guess you held true to
your word, but now I'm going to hold true to mine.*
  *Dub*

Dub was right; I had forgotten about him. For the
past five months I'd been consumed with Dino's and my
relationship. Then there was the pregnancy issue, which,
ironically, ended up bringing Dino and me even closer.

The night we got back to Columbus from Cincinnati,
we'd lain back and talked. I'd apologized for putting him
through everything.

"I can't explain why I am the way I am sometimes," I
had admitted to Dino. Maybe it was the painkillers I was
on, but I was truly opening up to Dino. "Half the time I
don't even think I'm mad at the person I'm lashing out at
more so than I'm mad at myself."

"But why? I don't get it," Dino had said as he lay next to
me in bed and stroked my hair.

I thought for a moment before answering, searching
for the right words to describe feelings that I could hardly
explain to myself. "Sometimes I just hate myself. I hate
the world, even. I feel like I just got dumped off in a life
that I didn't ask for . . . and I'm mad." I went as far as
slamming my fist down on the bed.

My mind went back to my childhood, and I shared with
Dino the lie my family had lived as far as my true pater-

nity was concerned. I thought about how my biological father hadn't stayed around and fought for me, fought to have me in his life. I thought about how much, growing up, I had hated my skin because it was so different from everyone else's in my family. I thought about how I had got teased because of it. I thought about how I had settled for crazy instead of love in the form of Dub because I didn't feel as if I deserved any better than that. Even worse, that maybe I didn't want better than that. Perhaps I just wanted someone to want me, someone to fit me into their life willingly, and if that came with a few kicks, punches, and scratches, then so be it. There was so much stagnant pain there, so much stagnant hurt.

"Sometimes I just don't want to be the only one hurting," I admitted to Dino, tears spilling from my eyes by now.

"It's okay," Dino said to me, his eyes watering. "I'm not here to hurt you. I'm here to love you unconditionally, for exactly who you are." He then kissed me on the forehead and said, "Things will get better. I promise."

For the first time since we'd met, we confessed our love for one another. My heart was filled 100 percent with love for Dino, or at least what I thought was love. He didn't give me butterflies in my stomach or anything like that. But our relationship was fairly new. There was time for the butterflies to free themselves from their cocoons.

We said that someday we would get married and everything would be all right.

"I talked my landlord into giving me more time," Dino said. "I promise everything is going to work out."

"I know it is," I said to Dino, wanting so desperately to believe that myself. I even managed to convince him that God would give us our baby back once we were married and ready to take care of it, just like the woman in the clinic had believed. But if Dub had anything to do with it, the only thing Dino and I would be doing together was getting buried.

After reading Dub's letter, which had been waiting for me at Nana's house after work, I allowed it to fall from my hands and onto the floor. I had to admit I was in shock. How could I have so easily forgotten about Dub's threats? And, even worse, how could I have gotten Dino all mixed up in this mess? Now, though he didn't know it, his life was in danger. So was my entire family's.

"Helen?" Nana said as she entered my bedroom. Her voice tore my mind from my dismal thoughts.

I jumped and grabbed my chest.

"What is it?" Nana asked as she walked toward me, noticing the letter on the floor. She asked with her eyes if she could read it as she knelt and picked it up. With my eyes and a nod of my head, I replied in the affirmative.

The room was dead silent while Nana read the letter. I watched the expression on her face do a dance of confusion, disgust, and even fear, although she tried to hide the last of her emotions. Nana was scared for me, for Baby D, and, more than likely, even for herself.

I didn't know what I expected Nana's reaction to be, but I guess I didn't expect what came out of her mouth next. "Come on. Grab Baby D and let's go," she ordered me as she exited the room to retrieve her coat, purse, and keys.

"Where we going, Nana?" I asked, ready to follow her to the moon if it meant Dub would not be able to get to us.

"To the police."

# Stone Number Thirty

Nana drove me to the Columbus Police Department, where officers directed us to the Franklin County Court-house after we informed them of the reason for our visit. Until Nana told me, I honestly had had no idea that Dub sending me threatening letters was even a crime.

At the courthouse we were steered to the prosecutor's office. After waiting two hours, we were called into the back by a prosecutor's assistant. Nana waited in the lobby with Baby D while I went in the back.

"So what is it we can try to help you with today?" the assistant asked, sitting at his desk with his hands clasped together.

"I don't need you to try," I told the assistant. "I really need you to help . . . period." I pulled Dub's letter out of my purse, along with the ones he'd written me in the past. I handed them to the assistant, my hand shaking the entire time.

"My, my," he said after reading the letters and initially being speechless.

"So can you help?" The tone of my voice was desperate. The look on my face was desperate. I was desperate.

"Has he physically harmed you?" the assistant asked.

"No, I mean, yes. I mean no, not while he's been in jail," I replied nervously. "But he used to abuse me all the time. That's how I know he's going to do everything he says he's going to do."

"Is that why he's in jail now, for hitting you?"

"No," I was sad to say, but then I perked up upon remembering something. "But he did go to jail once before for hitting me."

The assistant perked up as well, leaning forward. "And you pressed charges and he got sentenced to jail?"

My excitement fizzled out. "No. I dropped the charges."

"So there's basically just an arrest, no conviction?"

I nodded my head, and his gleam of hope seemed to fizzle out.

"So all we have here are these letters, huh?" He sounded as if he had to try a murder case with no dead body, no DNA evidence, only circumstantial evidence. The assistant thought for a moment before raising his index finger and asking me to hold on a second while he went to speak with one of his superiors. With the letters in hand, he exited the room, returning a few minutes later.

Excitedly, he plopped back down at his desk and began rummaging through his drawers, pulling out forms. He began to write on the forms as I sat in silence, watching him. Once he'd finish doing what he had to do with one form, he'd slide it over to me. "Here. Read this and then sign if you agree with everything."

I read form after form, which pretty much described my complaint. One of the forms contained excerpts from the letters. After I signed each form, the assistant made copies of the letters and attached them to the forms.

"There!" he said, as if he'd just built the most beautiful sand castle on the beach. "This will stop that lunatic!"

I sighed a breath of relief. At the time I didn't know how all those forms were going to stop Dub, but what I did know was that the assistant hadn't trivialized Dub's words, hadn't characterized them as nothing more than a jailhouse letter from an angry boyfriend.

"These are restraining orders," the prosecutor said, answering my unasked question. "What these documents will do is prevent Mr. Daniels from sending letters to your home or calling your home. The warden will also receive copies. Miss Lannden, you won't have to worry about receiving any more threats from Mr. Daniels."

"Thank you. Thank you so much." I was relieved as I stood and shook the assistant's hand. But then something hit me. "But he'll get out soon and won't have to write letters anymore. . . ." I knew the assistant knew what I was alluding to. Just because Dub couldn't write down his threats in letters anymore didn't mean he wasn't going to go through with what he'd already written.

"Typically, once guys like him are called out on this type of thing, they eventually get over it and move on. The fact that they know the law is involved is kind of like a wake-up call to them. So not to worry. You should be able to sleep a lot better now." His warm smile was reassuring.

"Thank you. Thank you so much," I said again, allowing his words to serve as a dose of comfort.

"No need to thank me. That's my job," he said as he escorted me back into the lobby and handed me copies of the filed orders for my records.

"So what did they say?" Nana asked me and stood up.

I showed her the papers. "They helped me file a restraining order prohibiting him from sending me any more letters or calling me."

"See, I knew there was something somebody could do about his threats," Nana said as she hugged me.

And just as always, Nana was right. Something had been done . . . for now. But I couldn't help but think about a case I saw on the news where a woman had been stabbed, along with her children, by her husband. She and her children were pronounced dead at the scene. She, obviously, hadn't been protected. I could only pray I would never encounter her fate.

***

"How's it going, Helen?" Keith, the mail guy at my job, asked me as he approached my desk with the mail cart.

I found Keith's questioning strange. It wasn't the question he asked. He always asked everybody how it was going. But today I noticed a different tone in his voice. He asked the question as if expecting a positive response from me to become negative and a negative response to become worse.

"I'm hanging in there, Keith. Why? What's up?"

Without saying a word, he removed a letter from the top of his pile and handed it to me. He didn't even look me in the face after that. He just scurried along to complete his mail route.

The letter was already opened, as that was customary at my job. Sometimes customers would address letters to the wrong person or department, so it was the mail room's job to briefly review any letters not marked "personal" or "confidential" and make sure they were directed to the correct person or department.

I had to look at the envelope for only a second to immediately recognize it as one of Dub's letters. I'd received one other letter at Nana's house since filing the restraining order. I figured it had been sent in between the actual filing and Dub being notified of the filing.

My heart began to race as I pulled the letter out of the envelope and read it. It was the most vulgar, threatening letter he'd sent me to date. It was so disgusting, I had to pull my trash can out from under my desk and vomit.

It had been over a week since I'd filed the restraining order. Certainly, he'd been notified by now that he would be violating the order by sending letters. The first paragraph of the letter cleared up my confusion.

*Oh yeah, and I got your li'l funky restraining order telling me not to write you or call you at your house anymore. Well, you stupid ho, it didn't say anything about sending you letters at work or calling your job, so . . . I'll be in touch. Literally, as I'm out of here in a week, anyway.*

*I hope you know, Helen, that reporting me to the warden only pissed me off more, which makes things a lot worse for you. You're still dead when I get out of here, but I'm going to torture you first. Just wait and see.*

*I'm going to cut your throat. Slice you from ear to ear. I can't wait to see the blood pour out. I'll probably have to just kill myself afterward, because you are not worth me spending the rest of my life in here. So once I kill myself, I'll see you in hell to torment you all over again.*

*Enjoy life while you can. Because in one week and counting, I'm out of here . . . and so are you!*
*Dub*

While reading the letter, I could hear Dub's voice say each and every word. I could feel his hot breath on my neck as he snarled the words through gritted teeth. I felt so trapped, I didn't know what to do. At that point, I just wanted to take my own life in a slow, painless manner before Dub got the chance to do all the bodily harm he anticipated doing to me.

"Helen, I need you to—"

I heard the sound of a male voice and felt a hand rest upon my shoulder. The next thing I knew, I was hunched over, crying my eyes out. I thought it was Dub's voice that I'd heard and Dub's touch that I'd felt. My mind was playing tricks on me.

"Helen, are you okay?" I heard the male voice ask, not recognizing that it belonged to my boss.

"Helen?" This time it was a female voice. "What's wrong? Are you okay?" I felt the woman's arms around me as she continued to ask me if I was okay.

I couldn't see who it was, because my eyes were so filled with tears. After a few seconds I felt her release me and bend down. I blinked away as many tears as I could and was able to make out who the woman was. It was Jina, my boss's secretary, and she was rising back up from bending down, having retrieved the letter, which had fallen at my feet. I watched her scan it and then hand it to my boss.

"Have a seat," Jina suggested to me, and then she helped me to get situated in my chair. "I'll go get you some water." She walked away as my boss stood there reading the letter.

"I'm sorry," I said, apologizing for making such a scene.

"No apology necessary, Helen, if your reaction is to the words on this piece of paper." My boss stood there, holding Dub's letter in front of me. "Is this what has you upset?" My boss had an appalled look on his face from the words he'd just read.

"Yes." I nodded. "It's from my ex-boyfriend. My son's father. He's going to kill me." Once again I lost control. I could see other employees peeking over into our area to see what was going on, but I didn't care. For once, I did not care what people thought. What would it matter, anyway, once I was dead and gone? "Oh, God, he's really going to kill me!"

"Calm down, Helen." He rested his hand on my shoulder. "Let's go into my office and talk about it," he suggested just as Jina returned with the water.

"Here you go, Helen." She handed me the water.

"Jina, I'm going to talk to Helen in my office. Can you please come and sit in?" my boss asked her. I could tell the last thing he wanted was to be in his office alone with a hysterical woman who was going nuts. The next thing he knew, I'd be accusing him of harming me or something. I didn't blame him for not wanting to take any chances, because at that moment, I had to admit, I wasn't in my right mind.

"So how long have you been receiving these types of threats?" my boss asked me once the three of us were secure behind the closed door of his office.

"He sent me several a while ago. He started sending them again, so I just got a restraining order against him," I replied. "I guess some jailhouse lawyer broke down the restraining order to him, and he realized that it didn't prevent him from sending letters here, to my workplace."

"Do you take these threats seriously?" my boss asked me. "I mean, obviously, you do, but I just need to hear you say it."

A confused look crossed my face, and I guess my boss detected it, as he began to explain his reason for asking.

"See, I need you to tell me this, because by doing so, you are officially putting your place of employment on notice about this domestic threat. By putting your employer on notice, your employer is now obligated to take every precaution necessary in addressing this situation in the workplace." My boss took a deep breath and then asked again. "Do you take your ex-boyfriend's threats seriously? Has he ever physically harmed you before, giving you cause to believe he would see his threats through?"

I swallowed hard. Answering my boss truthfully would mean having to tell him that I had allowed Dub to physically harm me. That I had stayed in a relationship for over seven years with someone who was mentally, sexually, and physically abusing me. I'd never had to do that before, confess outright to someone who knew me. Telling that prosecutor had been different. He didn't know me. Well, he knew me, but not like that. He knew me because of the hundreds of other women just like me who had occupied his office chair. Same story, different girl.

My boss *knew* me, though, and so I couldn't fix my mouth to confess it. What kind of stupid idiot would my job think I was? They thought they had hired someone smart, someone college educated who was in the process of earning their bachelor's degree. They'd probably fire me when they realized how dumb I was, after all.

As if Jina, who was sitting next to me, could see my anguish, she rested her hand on my knee for comfort. I looked up at her, and she nodded, as if to say, "You can do this, Helen."

I sighed and finally spoke. "Yes. Yes, I take the threats seriously, and yes . . . he has physically harmed me before."

Jina sighed just as deeply as I did, as if she'd been holding her breath, as if she somehow knew exactly what I was going through. Who knows? Perhaps she did.

Now that I had confessed to my coworkers out loud that I was a victim of domestic abuse, I had only one question. "So are you going to help me?"

"Yes." My boss nodded. "Yes, indeed. We are going to do everything we need to in order to ensure your protection while you're here."

And that was just what my boss did. He immediately called a meeting with the owner of the company to enlighten him about my situation. The receptionist and her backups were notified, as well as the mail room staff. The building security was even asked to be more vigilant. A description of Dub was given to everyone who might encounter him, as were emergency safety procedures. The very next day my company even installed an emergency call button under the receptionist's desk and a button that gave her the capability of automatically locking the glass double entrance doors to the office at her discretion.

I wouldn't call it a false sense of security. I appreciated the steps my job had taken to protect me. But I couldn't stay inside my workplace forever. I had to eventually go out into the world, a world in which I felt one day, and sooner rather than later, Dub would be waiting.

# Stone Number Thirty-one

"Helen," the receptionist said through the phone intercom, "you have a call on line three."

"Thank you," I told her, then waited for the call to come through. "This is Helen," I said, picking up after the first beep.

"Five days left and you're dead," was all I heard. It was all I had allowed myself to hear before slamming the phone down in its cradle as if it were a hot potato.

Dub's chilling voice had come through that phone like a killer's voice in a horror movie, just before the victim got killed. I couldn't believe it. Dub was, once again, taking advantage of the loophole in the restraining order, and he was using it to his advantage to the fullest. First, the letter to my job and now the phone call. He'd left me with no choice. I'd have to go back down to the prosecutor's office and see if there was a way to fix the restraining order to include my workplace. But with him being released in less than a week, did it really matter now?

My eyes immediately watered. Dub meant business. He wasn't going to let up. He was consumed with thoughts of killing me and my loved ones and wasn't going to let up until he did.

"Helen." I jumped when I heard the receptionist's voice blaring through my telephone intercom once again.

"Uh . . . uh . . . yes," I stammered.

"You have another call, on line one this time."

I remained silent for a few seconds. I was trying to think of a lie the receptionist could tell the caller as to why I couldn't take the call. It was too late; the call was coming through.

After the first beep I thought about allowing it to go to voice mail because I knew it wasn't anybody but Dub, but then I'd eventually have to hear his chilling voice on my voice mail. By the second beep, I'd convinced myself to just get it over with. The clock was ticking. Days were passing by. Sooner or later I'd have to face Dub. I needed peace of mind back. And fast.

"Listen, you bastard," I began in a low whisper, not wanting my coworkers to hear the language I was about to use. "If you are going to kill me and my family, just do it. Be a man about it and just do it, but don't be a coward, sending me letters and calling me on the phone. Do you hear me?"

There was silence on the phone. I assumed Dub was in shock as my standing up to him was a rarity. I hadn't stood up to him since I'd discovered the naked woman in my house. That had been the first and the last . . . until now. And although I was making a death wish, I felt good about it. I felt empowered, for lack of a better word. I quickly went from feeling empowered to feeling embarrassed when the voice on the other end of the line finally spoke.

"Helen . . . this is your aunt Lisa."

I burst into tears. For the first time in my life I'd finally stood up to Dub, or at least I thought I had, only to find that it wasn't even him on the other end of the phone. I couldn't take it anymore. I just couldn't. Not only hadn't I stood up to Dub, but now I'd definitely have to explain to my aunt what my rant was about. And through plenty of tears, I did just that. I told her all about the years of abuse, my escape from Dub, his letters, threats, and phone calls. "I just don't know what to do, besides plan my own funeral," I said, sniffing through the phone receiver.

"I feel so bad. I should have known. I should have done something." I could tell she was now crying.

"Please, Aunt Lisa, this is hardly your fault. There was nothing you could have done about it," I assured her.

She paused for a moment, sniffing and then blowing her nose. "You know what? You're right." Her voice lightened up just a tad. "Maybe there wasn't anything I could have done about it then, but that doesn't mean I can't do something now." Then I could almost hear the wheels churning in her head. "I've got an idea," my aunt Lisa said.

Once Aunt Lisa shared with me her plan on how to help me deal with my situation with Dub, I was on the fence. Going along with her idea meant opening myself up big-time. It meant taking a big risk, but the more I thought about Dub and his threats, which I knew beyond a doubt he would go through with, the more I realized I didn't have anything to lose. After all, what could be worse than losing my own life? So hesitantly at first, but eagerly at the end, I agreed to my aunt's idea. Her idea definitely trumped just running down to the prosecutor's office again.

"Come in," Nana said to the Channel Ten news reporter. It was now four days after I talked to my aunt Lisa. One day remained before Dub would be released from jail.

"Thank you," the reporter said as she entered Nana's living room, followed by a cameraman.

My heart raced, but there was no turning back now. I'd given my aunt Lisa permission to call the news station and tell them my story, how I had remained in an abusive relationship without even my family knowing. How most of my family would be finding out about the abuse for the first time ever as they watched it on the news.

"You must be Helen," the news reporter said to me when she saw me sitting on the living-room couch. "I'm Andrea Storm with Channel Ten News." She extended her hand.

I stood and shook her hand. "I'm Helen Lannden. Please have a seat." I sat back down and gestured for her to sit next to me. I felt like I had butterflies flying through my stomach. It wasn't a nervous fluttering; it was a feeling of anxiousness. Even though I was about to tell the entire world of my humiliating ordeal, my spirit felt at peace in doing so.

"Your aunt gave me some background on your story, but I'd like for you to tell me about your situation in your own words." She took out a pen and notebook. "You don't mind, do you?" she said in regards to her writing down what I was about to tell her. "I just want to talk with you before we begin taping to make sure I'm going in the right direction with the story."

"Oh, okay," I agreed. After all, the world would hear the story in my own words in a matter of minutes. Who cared if she had it down on paper as well? So I began to tell her about the years of abuse I'd suffered at the hands of Dub. I even told her about how he had shattered my car window, which ended in a trip to the hospital due to glass in my eyes. I dug up every single threatening letter Dub had written me and allowed her to read them.

Andrea took steady notes, but at certain points, when I caught myself off in a daze, talking, reflecting, and providing her blow-by-blow details of my mental, physical, and sexual abuse, her pen would remain frozen in her hand, as if she was too stunned to even write.

After about a half hour, Andrea closed her notebook. "Well, Helen, I think we have enough." She looked at me with such pity, almost as if she couldn't believe I'd lived through all that I'd shared with her. "As a matter of fact, I think we have more than enough." She thought for a moment. "Before we begin taping, do you have a photo of Dub?"

"I might," I said. That was when I realized that Dub, Baby D, and I had never taken pictures together. There were no family portraits, or even father and son pictures, for that matter, but then I remembered one picture that I did have. "Just a minute," I told Andrea as I went upstairs and retrieved my senior year memory book, which had been packed away ever since I moved into Nana's house. In the memory book was a prom picture of me and Dub. "This is the only one I have." I handed Andrea the picture as I sat back down on the couch.

Andrea admired the picture of the lovely couple smiling for the cameraman. All of a sudden she looked up at me. "Had he already been abusing you at the time this picture was taken?" I nodded. "Hmmm. I wonder how many mothers and fathers have their daughter's prom picture sitting on the mantel, with no idea that the very date in the picture is abusing her. Even worse, I wonder how many mothers and fathers have their son's prom picture on the mantel, with no idea that their son is abusing the very date in the picture."

I shrugged. Abuse wasn't something girls sat around discussing in the girls' locker room. It was the best kept secret I knew of. So whoever said that girls couldn't keep secrets was wrong.

"Well, let's get ready," Andrea said, looking at the cameraman, who had managed to set up everything while Andrea and I were talking. He gave her a nod, letting her know that he was all set. She then looked at me. "One last question, Helen. Why are you doing this? What do you want out of this interview airing? I mean, I know Dub is scheduled to get out of jail tomorrow, but he's locked up on unrelated charges. So what is your purpose for doing this?"

I didn't even have to think about the answer to that question. The answer to that question was what had allowed me to give my aunt the go-ahead to contact the media in the first place. I had literally felt as though I was living my last days on earth, so without flinching, I looked Andrea in her eyes and said, "I am going to be murdered, and I want the world to know exactly who killed me." I then turned to the cameraman. "I'm ready!"

# Stone Number Thirty-two

"I can't believe you did that! Why didn't you just tell me? I would have taken care of the situation. Now I look like a punk, like I can't protect my family!" Dino ranted and raved as he paced back and forth across Nana's living room. It was just seconds after my story had appeared that evening on the five o'clock news.

The morning Andrea came to Nana's, I'd taken off half a day from work. But right after we wrapped up, I'd headed back to the office, feeling like even if Dub came straight to my house once he was released from jail the next day and carried out every threat he'd ever described, I was going to live that last day free, which was something I'd never truly really been since getting trapped in Dub's clutches. He'd always held a piece of my mind captive.

Nana had called me and told me that the story had aired at noon, but with everybody at work, virtually no one had seen it then. Those very few who had made sure to get on the horn and let everyone know to tune in to the five o'clock news to receive the shock of their life, which was the truth about mine.

"Look, Dino, I'm sorry. But I felt as though this was my last resort," I told him.

"But you didn't even give me a chance. I'm sure I could have talked with Dub man to man and—"

My mom, who had come over to Nana's after seeing the story on the news, burst out laughing. "*Talk?* Boy, please, Dub don't do no talking. Trust me, I've dealt with that fool."

"I didn't want to tell you and have you all caught up in the middle," was what my reply to Dino was. I think that was one of the reasons why a lot of abused girls and women didn't tell what their mate was doing to them. They knew they got that crazy daddy, brother, or cousin who would do something they'd have to repent for later, or serve jail time for. Not telling was their way of protecting the people they loved. So they sacrificed themselves. "I was just trying to protect you."

"Protect me? From what?" Dino fumed. "Dub ain't nothing but a man just like me. I could have talked to dude, and if he tried to jump bad, then we'd take it from there."

Once again my mother burst out laughing as she headed back into the kitchen. Dino and I both heard her mumble as she shook her head at Dino's ignorance. "He just doesn't get it. He can't beat Dub."

Dino looked at me after my mother's comment. "Is that what you think too? That I can't beat him?"

I couldn't even stand there and think about lying to Dino about how I felt. I knew he was no match for Dub, not while he was in this relentless state. Dub had been shot, stabbed, and dragged by an automobile, and still he stood. He was like a real-life boogeyman.

"Answer me!" Dino exclaimed when I was taking too long to respond.

"You can't beat him, Dino. I mean, you're bigger than him and everything, but Dub's not going to fight, so I don't mean you can't beat him physically. What I mean is that he's crazy. You can't beat him at being crazy. The things he'd do to a person, you don't have it in you to do," I said, trying to reason with Dino without insulting his manhood.

"Unbelievable!" Dino flopped down on the couch. "So that's why you left me in the dark for so long. I mean, why should you tell me about this crazy fool when all along you felt in your heart that I couldn't protect you, anyway. Now I'm looking like a buster. Got my peeps calling me, talking 'bout, 'Y'all all right, man? Everything good with the family? You need some back up?'"

"Please don't try to make this about you," I said, trying to contain my anger as I watched him whine.

"Helen, it's for you." My mother peeked around the corner with the kitchen phone in her hand. I was so engaged in my conversation with Dino that I hadn't even heard the phone ring. "It's the news station."

I went and took the phone, wondering what the news station could possibly want. "This is Helen . . .Yes . . . Really? . . . Oh my God! Thank you! Thank you! Yes, I can be there. Thank you again so much," I said before I hung up the phone with Andrea. "Thank you, God!" I shouted as I fell to my knees. No, I wasn't a practicing Christian. No, I couldn't even consider myself a babe in Christ. But this all had to have been orchestrated by God. That much I knew . . . I felt.

"What it is?" Nana asked, coming out of her bedroom and into the kitchen.

"That was Andrea, the lady from the news that interviewed me," I answered. "She said the news station contacted the courts, asking them if there was anything more they could do to protect me from Dub. Come to find she got a call back from the prosecutor's office, which says that Dub sending me threatening letters through the U.S. mail is a felony, and they can charge him one count for each letter he sent that I can present to the judge."

"So what does that mean?" my mom asked.

"It means that if I can get down to the prosecutor's office ASAP, they can start the paperwork and present it to the judge first thing in the morning."

I was shaking with anxiety. I was anxious to get down to that courthouse. I made a mental note to call Andrea up later and thank her again. She'd contacted the courts, putting a fire under them and pushing them to do something more. She'd aired my story, so if Dub got out and harmed me, there was no doubt my story would come back to haunt the legal system, which I'd reached out to for help. They did not want that type of embarrassment.

I immediately headed to my bedroom and dug up every single threatening letter Dub had written me, along with the postdated, stamped envelopes, which showed he'd used the federal postal service to get them to me.

"Dino, do you want to drive me?" I asked as I cleared the corner and entered the living room, only to find the spot where Dino had been sitting empty. I went to the window and looked outside.

"He's gone," my mother said. "He left."

A small part of me could understand how Dino must have felt, but the bigger part of me was more concerned about protecting myself and my family, and Dino too, for that matter. So without harping on Dino's absence, I headed out the door to meet the prosecutor.

"What do you want me to do?" the judge asked me. "Keep him in jail forever?"

I couldn't believe the sarcasm of this man. After reading all those letters he'd been presented with by the prosecutor that morning, how could he not want to lock Dub up and throw away the key? Here this man was ready to just let Dub go on his merry way without so much as a fine. Something was wrong. Something was very wrong. That was when it dawned on me that the judge had received my case only that morning, and now it was only early afternoon.

"Have you read the letters?" I asked him. This man probably hadn't even read the letters, and yet he was ready to rule.

He paused. "No," he said in an almost inaudible voice that didn't hide his unease.

By now my eyes were filled with tears of both anger and frustration. I was angry because this man had been all ready to decide the outcome of the case—my fate—without even having taken the time to review the crux of my complaint. The crux of my fear.

I supposed the judge could read all these emotions circling in my mind like a tornado, as he decided to take a few seconds and read over some of the letters right then and there. Every now and then the expression on his face would change, as if he couldn't believe the words he'd just read. Then he would look at Dub, who stood at the defendant's table, with disdain.

I, on the other hand, had not looked at Dub one time in the courtroom. I could feel his intimidating presence. I could feel him staring me down with his eyes, which he was using as daggers. Just that morning I could imagine him as happy as a lark, knowing this was the day he was to be released back into society. This was the day he would be set free. I pictured him all packed and ready to go. So when the guards came for him, I was sure he hadn't had an inkling they would be bringing him to court for fresh charges. Unadulterated anger had to be writhing inside of him, like a worm trying to escape the hook of a fisherman.

I had always feared Dub, no doubt, but what I feared more than Dub at that moment was fear itself. I didn't want fear to force me to back down. I'd come too far. The light at the end of the tunnel was shining brightly on me. I couldn't dim it with the darkness that Dub held within himself. So I just kept my eyes on the judge and did something I hadn't done in a long time. I prayed.

*God, if you allow me to prevail in this matter, if you
make this judge see my side of things and help me . . .
God, if you save my life and the lives of my loved ones,
I'll give you my life. I promise that from this moment on
I will live for you.*

After one minute of praying and only one minute of
the judge getting the gist of the letters, my prayer was
answered.

"Mr. Dublen Richard Daniels, I find these letters to
be repulsive and threatening. Not only that, but I find
them to be a violation of the laws set in place by the state
of Ohio and the federal government." The judge sifted
through some other papers. "Had you not committed
prior criminal acts that involved violence, I might have
almost chalked these letters up to simple jailhouse
threats, but with your record, I can't take the chance with
Miss Lannden."

The judge looked at me as if he wanted to wink at me,
letting me know that he was on my side, after all.

I stifled the smile that was wrestling to make a courtroom appearance.

"I know you were probably incensed at the time these
letters were written," the judge continued. "And there is a
possibility that you didn't mean everything you said and
that you would never carry out these threats." He looked
down at the letters again and then looked at me. "But I'm
not willing to take that chance." Turning his attention
back to Dub, he concluded, "So, with that being said, I'm
sentencing you to twelve months jail time." The judge
slammed the file closed. "Plus the other four months from
your last sentence that you didn't serve. Since the last
eight months didn't give you time to cool off, maybe the
next sixteen will do the trick."

"Hallelujah!" I shouted, with tears of joy now streaming down my face. At the time I didn't even know that

"Hallelujah" was the highest praise to God. All I knew was that God had answered my prayers and I had to communicate my gratefulness in His own language.

In the midst of all the celebrating, as I watched the deputies handcuff Dub and take him right back to jail, I forgot one thing. I forgot about my promise to God. And it wouldn't be long before I forgot about God altogether. How I saw it, when I was in trouble, when I wanted something from God, I knew exactly what to say in prayer. But once God had done what I'd asked Him to do, I didn't know what to pray about. God realized this same thing about me too, so it would only be a matter of time before He gave me something else to pray about.

# Stone Number Thirty-three

Things really started looking up for Dino and me after Dub was sent back to jail. I couldn't say the same about myself and school. With all the drama going on in my life, my grades suffered tremendously. I ended up losing all my grants and scholarships. That really hurt, especially since I had only one semester to go in order to graduate. If I wanted to complete that final semester, I'd have to pay for it out of my own pocket. Considering that I was going to a private Lutheran college, I hardly had the money to do that. So I just put college on the back burner.

As a matter of fact, I put lots of things on the back burner . . . or should I say in the back of my mind? It was like I had this new life. After years of emotional and physical abuse, I had managed to completely disconnect myself from that life. I pretended as though it had never even taken place, that it had all been one bad nightmare, and now I was living a dream.

For the first time since I could remember, I felt free. There was no longer this imminent threat from Dub. Don't get me wrong. I knew I was definitely still on Dub's radar. If Dub had wanted to kill me before, I could only imagine how badly he wanted to see me dead now. I couldn't imagine spending all that time in jail and then, the day I thought I was going to go free, being rerouted to court on charges filed by my ex, and then being sent straight back to jail . . . for another year!

Hopefully, the judge was right and those sixteen months would be long enough for Dub to cool down . . . and maybe even forget about me altogether. But whatever twisted ways to kill me and my family that sprouted up in Dub's head, I'd never know about them, as the judge had made it very clear in his orders that Dub was not to contact me via phone, mail, skywriting, or by any other means, at any location.

"I still wish you hadn't felt the need to go public and had just come to me first," Dino kept saying the first couple of weeks after the Dub ordeal.

"Baby, I am truly sorry if what I did made you feel like less than a man, but in my heart, I'm not sorry for the route I took," I explained on one occasion.

All that stress with Dub made me appreciate more and more Dino and his good qualities, all of which Dub lacked. Strangely enough, the ordeal with Dub sort of lit a fire up under Dino to step his game up as a man and become a provider.

"Guess what?" Dino said before Baby D and I had barely made it through his apartment door one day.

"What is it?" I asked. His contagious joy and excitement had me sporting a mile-wide grin.

"I went out and got a job."

"Get out of here," I replied.

"Seriously. I start tomorrow. I realized that a settlement from my job is not realistic right now, so I went out and got a job."

"I'm so happy for you," I said, wrapping my arms around his neck and planting a kiss on his cheek.

"You and my landlord." Dino smiled. "He was the first one I told. I worked something out where I'm going to get him all paid up."

Although I'd never met him personally, Dino's landlord had to be a saint, his kind heart prohibiting him from putting Dino on the streets.

"The only thing about this job is that my hours are funky. I go in at nine at night and don't get off until three in the morning."

"It's only part-time?" I tried to maintain my excitement after hearing he'd be putting in only six hours of work. Looking on the bright side, if the job paid well, then perhaps six hours was all he needed to put in in order to get a decent check.

"Yeah, but it's better than nothing. I had to get a job." Dino's last statement almost made it seem that someone had stuck a gun to his head and had told him to go out and get a job or else.

"Yeah, you're right," I agreed.

"Do you have to wear a uniform?" Baby D interjected. "Like police and mailmen do?"

"As a matter of fact, I do," Dino said before disappearing into his bedroom. He returned with his uniform over his arm. "See, here it is." He held it up, showing it off to Baby D. It consisted of dark blue pants and a blue- and white-striped shirt. There was a picture of a little redheaded white girl with pigtails on the corner pocket of the shirt.

"Cool," Baby D replied, touching it. "Does this mean we can all get free Frosties? Because I like . . ."

Baby D was talking, but I wasn't listening. I was still stuck on the fast-food restaurant uniform Dino was so proudly showing off. I had to do a double take. Was this big, overgrown man really excited about the fact that he'd just landed a job at a fast-food joint? I mean, if he were a teenager looking for a job to support his tennis shoe addiction, that would be another story, but this man was only two years younger than me, which made him twenty-two . . . and not only was he a man, but he was my man! I couldn't wrap my brain around it in order to get excited.

"Burger King, huh?" was all I could say.

"No, Mom. Wendy's," Baby D said, correcting me, rolling his eyes.

I guess Dino saw the disappointment on my face. "Look, Helen, I know it's not much. It's not office work in corporate America, like you're doing, but it's a job. You never know. I could end up becoming a top manager." He smiled and placed the paper hat on his head.

Why was this sounding like that old McDonald's commercial where the whole neighborhood was proud of Calvin for getting a job at the fast-food restaurant?

"So, just hang in there with me, all right?" Dino rubbed my cheek and smiled.

That darn smile of his made me smile, and the next thing I knew, I said a cheerful and meaningful "Okay."

For the moment, I was glad that Dino would have a little somethin', somethin' in his pockets. His working at Burger King—I mean Wendy's—couldn't be too bad, that is, as long as no one found out.


"Did I see Dino working at Wendy's?"

It was almost shameful when a girl from work came over to my desk and asked me that question. Folks had seen Dino drop me off and pick me up from work a couple of times. I'd allowed him to use my car while I was at work so he could go look for work. Never had I imagined that he would find work at a fast-food joint and that my coworkers would spot him.

I wanted to melt like the Wicked Witch in *The Wizard of Oz* when Dorothy threw water on her. Instead, I simply replied with the truth. "Yes, he works there now on the side." Well, almost the truth. Wendy's wasn't his side job. It was his *only* job, but I'd led her to believe it was just a second part-time job he'd picked up for extra money.

"I was just making sure, because my boyfriend and I stopped in there and I told him, 'I think that's the guy Helen's seeing, the one she brought to the Christmas party.'"

"Yep, that was him." I hated saying it once again, forgetting all about the fact that Dino had accompanied me to the office Christmas party. He had put on such a show with his old-school dance moves, I imagined he was more than recognizable to my coworkers, even in his work getup.

"Well, girl, at least you got a man that's willing to work. I can't get my boyfriend off the couch," she joked.

We each laughed, and I immediately felt more at ease. Here, I thought she was coming over to rub in my face the fact that I was dating someone who worked in a fast-food joint, and she'd ended up confessing that her man didn't even work at all. I could tell she was real people. And that right there was the start of a new friendship.

Bianca, the girl from work, and I exchanged phone numbers and started hanging out. We had so much in common that it wasn't funny. Although she had her friends that she'd hung out with since high school and I had Synthia and Konnie, she and I were more alike than anybody. We even shared the same birthday.

She and I ended up doing stuff together almost every day, and that was easy since we worked together. But we even found reasons to hang out after work. I'd invite her to all my family's events, and she'd invite me to hers. My family took to her immediately. And, of course, Dino liked her. Dino liked everybody. That was another quality he had that I admired: he saw the best in everybody. Even me, go figure. I had a hard time seeing anything good in myself. The way I saw it, anything good that might have been in me, Dub had beaten out.

Hanging out with Bianca brought out another side of me. She was full of fun and full of life. She had this shine about her, a shine that made all those around her want to shine too. I had never laughed as much as I did when I was with Bianca. Since Bianca didn't have any kids, she kicked it nonstop, and soon enough, so did I.

"You going out again?" Dino asked as I began getting dressed after putting Baby D to bed.

"Me and Bianca are just going out for a quick drink," I replied, ignoring the tone in Dino's voice, which sounded a little disappointed about the fact that I was about to leave. "You know I don't drink all like that, so I won't be long."

"But it's the middle of the week. And it's my night off."

"And?" I said, slipping my sheer, long-sleeved black bodysuit on over my Victoria's Secret black lace bra.

"Are you going out for a drink, or are you going out to get dudes to buy you a drink?" Dino looked my outfit up and down. "And why are you wearing that out with Bianca? You and I used to go out all the time together, and you never dressed like that when you were with me."

I simply shrugged and slipped on my black dress pants.

"How did you know I didn't have plans to go out?" Dino nodded toward the room in which Baby D was sound asleep. He was hinting at the fact that if he had had plans, there would be no one at home to watch Baby D. "How did you know I wasn't going out to have a drink with one of my boys?"

"Because you always broke," I spat. "Where would you get money to go out? But if leaving Baby D here is a problem, just let me know. I can take him to Nana's."

Baby D and I hadn't been to Nana's since Dub went back to jail. Appreciating Dino all the more, I had stayed up under him.

After meeting Bianca, though, that all changed. I discovered that I could be a different person when I was out hanging with her. When I was out with Bianca, we always seemed to attract attention; we were like magnets to a good time. I had had no idea how popular Bianca was in the streets. Not because she had a bad reputation or anything, but because she was just so fun and likable, everybody knew her. All the popular people I recalled hearing about in high school, even those who didn't attend my high school but were from one of the main high schools in Columbus, Bianca knew.

Bianca and I never went anywhere where she didn't know somebody and where somebody didn't know her. And because of Bianca's status, I soon enough began to know all these people as well. People who I had never imagined hanging out with back in high school, I was hanging out with now. It was incredible. It was like a rebirth, like even though I was older now, I was getting to live out my high school days. While I was being born again and coming into the world, unbeknownst to me, something else was being born as well. . . .

# Stone Number Thirty-four

"A baby!" I couldn't believe the words that had just come out of Dino's mouth. I guess he figured I wouldn't believe him, so that was when he whipped the picture out of his wallet and laid it on the table in front of me.

"Her name is Jontay," he said. "I . . . I . . . wasn't sure she was really mine. That's why I didn't say anything until now."

Speechless, I just sat there, staring at the picture.

Dino decided to keep talking. "She's four months."

"Four months?" I finally found my words. "You mean to tell me, all this time we've been kicking it, you've had a baby on the way?"

"Like I said, I didn't know if she was mine or not. My girlfriend from back home and I had broken up. I moved to Columbus, and then she called me, talking about she was pregnant. At first, I didn't even think she was really pregnant. I thought that was just a trick for her to get me back and to let her come here to Columbus with me."

"So when did you find out that she was really pregnant? Was it before or after you met me?"

Dino put his head down. "Like a couple weeks before."

"So, you didn't think that during all of our getting-to-know-each-other conversations you could have mentioned that you might have some girl back home in New York pregnant?"

"I still needed to find out if the baby was mine or not. If it wasn't mine, I didn't see why I should even bother mentioning it and risk you not being interested in me. Even when she was born . . . I mean, she looked like me, but I still couldn't be sure. I just stood there outside the hospital nursery and stared at her for a long time, trying to—"

"Wait a minute." I stood up. "Are you saying that you were there, at the hospital, when this child was born?"

Dino nodded.

"I don't remember you going to New York."

"Uh, the baby wasn't born in New York. The baby was born right here in Columbus."

I began to laugh nervously to keep from crying, not tears of pain, but tears of anger. I had promised that if this fool had been so broke because he was living a double life, I would . . .

"She ended up moving to Columbus, anyway, when she was about seven months into the pregnancy. A cousin of hers and his wife live here, so she talked them into letting her move in with them."

"So let me get this right. For the past few months your maybe baby mama has been living in the same town and you have not said one word to me about this?"

"She's not a maybe baby mama. Jontay is mine. The welfare office made Tabatha seek child support, which involved a paternity test to prove that I was the father. She's mine, Helen."

Although Dino and I had made it a point not to really talk about our exes, I recalled him mentioning Tabatha's name a time or two, only to talk about how evil and mean she was. Other than that, he never mentioned her, so I assumed she wasn't anybody special, nobody he had truly been in love with and had bonded with. Here, all the while they had shared a bond that he and I didn't have. Then it dawned on me that once upon a time he and I had had a chance to share that same kind of bond, but I'd destroyed it.

"You mean to tell me that knowing there was a possibility you had a baby on the way, you wanted me to have a baby by you too? Ooh, I am so glad I got that abortion, I don't know what to do. God knew all this mess was going on and that you didn't need another baby."

"God didn't have anything to do with the decision you made all by yourself to get that abortion," Dino was quick to say. "I was trying to be a man about it, take care of my responsibility, but you were hell-bent on going through with that procedure. The same way I was trying to be a man about taking care of the one that was growing in your stomach, I'm now trying to be a man about taking care of the one that is here."

"So that's why you all of a sudden became so bound and determined to start bringing in an income that you stooped to working at Burger King?" I spat.

"Wendy's," he said, correcting me. Dino looked at me with so much hurt in his eyes. "*Stooped?* Is that what you call it?"

I could tell that I'd hurt his feelings with my choice of words, but I was too angry to even care. I think I was born angry. Mad. Mad at the world. Wouldn't know happy if it smacked me in the face, because I probably didn't want to know happy. Not really. Hurt, anger, and pain had become my best friends. They'd feel betrayed if I let happy in, if I let happy get too close to me.

"Well, what else would you call it? A grown man working at a fast-food restaurant? I mean, I could see if you were the store manager or something, but you ain't in charge of nothing but fries. For a minute there I was almost flattered, figuring you'd finally gotten off your butt to do something to earn some money instead of being a leaching bum, but now I realize that you did it for one reason and one reason only, you getting hit by the system. You gotta pay that broad child support, don't you?"

He paused for a moment. "Of course I have to take care of my baby," Dino replied.

"Oh, no, my brother, don't try to play me." I shook both my head and my index finger at him. "After getting those results to the paternity test, welfare ordered you to pay them some child support, didn't they? Threatened to take your butt to jail, huh?"

"Even if they hadn't ordered me to do so, I still would have. I don't need no system telling me that I have to take care of my baby."

"So not only are you dang near bringing in a minimum-wage check, but it's getting hit by child support?" I asked, not expecting an answer. Dino didn't give me one, either. "Wow. This is just too much."

"I know, but there's nothing I can do about it now. Unlike you, she didn't kill the baby."

Talk about nails down a chalkboard. Now I was outraged. Even though Dino had made the comment with absolutely no venom in his tone, and the comment was indeed a fact, I still blew up. "Don't you dare try to turn this thing around on me. Don't you even try to refocus the situation on something I did in the past. You are wrong, and you know you are wrong. You lied by omission. You kept secrets!"

Dino threw his hands up. "Okay, so what if I had told you what all was going on? Would that have changed anything between us?"

"I don't know, but at least I'd have a choice in the matter on whether this is something I wanted to entertain or not," I lied to him, knowing darn well that had I known he had a baby on the way when we met, he would have never had a chance with me. Telling the truth about myself, I was only half a mother to my own son, so there was no way I saw myself as being a mother to some other woman's child.

"Look, I'm sorry," Dino said, throwing his hands up in defeat. "I'm sorry for not letting you know what was going on before now, but I'm not sorry that Jontay is here."

All I could do was look at Dino and reply, "Well, I'm sorry too . . . about everything."

"Girl, you are lying!" Bianca said as she and I sat in Cheddar's Casual Café for lunch.

I had e-mailed her when I went to work the very next morning after Dino gave me the news about his baby and had asked her to lunch. I'd told her there was something I had to talk to her about. The dude she was dating had a three-year-old son whom his baby mama had been pregnant with when she started dating him. I needed some advice from her about what to do.

"I wish I was lying," I replied, stirring my Coke with the straw.

"Well, at least in my case I knew what I was getting into. I knew my man had a chick knocked up." Bianca took a bite of her mozzarella stick from her Triple Treat Sampler, her favorite item on the menu.

"But didn't you worry about him having to spend time going to visit the baby and stuff, which means he has to be around the mama too?"

"Girl, please, whenever he went anywhere near that baby mama, I made sure he took a part of me with him."

"How so?" I asked, confused.

"I made sure I always sent the baby a gift with him, and I would tell him to tell the baby right in front of the mama, 'This is from Bianca.' I needed for him to constantly remind her that even though she was the baby mama, I was his woman. Girl, I'd send the baby cards signed by both me and my man. I'd cut out diaper and wipe coupons and tell him to make sure he gave them to

her and to tell her that I was the one who thought enough
about her wallet to cut them out. I kept my name in his
mouth while he was around her. I had to let that chick
know that baby or no baby, I wasn't going nowhere."

"You crazy." I chuckled.

"Yeah, but I won. She had thought that having that
baby was going to bring her and my man closer, that she'd
be able to steal all my man's time so that he wouldn't have
any left for me. I proved her wrong. He'd tell me about
the little comments she'd make about them, hoping they
could be a real family once the baby was born. Well, I
nipped that in the bud quick, fast, and in a hurry. I was
not about to feel like some quitter or loser and give any
broad on the planet bragging rights that she'd stolen my
man from me. No way, no how."

Until then, I honestly hadn't looked at things like that.
In all actuality, I really had wanted Bianca to back the
decision I'd already made to let Dino go. But that was
before she started throwing words like *quitter* and *loser*
around. I didn't want to be a quitter, and I certainly didn't
want to be a loser.

"Look, let me tell you this," Bianca said. "Whatever you
do, don't let the baby mama win. Do not let her get the
'w,' the win. Do whatever you have to do to make sure she
doesn't win." Those were her last words of advice to me
before she demolished her Triple Treat Sampler.

I allowed Bianca's words to get my adrenaline going.
From that moment on I was bound and determined to do
whatever I had to do not to let Dino's baby mama walk
away thinking she'd won by having that baby of hers. But
at that moment, I had no idea just what lengths I'd go to,
to ensure that I walked away with the "w."

# Stone Number Thirty-five

"I do," I said, with tears in my eyes.

"Me too," Dino said, and everybody in the sanctuary let out a chuckle.

I couldn't believe that after knowing Dino for less than a whole year, I had just committed myself to him until death did us part.

As the preacher read the vows for Dino to repeat, Dino stood there holding my hands, trembling, with tears in his eyes. Tears had filled my eyes as well.

Unfortunately, the tears in my eyes weren't tears of joy. I mean, I was happy . . . I guess. I wasn't consumed with the feeling of being in love on my wedding day, a feeling I'd dreamed of as a little girl. I'd dreamed of a love that would break the curse of hate I felt had consumed me. I'd dreamed of the most powerful, mightiest love that could crush through all the bitterness I was filled with.

My tears were mostly tears of pity. I pitied Dino. I felt so sorry for him. He was in love all by himself. That boy honestly loved me. In spite of me and my ways, Dino loved me. I could see it in his eyes when he said, "I do." This moment, this very moment, his eyes told the world he would treasure his wife for as long as he breathed. It was the look in a man's eyes that every woman would kill to see on her wedding day.

I loved Dino back. Really, I did. I had mad love for him. I just wasn't sure I was in love with him enough to want to spend the rest of my life with him as his wife. I wasn't sure if I loved him as much as I did because he wasn't Dub or because of who he actually was.

Although I hadn't been to church in quite some time prior to Dino's and my nuptials, the church I had been attending was where the wedding was held. It was a nice-size sanctuary that sat around three hundred people. It had a huge vaulted stained-glass ceiling, and when I looked up, I truly felt as if I was getting a sneak peek into heaven. But what I loved most were the beautifully painted angels that decorated the walls of the church.

On that day, it served as nothing more than a building. There was no anointing in our union. Even the minister who married us could discern it, especially after getting a chance to dive inside our relationship a little after I signed us up for counseling sessions.

After the first session she was on to me. She could see right through me with all my talking over Dino whenever she asked him about things he saw in me that he didn't care for.

"Sometimes she yells and fusses and says—"

I cut him off quicker than Michael Myers and Jason put together could have cut one of their victims. Why was he telling this woman about my yelling and fussing?

I knew there was this ugly beast inside of me that sometimes lost control, but that was my business. It was my demon. It was like this thing would just take over me. It would handcuff and muzzle me so that I couldn't stop it from doing whatever it was it wanted to do . . . from hurt whomever it wanted to hurt. No matter how painful it was for me to just stand by and watch. It felt like a sickness, like a disease there was no cure for.

One time I had an episode of screaming at Baby D, who was now in second grade. I had screamed at him for about two hours, and afterward I had prayed to God to just let me be nice for one week. Let me not snap off and lose control. It was probably what someone trying to rid themselves of a cigarette addiction would pray. If I could control myself for one week, then I could do it for two and then three and so on. But my prayers were never answered. Perhaps they were, but I just was too busy yelling to hear the answer.

One day I shared my feelings with my mother. After that she started spending more and more time with Baby D. She basically relieved me of him, so to speak, because eventually all his clothing and belongings ended up at her house. He was safe from my vicious tongue there. While he was gone, I was hoping not having him around would allow me to change a little. It allowed me to change only the person whom I directed it all at, which was Dino. And now he was ratting me out!

I began talking over Dino, with a fake smile plastered on my face.

"I just talk loud," I said, reasoning with the minister. "My whole family is loud. Our voices carry."

The minister tried her best to get back to Dino's concerns by ignoring me completely and staying focused on Dino. "So you don't like when she yells and fusses?" she repeated. "How does that make you f—"

I talked over her as well. "I used to get in trouble all the time in class for talking loud." I chuckled.

Now, at the altar, I was even talking over God's "Please don't" with my own "I do." Seeing that I was a big girl and insisted on doing my own thing, God let me be. And with His absence, God was nowhere in the midst of this marriage. Even He knew my heart and refused to show up and bless such a mess.

I felt so bad knowing that my "I do" and Dino's "I do" didn't mean the same thing. His "I do" meant just that. Mine meant 'I really shouldn't, but I will.' Dino didn't deserve that. He didn't deserve me. He deserved much better.

Dino would have given me the world if he could have. He was romantic, liked holding my hand or putting his arm around me. He opened doors for me. Anywhere he got invited, he invited me, whether he thought I wanted to go or not. He loved hanging out with me. He wanted to show me off to the world like I was Miss Universe. Like in D'Angelo's song, I was his lady and he wanted the world to know. Like Maxwell, he felt fortunate to have me.

The way Dino felt about me was exactly how I had always wanted a man to feel about me. It was the fairy tale. Well, almost the fairy tale. The only thing that wasn't part of the fairy tale was the proposal. Dino didn't get down on one knee and propose in some special way. But I know he would have . . . had I let him.

See, I had thrown Dino this really nice birthday party at a party house and had invited all his friends and family and mine. I was going to do it up. I even made sure that Dino invited his baby mama's cousin, whom she was living with, and his wife. Word needed to get back to her ASAP about what was going to go down at the party. If she had any ideas about trying to get back with Dino, after tonight they would be crushed. Like Bianca had instructed me, I was not going to let her get the "w."

While Dino wasn't that financially stable, at least his hours at Wendy's had increased to full time and he'd gone on two interviews at a bank. He'd also gotten lucky with a lottery scratch-off ticket, winning five thousand dollars, which he turned over to his landlord. In addition, he was getting caught up on his rent from monies from his paycheck. And, of course, we were living together now, so I had income to chip in and help out. I was going to be the wife, which trumped the baby mama. Things were looking much brighter. Dino was a good guy, much better than Dub. I couldn't see myself getting a better guy. So why not just marry him and allow our relationship to fully blossom?

After about an hour into the party I had the DJ stop the music so that I could make a toast to Dino.

"First, I just want to thank everybody for coming out. I know it's a blizzard out there, but thank you, guys, for pressing your way through. It really means a lot to me, and I'm sure it means a lot to Dino." I looked over at Dino, who nodded in agreement with a smile. "Dino's a special guy. That's why I wanted to throw him this special birthday celebration. If anybody deserves it, it's my baby."

"Awww." Dino playfully blushed and then kissed me on the cheek.

"Y'all know it's the truth. Dino would give you the shirt off his back if you needed it. He'd give you the last bite off his plate if you were hungry." I looked over at Dino and jokingly rubbed his pudgy belly. "Well, I don't know about that last one."

Everyone started laughing.

"No, but seriously," I continued. "I couldn't have asked for a more loving, kind, caring gentleman in my life. I can see myself spending the rest of my life with Dino." I turned and looked into his eyes. "As a matter of fact . . ." That was when I reached into my pocket and pulled out a box. "I want to spend the rest of my life with you." I opened the box, which held a beautiful gold band with diamonds around it. "Tarino 'Dino' Morton, will you marry me?"

Dino was in complete shock, as was everybody else in the room. I had kept this entire thing under lock and key. I hadn't told a soul. It wasn't that I didn't want someone slipping up and telling Dino. The truth was, I knew darn well I had no business asking this man to marry me, and a real friend would have talked me right out of it. Then I wouldn't be able to get the "w."

The whole proposal thing wasn't something I wanted to share with people. I was almost embarrassed that I was doing this. But I did not want to lose to his baby mama—no

way and no how. I refused to take the "l" to any woman. So
before he could even think about leaving me to get back
with her, I had to lock him in good. Did I love Dino? Yes.
Enough to marry him right now? Well . . . But none of that
mattered. In my mind, time was of the essence. The clock
on the scoreboard was ticking. And before the game ended,
I had to make sure I made the winning shot.

And so, just a few short months later, when the minister said, "I now pronounce you man and wife," Dino was
locked in, all right. But even worse, I was now locked in
too.


"You going out again?" Dino asked me as I came down
the steps, dressed in next to nothing. "And you're wearing
that?"

I had on some thin white pants with a lacy white
bodysuit and some white stilettos. Underneath the see-
through lacy bodysuit, I wore a lacy Victoria's Secret bra
and a matching thong. I loved dressing like this. I loved
showing off what my mama gave me.

"I told you I was going out," I reminded Dino.

"You taking the car?" he asked. The car I had when
Dino and I first met had died on me. It had got so worn
out taking both Dino and me where we needed to be,
not to mention the way Dub had worn it down as well. A
couple, two kids, and no car was not going to work. We
needed transportation. I had practically no credit, and
Dino's wasn't good enough for us to get a nice new car.
So we scraped our pennies together and got the best one
that we could.

"Lori's coming to get me."

Lori was the wife of his baby's mama cousin, whom
she lived with. She was Tabatha's twenty-seven-year-old
cousin-in-law. Ever since the birthday party when I pro-

posed to Dino, Lori had been like my best bud. She wasn't from Ohio and had no family here. She'd shared with me that she resented Tabatha for moving in with them, along with her baby, and practically taking over their house. If you asked me, there was really only one reason why Lori had befriended me—to get under Tabatha's skin. It was probably safe to say that I had befriended her for the same reason.

Being a stay-at-home mom, Lori's five-foot-two-inch, 160-pound frame didn't get out much. The couple of times she went out with me were her only outlet besides trips to the local grocery store. Her husband, on the other hand, was always out with his boys, so Lori loved the opportunity to switch places with him and have him sit at home and take care of the kids. She said it was like taking a vacation from the person she really was. I could relate, especially on nights like tonight ,when I was going out to kick it, almost forgetting the fact that I was somebody's wife and mother too.

I looked down at my outfit. "What's wrong with what I have on? When I wore it to the cabaret that one time, you said you loved it."

"Yeah, that's because you were with me. I'm not about to allow my wife to go out of the house, looking like that, without me."

Had he just said he wasn't going to *allow* me to do something? Oh, he definitely had the wrong one. We'd been married for only three months, and if he thought he was going to start telling me what I could and could not do, he had another think coming. And I was about to give it to him. But before I could, the doorbell rang. That negro was saved by the bell, literally.

I rolled my eyes at him and went to open the door.

"Hey, girl," I said, greeting Lori as she stepped inside our apartment.

"What's up?" she replied to me and then turned her attention to Dino. "What's up, Big D?"

"Oh, nothing too much." Dino stood to greet and hug Lori. "What's that husband of yours up to?"

"Nothing. At home with the kids so I can go and get my drink on. It's been a long week with those bey-beys. I need a drink. A strong one." She laughed and then looked at me. "You ready, girl? You look too cute."

"Yeah, I'm ready. Thank you," I replied. "I just have to head up the stairs and get my purse. I'll be right back."

I darted up the steps and went into my bedroom closet. I needed to retrieve my little white clutch-like purse. I didn't want to carry my everyday purse, because it nowhere near matched my outfit and it was too big.

"Oh, God! You scared me," I said as I went to exit the closet with my purse in hand. I hadn't even heard Dino come up the steps. He was just standing there in the closet doorway. "What's up? You need something before I leave? There is leftover meat loaf in the fridge and—"

"I don't need no food." Dino cut me off with a sharp tone. It surprised me because Dino had always been soft-spoken, except for that time he went off about that abortion. "But what I do need you to do for me before you leave is to change up out of that outfit."

I looked at him for a moment like he was crazy, then let out a chuckle. "Boy, you crazy." I went to brush by him, but he grabbed my arm. I looked up into his eyes and knew he was not joking around. There was this look in his eyes. I'd never seen it before. Correction. I *had* seen it before, but not in his eyes . . . in Dub's.

I immediately snatched my arm out of his grip. "Dino, you trippin'."

"No, you trippin' if you think I'm going to let my wife leave out of this house in all this see-through crap. You're practically naked. Some of my boys might be out and see you. I ain't gon' let you embarrass me, running around looking like a stripper."

"Oh, really? So that's how you feel now?" I was truly stunned by Dino's words. He'd never questioned what I wore before. Of course, this was one of the most risqué outfits in my closet, but still, I'd never seen him act so possessive. Was this the married Dino versus the "just kickin' it" Dino? I knew I had to get out of there before things got crazy, so I walked over to my everyday purse and started taking out the things I needed for the night and putting them in my white purse. I pretended as though Dino wasn't even standing there. I was just going to do what I needed to do and get out of there.

The next thing I knew, Dino yanked both my purses away from me and threw them across the room. My stuff went flying everywhere.

"Are you crazy? What has got you buggin', Dino, for real?" I marched over to get my stuff together. I was still determined to just get on out of there and enjoy my night.

"Did you hear what the freak your husband said?" Dino threw his big body in front of me. It was like a brick wall, stopping me in my tracks.

Now, Dino rarely got fly at the mouth like that. Again, I stared at him in nothing but complete shock. Who was this dude, and what had caused him to act this way?

"An outfit? You are really losing it over an outfit? Dino, seriously, I look good. No matter what I throw on in that closet, dudes gon' be checkin' for me regardless, so let's just keep it moving."

As soon as I brushed by him and started to pick up my stuff, I once again felt Dino grab my arm. This time he slung me back so hard that I landed on the bed but rolled off onto the nightstand. The nightstand toppled over, and everything on it crashed to the floor.

"Are you crazy?" I shouted, shocked as all get out. I had never expected in a million years that Dino would ever, ever put his hands on me in an aggressive manner.

This mess was like déjà vu, only instead of Dub, it was now Dino. I didn't know what was about to go down. I was just glad Baby D was with my mom and not at home to witness it, but what I forgot was that there was still a witness.

"What is going on? Is everything okay?" Lori looked horrified as she stood in the doorway.

"Everything is okay," I said, getting up off the floor and brushing myself off. "I just need to get my purse so we can go." I tried to play the scene down, but Lori knew something was up. I could tell by the concerned look on her face.

"So you just gon' act like I didn't say anything?" Dino snapped.

I ignored him and just gathered the items I needed and shoved them into my white purse. "Come on, Lori. Let's go."

"You can go after you change up out of that ho-looking outfit," Dino said, jerking me by my arm and pulling me back into the bedroom and over to the closet.

"Dino, stop it!" Lori and I said to him in unison.

Our words fell upon deaf ears, as he bear hugged me and dragged me over to the closet and began pulling out random items of clothing. "You can wear this. And what's wrong with this?"

"Dino, stop it!" I cried, trying to squirm out of his arms. He had me in a death grip. I felt suffocated. All of a sudden I just started having flashbacks of Dub and all his abuse. I couldn't breathe. I needed to break lose at all costs. The next thing I knew, my hand rose and I decked Dino right in the face. Now he was the one who was stunned. He released me and then drew his fist back out of instinct. I looked at him with such fear. I thought he was going to lay me out. He was looking back at me with the same fear I had in my eyes. He, too, thought he was going to lay me out. That scared him. Dino knew as well as I did that he wasn't that type of guy.

Dub hadn't been that type of guy when I first met him, either.

*Oh, no.* Was I about to create another monster? Why hadn't I just changed the stupid outfit? Maybe now that I was in a much healthier relationship than the one with Dub, the challenge was to accept boundaries.

# Stone Number Thirty-six

I walked in the apartment after my night out with Lori, during which we did nothing but talk at the bar about Dino's and my fight. Dino was sitting there, waiting on the couch in the dark. I knew that might look bad to the average person, but I knew Dino. He wasn't sitting there, waiting to pounce on me. He was sitting there, waiting to . . .

"I'm sorry," he wept.

He'd been waiting to apologize.

He got up from the couch and raced over to hug me. "Baby, I'm so sorry. I have no idea what got into me." His shoulders were heaving up and down.

*Is this big ole bear crying like a baby?* I asked myself. I couldn't get past all the tears, snot, and slobbering to get to the actual apology. "Babe, are you drunk?" I asked him.

"No. You know I don't get drunk," he said, pulling away and looking at me like I was crazy for even asking that question.

I walked over to turn the lamp on. I looked around the room for any signs that he'd been drinking, smoking, or something. There was nothing. I looked at his eyes. They were red, but not from being high. They were just red and puffy from crying.

"The way I acted was uncalled for. I promise to never disrespect you like that again." Dino walked over to me and put his hands on my face. "I can't believe I put my hands on my beautiful, precious wife." And that was when he broke down again, squeezing me tightly in his arms.

I didn't know how to receive his apology. Heck, after Dub would hit me or yoke me up, he would never apologize, except for that first time he hit me, of course. After that, there were no apologies, which made me feel like I might have deserved the abuse. Dub would either force me to have sex with him or call me a bunch of vulgar names after he hit me. That was what I was used to. Not this heartfelt, wimpy stuff. Or maybe, just maybe, this was me and Dub all over again, only now it was me and Dino. Would Dino make a habit out of this until it became our new normal?

Did I like getting knocked upside the head? No. But I was used to a little more aggression than what Dino was displaying. For someone as big as Dino, who, by the way, had been getting bigger by the minute, he was acting real soft, which I had discovered was a major turnoff.

"Just tell me you forgive me," Dino pleaded, wiping the snot from underneath his nose with his hand.

*If it means you'll stop crying, then yeah, I'll forgive you.* I thought that in my head, but I didn't want to hurt his feelings by saying it out loud. Call me bipolar, not to make light of those who had actually been diagnosed with it, but sometimes I could snap off in a heartbeat, but other times I just wasn't up for the fight that I knew snapping off could sometimes lead to. So I just gave him a simple, "Yes, Dino, I forgive you." I then headed up the stairs. "I'm drained. I'm going to bed."

Dino turned out the lights and followed me up the steps. He got in bed, while I got my pajamas on and then climbed in bed after him. I purposely lay with my back turned to him. Then he purposely got close up on me and spooned me.

"I'm sorry," he whispered, then apologized repeatedly, soft kisses landing on my neck following each apology.

Okay. Now, this was the Dub way. Fight and then be ready to have sex. This was what I was used to, but it wasn't what I wanted to do. So the same way I used to try to fight Dub off of me, I would do with Dino. Although Dino equaled about four Dubs, I'd been fighting all my life practically, and so I'd at least give him a run for his money.

"Stop, Dino. I'm tired. I'm not trying to do that tonight."

"All right, baby. I understand." He gave me one last kiss and then just rested behind me, still spooning me.

I waited for him to start kissing me again, to start rubbing up against me, something. Dub had never relented that easily. Dub had never relented at all. The next thing I heard was Dino snoring in my ear.

What? Just saying no to him had actually worked. I was both ecstatic inside and a little puzzled. Did Dino giving up so easily mean that I wasn't that attractive to him? That he could take it or leave it? Did it mean that I wasn't worth fighting for? Because all I knew at that point was fighting.

I didn't allow the battle to go on in my mind much longer before I fell off to sleep. Even then, my sleep wasn't interrupted by Dino taking from me what I had denied him. Was I dreaming? I had to be, because this had not been my reality. If I was dreaming, it wouldn't be long before somebody woke me up out of it.

"It is really jumping in here. There are way more people at this cabaret than there was at the last one," I said as I looked around the rental hall.

The place was decorated with eight-foot-long tables dressed in black and red tablecloths. There were bottles of champagne in ice buckets at each end of every table, and candles served as centerpieces. This cabaret had a really nice ambiance going on, and the crowd was a slightly older crowd than Dino and me.

Dino had a cousin who would get together with him and a couple of his frat brothers and throw cabarets a couple times a year. We always supported him because the price was right, the atmosphere was right, the food was always on point, and drinks were included in the ticket price. And did I mention the DJ was on point?

"Let's find us a seat and grab a drink and some food before it's all gone," Dino said, taking my hand and walking me around the room. "Hey, there go my peoples." He pointed to where his cousin's wife was sitting, along with a couple other members of his family who I had met before.

We made our way over there and greeted everybody with a hug. Folks were already buzzing and feeling right, so Dino and I joined in the fun. We'd been there only about twenty minutes when one of our favorite songs came on.

"Come on, baby. You know I got to go show off my beautiful wife and her dancing skills." Dino took me by the hand and pulled me out of the seat. He then placed his arm around my waist and escorted me to the dance floor.

Even if I wasn't the most beautiful woman in the room, Dino always treated me as if I were. He always did everything in his power to make me feel like I was. I guess that was why I never had any doubts about Dino's loyalty and love for me, never got jealous, never felt a need to check up on him, question him, or anything of that nature. He made me feel so loved and so special that he never gave me a reason to put his love and dedication toward me under a microscope. I wasn't consumed with thoughts of what he was doing or who he was doing it with. He made it his business to make me feel as though he and I were one. That I was the center of his universe.

And even though he was younger than me, he was mature in years when it came to how he was supposed to make his woman feel.

Somewhere along the line, though, I guess I hadn't done the same by making Dino feel like he was the only man in the world.

"Y'all was out there cutting the rug," his cousin's wife said when we returned to the table after dancing to a couple of songs. "Y'all look so cute together, so in love. Like the perfect couple."

"We are perfect." Dino smiled. "She's perfect for me, anyway."

I lifted my glass of champagne and clinked it with his glass of soda. "Cheers," I said, then joined him in the toast.

Before I could even remove my glass from my lips I heard someone say, "Helen, is that you?"

I turned to face the figure that was standing by the table.

"Girl, it *is* you."

"Oh, my God! Franklin? Boy, I have not seen you since high school. Look at you." I stood up from the table and leaned in to give my old high school friend a hug, while Dino sat there next to me. I didn't think anything of it. It was just a friendly hug with a pat on the back with an old high school friend. There were no sexual intentions involved on either part.

"Look at you," he shot back. "Lookin' good, girl." I was several pounds lighter than the high school version of me.

"Thank you." I looked around. "Who are you here with? You got a girl? Married now? You know you was a playa playa back in school." I winked and joked with him.

"Naw, I'm here with Brady and them." He pointed to the back of the room.

I turned to see his running buddies from high school. They waved when they saw Franklin pointing and me looking back at them. I waved back with a big ole Kool-Aid grin on my face.

"You married?"

"I most certainly am," I said, just as proud as I could be. I then turned to Dino. "Franklin, this is Dino, my husband," I said, introducing them. "Dino, this is Franklin. We went to school together."

Franklin happily extended his hand to greet Dino. I was shocked when Dino's usually lively, perky self didn't even bother to shake Franklin's hand. He just hit him with a head nod instead.

It felt like the entire room just all of a sudden stood still while Franklin's hand was left hanging.

Franklin cleared his throat at the awkwardness of the moment. "Well, um, I'ma go on and head back with my boys. I just wanted to come check you out."

"All right, Franklin. It was good seeing you." I slid back into my seat, embarrassed as all get out. It had been a couple weeks since Dino had embarrassed me in front of Lori, and now here he was, acting a fool again.

I tried to change the mood by lifting my champagne glass. "Let's toast again." I held my glass up in Dino's direction.

"Naw, you cut off." He pulled my hand down in a quick motion, causing the champagne to spill down my arm.

"What is wrong with you?" I cut my eyes at him and then took a couple of napkins that his cousin's wife was extending to me. I began wiping the liquid off my arm while his cousin's wife began sopping up the table.

"How are you going to cut me off when this is only, like, my second glass?"

"Because you're already drunk," Dino said. "You must be drunk to sit here and hug some dude all up in my face.

You got me sitting here, looking stupid in front of my peoples while you flirting with old boy—"

"Baby, cuz," his cousin's wife interrupted, "it ain't her that got you sitting here, looking stupid. You doing a great job at that all by yourself."

I couldn't help but chuckle when his cousin's wife and everyone within earshot burst out laughing.

"Forget this. We out of here!" Once again Dino grabbed me by my arm and pulled me up.

My poor arm had had enough. I had had enough. I didn't want any trouble up in there, so I snatched my arm away from Dino and just willingly walked out with him on my own. By the time I reached the car, tears were streaming down my face. As I got in the car, I knew exactly where Dino and I were headed. I was afraid that this was only the spark of something that could ultimately turn into an all-out inferno. I had been down that same path before. Only this time I wasn't sure if I could go along for the ride.

# Stone Number Thirty-seven

"What is this?" Dino entered the dining area, where I sat eating a bowl of cereal while staring out the patio door.

At the sound of his voice I turned to look at him. He was holding up my wedding ring set, which I had laid on the nightstand on his side of the bed that morning.

The night before, while we drove home from the cabaret, I'd made my decision to get out of a marriage I should have never gotten into in the first place. I knew that after being with Dub, I hadn't taken the time to get rid of all the junk that had built up inside me over the years. There was so much pain and hurt. I thought it was almost intentional that I went from one man to the next. That way I was able to carry the hurt and the pain, which had become permanent fixtures in my life, into the next relationship.

I was apprehensive about letting the pain and the hurt go because they were all I ever knew, and I guess I was afraid of the unknown. The pain and suffering were comforting because I knew how they felt and how to act with them. I had to be honest with myself and admit that this was one of the reasons I had made the decisions I had made throughout my life to keep going back to men and to remain in situations I wasn't pleased with. Plain and simple, I was afraid to be happy.

"What does it look like?" I stated plainly and then directed my attention back to my bowl of cereal.

"I know what it is, but what does it mean?" Dino sat down in the chair next to me.

"Dino, I should have never married you," I began. "It was too soon, and it was for all the wrong reasons. We didn't even get a chance to know each other. I mean, to really get to know each other, to learn each other's ways."

"But, Helen, I don't care about your ways. I love you. I love all of you. The good, the bad, and whatever else there is to come. I meant those vows."

I was listening but still eating my cereal.

"I'm in love with you. I've never felt this way about another woman in my life. Don't I show you that? I mean, I know I've snapped a couple of times here lately, but that's just because I love you so much. I don't want to lose you. I try to lavish you with all the love and attention possible so that you don't feel the need to seek it elsewhere. That's why I snapped about the outfit that night. I know how women are. They wear certain things to get attention, to get noticed. They feel like that validates them as a woman. So I got a little pissed because it made me feel as though my validation wasn't enough, that you needed to go out there and be validated by everybody else."

Again, I just listened. And, I admit, he had made some very valid points. He was right; I did have this need for validation from men. Maybe it was because my own biological father had never validated me that I needed this stamp of approval from men. Though I had never thought about seeking out my biological father to get his side of the story, to question him as to why he didn't play a part in my life, perhaps buried somewhere deep within me was that abandoned little girl. A little girl who needed her biological father to know that just because he didn't want her didn't mean other men didn't.

I didn't know. My life was full of so much mess, I hardly ever thought twice about my biological father, about the whys and the what-ifs. But what I did know was that eventually that need for validation would land me in a really dark place. But for now, with Dino, the sun was about to set, and that was dark enough.

"And then, when dude at the cabaret came over . . ." Dino shook his head. "I know I was acting like Martin Lawrence said in one of his stand-up routines—crazy and deranged." He chuckled. "But I get it now. I get that you are my wife. That we took vows. That the piece of paper that says we are married is more than just a piece of paper. It's more valuable than any notes of currency in the world combined, and that's good enough for me."

My eyes filled with tears. Dino was saying all the right things. He was saying exactly what the leading man in any bestselling romance novel would say. He was saying exactly what any leading man in a "happily ever after" fairy tale would say. I'd always dreamed of hearing those words from the man in my life, namely, my husband. But this was all wrong. I was not the woman whom Dino should have been saying those words to.

I had thrown fate a curveball when I proposed and married Dino. It wasn't written, but I had still decided to pencil it in. Well, now it was time for me to face the music, be a big girl, and pull out my eraser to erase it all. I knew it was going to hurt Dino, but he would be better off. I'd already wronged him by marrying him just so his baby mama couldn't have him. To stay married would have robbed him of his true destiny. I had to let him go.

I finally spoke, placing my spoon down in my bowl. "I hear you, Dino. And I know with every fiber of my being that you mean every word you are saying."

I turned and looked at him. I could see the pain in his eyes, and it hurt me. It hurt me that I had robbed him of what felt like the longest year plus of his life. Dino was still in his prime, though. He was still ripe like a banana. He could and he would find someone deserving of him.

"I bring out the worst in you, Dino. I make you feel insecure because there is no reciprocity on my end. I just can't give you what you give me, and you really do deserve that."

"Girl, I'll take what you can give me. Like you said, we really didn't know each other that well before we got married. But we have the rest of our lives to do that, to get to know one another. Let's just roll with it. We can get through whatever comes at us, and I'm sure it will only make us stronger."

This was hurting my heart. Dino was wasting his words on me. He was wasting his heart . . . on me. I'd rather have stolen his wallet than stolen all this love that he was giving to the wrong person.

Dealing with Dub had been a nightmare, so meeting Dino had been like this dream come true. I had jumped headfirst into the deep end without a life jacket, knowing I wasn't that good of a swimmer. Before I got in any deeper, it was time to request a lifesaver and be pulled back to shore. I was drowning. It was one thing for me to jump into the unknown and risk drowning, but it was another thing if I took Dino with me.

Deep inside I'd always felt that I was the one who turned Dub into a monster. Had it not been for me, could Dub have turned out to be someone other than who he was? Someone sweeter? Someone kinder? I could not take that risk with Dino. He was better off without me.

"Dino, baby, I do love you, but trust me, you deserve far more and far better than I will ever be able to give you. You are a wonderful person, and that wife God has for you is going to appreciate every morsel of it. But I am not her, and I won't block anyone's blessings." I stood up, kissed him on the lips, and headed upstairs to pack.

It was back to Nana's I went.

\*\*\*

"You okay?" Nana asked me as I unpacked my things.

I nodded, sniffing while I walked over to the closet and hung up some of my clothes.

Nana just stood there. She knew I'd talk eventually. I just had to catch my breath from all the crying and emotions.

"You miss him already?"

I had to be honest with Nana. I shook my head. "Not really, Nana. I miss the lost time. I just feel like I've wasted so much time. It makes sense what you used to tell me." I looked at Nana.

"That you can never get back time, so you should cherish and value every minute?" Nana said.

"Yes," I cried. Now I knew exactly what Nana had meant by that. Not only could I not get my time back, but Dino and I hadn't even made it six months in marriage and now I'd have to tell everybody about our divorce. I felt like such a failure.

There were times when Dino would call me and beg me to give our marriage a chance. "I'm not going to let you leave me. I'm not going to sign divorce papers," he would say. "We can work this out. Baby, let's just work it out. Come back home, please."

I couldn't tell you how many times I was tempted to just go for it. Who knew if I'd ever meet another man who loved me that much and wasn't ashamed to tell it, show it, or make it known to the world? But I had to trust my decision on this one. I'd have to trust that someday I would get my fairy tale. That I would appreciate it and be able to be the princess the leading man so deserved. But for now, I had to move out of the way of someone else's fairy tale in Dino.

It wasn't but a couple months after I filed for divorce that I ran into Lori in the grocery store. "You know her and Dino are back together again. She moved out of our place and in with him." Lori began doing a praise dance. "Hallelujah, finally no house guests. Now me and my husband can finally have sex as loud as we want to," she joked. Lori never was one to be diplomatic with her words. I was sure when she added that last line, her intentions were to make me laugh instead of cry.

I laughed, but on the inside I was crying. The sad thing was, I didn't know why it was so upsetting to hear that Dino and Tabatha had ended up together, after all. Was it because a part of me deep inside really wanted to be with Dino? Or was it because at the end of the day, Tabatha walked away with the "w," leaving me feeling like the biggest loser ever? Some said that it didn't matter whether you won or lost. It was how you played the game. I begged to differ.

After loading my groceries into the car, I climbed behind the wheel, still thinking about Dino getting back with his baby mama. I started to get a little teed at the fact that Dino couldn't even wait for our divorce to be final before he went crawling back to her. But wasn't that the whole point of my divorcing him? To give him a chance at true love? Maybe Tabatha was really his true love, and I had just gotten in the way, first by accident and then on purpose.

Although I'd long started my engine, I'd yet to drive away. I sat there so consumed with emotion that I didn't even know which direction to go in, both figuratively and literally.

How did I get here in life? I thought it. And then I said it. "How did I get here in life?" And, then, as if some booming voice was going to reply, I waited for an answer.

# Stone Number Thirty-eight

"Thanks for the ride," I said to Bianca as I closed the passenger door and headed into Nana's house. Baby D was still staying with my mother. It was a big help because mentally, I still wasn't where I needed to be in order to raise him in a peaceful environment. I was not yet at peace with myself.

I did end up enrolling in school to finish my very last semester. Because I'd lost and exhausted my scholarship and grants, I had to take out a fifteen-thousand-dollar loan. I didn't have much of a choice. It was either that or let my completed semesters be in vain and never get a degree. But it was hard working and going to school, considering I was back to using public transportation and hitching rides.

The one thing I hadn't counted on when I divorced Dino was that he would take the car. So here I was, without my own place, still living with Nana, and now without a car. I felt like a loser in more ways than one.

"Hey, Helen," Nana said as I walked in the door. "I'm making your favorite dinner." She smiled. That wasn't unusual; Nana was almost always smiling. But something was peculiar about this smile. It seemed feigned, forced even.

"Spaghetti pie?" That was my favorite.

"Garlic toast and salad," Nana replied and then walked over and gave me a hug.

Now, Nana very seldom greeted me with a hug whenever I walked through the door. Not only that, but the hug was quite long. I thought I was the one who ended up pulling away.

"Nana, what is it?" I just came right out and asked. I was done playing games . . . with everybody.

"Why do you think something is wrong?" A nervous chuckle followed.

I exhaled, placed my purse on the bottom step, and then walked over and sat in the chair next to Nana's favorite chair. Nana made her way over to her chair. She sat there with her hands folded in her lap. She fidgeted with them for a moment before finally speaking.

"Aunt Martha is sick," she said sadly. Aunt Martha was her older sister and lived out in Florida.

"Oh, no. That's too bad. So you have to go see her or something?"

Nana nodded.

"When are you leaving?"

"Next month." Nana wasn't looking me in the eyes. She was looking down at her fidgeting hands.

"Next month?" I asked, confused. "Won't she be better by then?"

Nana didn't reply.

This overwhelming feeling started to come over me, and then I got this funny feeling in my stomach. "Well, if you're leaving next month, when are you coming back?"

Nana swallowed so hard, it sounded like the gulp was coming from my own throat.

"I'm not," she mumbled.

"Huh?" My eyes watered, and I didn't even try to stop them. I knew what was coming next.

"Aunt Martha asked me to move to Florida to be with her, and I said yes." Before I could reply, Nana went into explaining herself. "You know she doesn't have anyone else to take care of her. Sure Aunt Ann lives in Florida, but she's too busy taking care of Uncle Matthew. I can't put the burden of Aunt Martha on her too. Besides—"

I had to cut Nana off. She was about to work herself up into a heart attack. "Nana, you don't have to explain your move to me. It's okay. I get it. If Lynn needed me, I'd do the same for her."

Nana exhaled so loudly, I thought the lamp next to her might topple over. "I've already talked to a Realtor. The house is being listed in a couple days. You can stay here until it sells."

So that was the whammy. That was why she'd prepared my favorite meal. It was kind of like the Last Supper. I was being kicked to the curb.

"You're selling the house?" I didn't understand. Why couldn't she just let me stay there and rent it from her?

"Yes. I don't want to have to worry about it all the way in Florida. Even if I rented it out, I'd still have to worry about the upkeep and maintenance." She looked around the room. "And this house is just too old for that. Anything can give at any time. Why, it would be too much for you even."

Guess I got my answer. And just like that, not only did I not have a car and my own place, but I didn't have anybody's place. Nana's house ended up selling after only two weeks on the market, which was two weeks before she was set to leave for Florida. According to the closing agreement, Nana had thirty days to vacate the home, which technically meant I had thirty days to vacate, because Nana would be long gone.

Before heading to Florida, Nana ended up helping me get my own apartment by cosigning a lease for me. I probably could have gotten it on my own if I hadn't gotten my new car first. It wasn't brand-new, just a nice little Toyota to help get me from point A to point B. But by the time the apartment complex pulled my credit report, the car was already on it, which didn't look good for my debt ratio.

Nana had vowed that she would never cosign anything for anybody after she cosigned on a car for one of my uncles and ended up having to pay off the balance when the loan went into default. But I think Nana felt responsible for me having to move out in the first place, so she obliged without a second thought.

"I promise, Nana, you don't have to worry," I told her. "If I don't pay anything else, I'm definitely going to pay my rent."

That lasted all of about four months. It was already pretty rough keeping my head above water while paying rent, utilities, a car note, and car insurance, but when that student loan became due, I simply could not manage. I'd graduated with a bachelor's, but now it was time to pay for it.

I ended up going to one of those cash advance places to take out a loan, but all that did was put me in this viscous cycle of robbing Peter to pay Paul. I would go to one cash advance place after another, taking out one loan to cover the last loan and so on. Before I knew it, my answering machine was filled with messages from the cash advance place and all my other debt collectors. I'd dug myself into a deep hole that I saw no way of getting out of.

"Why can't I win for losing?" I cried out, overwhelmed with all the collection calls and paper bills that sat before me. I needed money, quick money, because I needed all my problems to go away quickly.

I ended up going next door and borrowing my neighbor's paper in order to check out the want ads. I was set on finding a quick way to make cash, such as babysitting, dog walking, whatever. I just needed money now, quick, fast, and in a hurry! I was past the point of having to go through some long, drawn-out interview process, only to then have my first paycheck held.

*Dancers needed! No experience necessary! Cash every night! Start tonight!*

I picked up the phone and dialed the number that was listed on the ad.

"Club Shake 'Em Up. This is Troy speaking," a guy answered.

"Uh, yes, hi. I'm calling about the ad in the paper, the one about dancers needed."

"Yes, I'm the manager. You interested?"

"Yes."

"Anyway, you can come in today for a quick interview?"

"Uh, yeah, well, sure." I was a little thrown off, but happy he wasn't beating around the bush. After all, I did say I needed this thing to move quickly.

"Good. What time can you be here?"

"Uh, I can come now," I said enthusiastically.

Troy gave me the address. I jotted it down and then hung up the phone, promising I'd be there in the next hour.

I raced to my closet and tried to find something sexy to wear to my so-called interview. I ended up piecing together a pair of thin white pants, a lacy white bodysuit, and some white stilettos. Underneath the see-through lacy bodysuit, I wore a lacy Victoria's Secret bra and a matching thong. I chuckled at the irony of Dino once saying it looked like a stripper outfit. *If the shoe fits . . .*

I put on my Mary Kay cosmetics, pulled my hair back in a nice, neat ponytail with a couple of strands purposely left out, and then I headed to Club Shake 'Em Up. It was clear on the other side of town, but there was no traffic, so I was there in under a half hour.

When I got out of the car, my knees almost buckled. I was so nervous. Here I was, somebody's mother with a college degree, about to go apply for a job as a stripper. This was surreal. *Do you really want to do this?* a voice in my head asked right as I made it to the door, placing my hand on the doorknob. I paused, then heard the voices on my answering machine of those who had made all those threatening collection calls.

I took a deep breath and answered out loud, "No, I don't want to do this. . . . I have to do this."

Before I knew it, I was on the other side of the door. I walked back out a few minutes later with my new work schedule in hand as the newest dancer at Club Shake 'Em Up.

# Stone Number Thirty-nine

"What the . . ." I cursed upon pulling up in front of my apartment door and seeing a paper taped on it. I got out of my car and walked up to my door, only to find an eviction notice plastered across it. I was like a woman waiting on her period after a night of unprotected sex. I kind of expected it but wasn't sure when it would come. After all, it had been a couple of months since I had last paid my rent in full. I mean, I had put some money on it like it was a nice outfit I had in layaway that I couldn't afford. It was a good faith effort on my part, but not good enough to hold off their threat of eviction.

I ripped the eviction notice off the door, cursing again, only to find that underneath the eviction notice was a disconnect notice from the gas company. "God, you've got to be kidding me." I'd been paying bits and pieces on the gas bill as well. Couldn't they have at least given me a break? I guess Columbia Gas has no layaway plan, either.

I could only guess at how many people had walked by and seen the notices. Even now as I stood there, I felt eyes burning my back, watching me, heard people laughing and snickering at the broke chick in apartment F. *F* for *failure*.

I made sure I ripped all remnants of both papers off my door and then went into my house. I closed the door behind me and just stood there. I felt so lost and confused. I was trying my best to handle all my bills, but it just wasn't working out in my favor.

I earned three dollars an hour dancing at Club Shake 'Em Up. I knew that sounded like cheap labor, but the bulk of a dancer's money was supposed to be earned in tips and drinks. Drinks for a dancer at Club Shake 'Em Up started at ten dollars and could go all the way up to one hundred dollars. The dancer received a forty-cent commission on every dollar a customer spent on her for drinks. The ultimate goal was to get customers to buy you as many drinks as possible.

Even with the commission I earned on drinks, the tips, and my modest hourly wage, the money was still not coming in fast enough. Granted, I had been working there only two weeks and hadn't really had time to get any regular customers who were willing to spend a car note on me. Yes, the money was fast, somewhat easy, and pretty decent, but the money I made from dancing had to be put right back into dancing. What I meant by that was that I couldn't just show up to work in cute bra and panty sets. Costumes were required. I hadn't taken into consideration at all the fact that I would need dance outfits to perform in.

If everything turned out in my favor, though, I wouldn't have to do this any more than two or three months or so, to at least get my head back above water. But right now I was drowning in bills and needed a life jacket quick. Still, I was confident I'd make my way back to shore in time. I was gonna be in and out of this game before the waters got too deep.

My head began to throb as I put my back against my door and just slid down to the floor, the tears sliding down my face simultaneously. "God help me!" was all I could say. This pity party couldn't last too long. I had to be at the club in an hour.

\*\*\*

"So what's it gonna be, Ma?"

I could tell by his tone that Damon was getting a little impatient. I mean, in his mind, what was there to think about? He was offering me five hundred dollars not just to dance for him, but also to hook up with him tonight? He was as fine as all get out and paid! Heck, most women would be willing to let Damon hit it for free, so why was I tripping?

The second song to my set came on. As R. Kelly's collaboration with the late, great Notorious B.I.G. was playing, I swayed my hips across the stage, almost in a trance. The irony of the lyrics and my situation at hand almost made me laugh out loud. But this was no laughing matter. I had an eviction notice on my door, my gas was off, and an opportunity to change all of that by morning was staring me in the face.

Damon gave me a wicked grin as he extended the five-hundred-dollar bill to me. I knew it wasn't just a regular tip. It was a proposition, and I was sure if I passed it up, I'd kick myself for refusing in my cold shower tonight. I closed my eyes. I needed to shut the rest of the world out and think in peace.

*This is a bigger one-night come up than I could have ever expected dancing in this club,* I thought to myself. *Even though I'll be able to do good things with this money, like keep a roof over my head, is all money good money?* For every thought I had with positive reasons for taking the money, a negative one followed and crossed it out. Within seconds my mind was caught up in a tornado.

The next thing I knew, I saw my hand taking the bill from Damon's hand.

# Stone Number Forty

"This is a really nice place you have here," I said, complimenting Damon as I stood in the middle of the living room of his luxury apartment located in Reynoldsburg, Ohio, a suburb of Columbus, Ohio.

"Thank you," he replied. "Can I fix you a drink?"

"No, I'm fine. I think I've had enough drinks for one night." I smiled.

"Cool. Well, then, you just have a seat right here." He bent over and patted a spot on his white leather couch, which sat on the fluffy white carpet that covered his floor.

I took a seat.

"I'll be right back."

He disappeared up the steps. He had been gone for about ten minutes when I heard the sound of a toilet flushing. A few seconds after that he reappeared.

"You all right?" he asked, twitching his nose, then taking his hand and wiping it.

"I'm fine." Believe it or not, I was fine. Not the least bit nervous. Damon was a regular at the club, he had money, he had a nice, clean place, and that Corvette he drove us over here in was off the chain. I'd made up my mind that he was no serial killer. As a matter of fact, he just could be my Richard Gere.

Damon grabbed a remote and turned on his stereo system. One of Jodeci's songs played as Damon poured himself a shot of a dark liquor, downed it, then came and sat by me on the couch. "Dang," he said, then started feeling around his pockets.

"What's wrong?" I asked, noticing how quickly he was becoming agitated. He ignored me and just continued patting himself down. Next, he started digging down in the couch. I watched him as beads of sweat began to form on his head. "What's wrong? What did you lose?"

Damon stopped and looked at me like it was his first time remembering that I was even there. "You have it, don't you?" he growled at me.

"What?" I was stunned. Damon had undergone this immediate transformation. He was no longer a sweet, smooth, debonair type of dude. He was now this clammy, aggressive creep.

"Give me that!" Damon snatched my purse, which was sitting beside me, and started throwing everything out of it.

"What are you doing?" I stood up.

"You got me? You tricked me, didn't you? All the tips, the drinks I bought you, the five hundred dollars, that just wasn't enough for a whore like you, was it? You had to go and steal my wallet."

"Dude, is this a joke?" I asked as a matter of fact, letting a laugh slip out, because this had to be a joke.

"You think this is funny, huh?" Before I could react, Damon's hands were around my throat, choking the life out of me. After what seemed like forever, he removed his hands from around my throat, pushing me back onto the couch. "I had three thousand dollars in my wallet, so now, instead of working five hundred dollars off, you owe me three thousand worth."

I watched as Damon stripped down until he was buck naked. I was paralyzed. I couldn't move. I was not even sure how I was able to breathe. I closed my eyes and did something I hadn't done in a while. In fact, I couldn't even remember the last time I had done it. I began to pray.

Just like in movies, my life began to flash before my eyes. I saw Lynn and myself drawing and playing hopscotch as little girls. I saw my cousin and myself playing with our Barbie dolls at my grandparents' house. I saw myself comforting Lynn in high school when she found out she was pregnant. I saw Lynn comforting me in the hospital after I gave birth to Baby D. I saw Baby D laughing, playing, and pointing at his favorite cartoon characters while he watched television. I saw Dub and myself in the park, talking. I saw Dub beating me and holding me a prisoner in my own home. Next, I saw myself that day in court when I was set free from Dub. I saw Nana and myself garage saling. I saw Dino and myself on our wedding day. I saw Dino and myself arguing, and then I saw myself filing for divorce.

Finally, I saw this casket and all these people surrounding it. I saw my mother, my father. I saw Rochelle, Synthia, Konnie, and my aunt Lisa. Practically the only person I didn't see was myself. Then it dawned on me. If I wasn't one of the people surrounding the casket, then that must mean only one thing: I was the person in the casket.

"No!" I shouted. "No!"

"Dang, calm down. That's all you had to say."

I opened my eyes to see Damon sitting on the stage in Club Shake 'Em Up. In the background I could hear the R. Kelly and Notorious B.I.G. song fading out. I looked around frantically, trying to figure out where I was.

I could hear the song "The Rain (Supa Dupa Fly)," by Missy Elliott, starting to play.

"You done made your money. Get off the stage and let me make mine."

I looked up at Angel, who smiled and winked, then proceeded to work her body to the song as if I was no longer standing there.

I was here. I was still in Club Shake 'Em Up. On the stage. I wasn't in Damon's apartment. Even better, I wasn't in a casket.

"Thank you, God," I murmured, the words escaping my lips almost subconsciously.

Next, I turned and looked at Damon, who was extending the five-hundred-dollar bill to me. I hadn't taken it. I hadn't sold my soul for five hundred dollars.

"Thank you, God." This time it was a conscious choice.

This overwhelming feeling came over me. I looked down at the bill, and then I looked into Damon's eyes. After about a five-second stare down, Damon shrugged his shoulders. Next, he tucked the bill back into his wallet, finished up his Hennessy, then stood. He gave me this one last look, his eyes questioning, "Are you sure? Going once, going twice . . ."

Then he was gone.

I quickly turned around, almost doing a sprint. The pole that I had almost run dead smack into stopped me in my tracks as I stared at it. Just moments ago I'd complained to myself how wrong the cleaning man was for making the pole so sparkling clean. On second thought, maybe it was me who was wrong. Deep down inside, maybe this side of myself was exactly who I was supposed to see. After all, how could I clean up a dirt spot if I had no idea that it was there? Looking at my reflection in the pole, I realized that maybe the pole wasn't so clean, after all.

I hurried off the stage and into the dressing room. I brushed past another dancer who was coming out and headed straight to my locker. I began pulling all my belongings out and stuffing them into my duffel bag. In one swoop I cleared my dressing table of all its contents, scooping them into my duffel bag as well. I snatched up any costumes, shoes, hair accessories, whatever, and stuffed my bag to the point where it wouldn't close.

I sat down at the dressing table for a minute in order to catch my breath. My chest was heaving up and down, I was breathing so hard. Before I stood up, I happened to catch my reflection in the mirror. Until looking at myself in the mirror, I hadn't even been conscious of the fact that I'd been crying. Even then, tears continued to pour out of my eyes.

"How did you get here?" I asked the girl in the mirror, truly expecting an answer. I swallowed hard and then took a deep breath, thinking back to how just moments ago my life had flashed before my eyes.

*My life?*

Was that what one would call my years of existence here on earth? A life? It had been full of struggle and pain. Was that really living? And now that I'd overcome so much, was I really still that stupid, where I'd continue to make the same mistakes and get the same results, which was exactly what I'd done for so long?

"On earth as it is in heaven." That scripture, prayer, or whatever it was, instantly came to my mind. I knew there was a Bible term for it—revelation, or something like that—but I got it! I got what that meant. It meant that God wanted me to live life here on earth just as He would have me live in heaven. He did not mean for me to have a miserable existence on earth and wait to get to heaven to live life abundantly and happily, with peace, love, and joy.

"You are dead." Those words escaped my mouth and hit the reflection in the mirror like daggers. The person I was looking at had been a dead woman walking. And look where that long walk had gotten her.

"I don't know how you got here," I said to my reflection. "You can stay if you want. But me . . . I'm out of here!"

On that note, I stood up and exited the dressing room, heading for the exit doors of the club.

"Hey, Almond!" I heard Candace shout out. I ignored her. "Almond," she repeated.

I had to stop in my tracks and remind myself that I was Almond. That was my stage name. My skin reminded me of the color of an almond covered in that dark chocolate on the package of one of those Almond Joy candy bars, and that was how I came up with my stage name.

"You're forgetting your drink commission." Candace was waving a few bills in her hand.

I took one step toward Candace.

*You don't need it. You don't need money. You just need me.*

I heard those words loud and clear. It wasn't some booming voice that put fear in me. It was a soft, calm, loving, peaceful voice deep within a part of me that I couldn't explain. It didn't take someone born on a church pew to know that it was God. So many times in life God had tried to speak to me, to direct my path, but I'd refused to listen. All those other times I'd been too busy running to stand still long enough and truly take in what God was trying to tell me. God had never been able to get a complete sentence out before I'd already taken off running. But now, for the first time, I was standing still. There was no longer anyplace to run. Every direction I'd tried to take myself in before had taken me to a dead-end cliff where I struggled to keep my balance. No more. The devil had me cornered. It was now a matter of life and death. There was only one place my flesh could lead me, and that was over the cliff, and that meant death.

I looked around the club.

Was I ready to die?

I took one step back.

I inhaled a deep breath.

I'd made up my mind.

"Give it to her." I nodded toward the dressing room.

"But it's yours," Candace said, with a confused look on her face.

"I know, but I ain't me no more. So give it to her." I nodded once again toward the dressing room, toward the girl I had left in the mirror. I then proudly walked out that door, knowing exactly what I was leaving behind . . . and it wasn't just the money.

I chose life!

# Stone Number Forty-one

The women in the New Day Temple of Faith Singles Ministry had never been this hushed during one of the meetings. There was usually some type of chatter or back-and-forth banter regarding the men in their lives or the lack thereof. Even if someone was giving a praise report or testimony, there was still some type of amen or someone adding their two cents to the kitty. Not this time. It was as if after hearing Helen's story, the women were absent of dialogue.

"You wanted my story, and now you have it. The whole twenty-six years," Helen told them, breaking the silence. She stretched her arms in the air and then allowed them to drop back down to her sides. "So now what? You gonna kick me out? Gonna ban me from the church?" Helen said defiantly.

This was pretty much what Helen had expected of her so-called church family. Never in her life had she ever really felt as though she fit in, not even with the family she grew up with. So why should anything be so different now? The only difference, though, now was that Helen knew if they threw her out on her tail, she'd land in God's lap. She'd been battered and tossed by life's raging sea, but whether she wanted to admit it or not, God had always been right there with a life jacket. There was no other explanation for how she'd made it this far. It certainly could not have been on her own strength.

Still, no one spoke.

Finally, Mother Doreen cleared her throat and then said, "How did you end up here, Sister Helen? I mean, literally, how did you end up here at New Day?"

"Well," Helen began, "the night I left the club for the last time, I got a flat tire on the freeway as I headed to my house." Helen thought back to the night as she continued to explain. "I remember saying, 'Lord, I did the right thing, and now here you have me stuck out here in no-man's-land in the middle of the night to be kidnapped, raped, and chopped up into little pieces, anyway. I might as well have stayed with Dub.'" Helen let out a chuckle. "Not that I probably hadn't deserved just that type of demise. After all, it wasn't like God hadn't come to my rescue before. Me shouting 'Hallelujah' at the time and then promising to turn my life over to Him, which I never actually did."

Mother Doreen let a gentle, knowing smile cross her face, letting Helen know that she wasn't alone. She had heard that story before, maybe had even been in the same position herself once upon a time.

"But then this couple came along." Helen shook her head as her eyes began to moisten. "And they actually offered to help." Her voice was laced with disbelief, even though she knew it firsthand to be true. "I . . . I couldn't believe God was sending me help once again. God still wanted to help me." She pointed to her chest as a tear fell. "All the promises I had made to God and had broken, yet He still was there for me. He still cared about me and came to see about me."

"Look at God," Tamarra mumbled softly to herself, reminded of how, no matter what, God was a God of second chances.

"The couple, I know, was sent by God," Helen continued. "The man, he put my spare tire on, while his wife stood with me and conversed. He had my car back up and running in no time without incident. I knew they were a nice, churchgoing couple, because before they left, the woman held my hands and prayed for me. I tried to pay them, but they wouldn't accept anything. They told me that coming to visit their church would be compensation. I knew that was nothing but God trying to cash in on the debt I owed Him—"

"No," Mother Doreen interrupted. "Jesus already paid the price. That was God letting you know that He hadn't brought you that far just to leave you stranded there."

Helen smiled and nodded at Mother Doreen's revelation. "That very next Sunday I was here. The message that day was so moving that it moved me right on down the altar to join the church."

Helen looked around the room, into some of the women's eyes. "I know what some of you are thinking, that joining the church has obviously done nothing for me. But you are all wrong. It has. Believe it or not, I'm so much better than I might be had I not joined the church. It's just that . . ." Helen's words trailed off as she got choked up. "I'm still in so much pain. I hurt so bad inside, and sometimes that hurt wants out and wants company. It wants other people to hurt too."

Tamarra spoke up. "I hear what you are saying, Sister Helen. I've harbored so much pain inside that you wouldn't believe. But hurting other people is not part of the healing process."

"And just joining a church, be it as it may, a great start," Paige said, jumping in, "is not enough."

"You should know," someone said in a low, condescending tone.

Paige turned around to find the culprit, but Mother Doreen, sensing something was about to jump off, interrupted.

"Paige is right, Sister Helen." Mother Doreen stood up and walked over to Helen. "I know you joined the church, but have you been . . . saved? Have you ever spoken with your mouth and believed in your heart that Jesus Christ is real? That He is the Lord? That He died at Calvary for the remission of your sins? That He rose from the grave and now sits at the right hand of the throne in heaven with our Father, God?"

Helen's eyes filled again with tears just hearing Mother Doreen say those words with such conviction and truth. She shook her head.

"Well, have you?" Mother Doreen asked. "Do you really, truly believe that?"

Helen nodded. She did believe. Looking back over her life—in the form of standing there, divulging every nook and cranny of her grainy past—Helen knew it was nothing but a simple and long overdue earnest cry for help. And today, without a shadow of a doubt, God had indeed heard her cry. Just like always, He'd sent her help. This time it was in the form of these women of New Day Temple of Faith. And on this day, the same way that God had received Helen with open arms in spite of her blemishes, she was going to open her arms and receive Him.

"Mother Doreen," Helen said, trembling, "you have been right about a lot of things you've spoken, but there is just one thing you are wrong about." Helen swallowed and then said, "I do owe God. I owe Him my life . . . and I'm ready to give it to Him."

"Amen!"

"Praise God!"

"He's worthy!"

Now, those were the customary sounds that echoed throughout the room at a New Day Singles Ministry meeting.

"Then, child," Mother Doreen said, placing her hand on Helen's shoulder, "let's give God what you owe Him. Let's get you saved!" Mother Doreen turned to get her Bible, then paused. She turned back to face Helen. "That is, if you want to be saved."

"Yes." Helen could barely get the word out through her tears. "I want to be saved."

Mother Doreen retrieved her Bible and began to read scriptures to Helen regarding one's soul being saved. "Lift your hands up to God in surrender, my dear child," she told Helen.

Helen lifted her shaking hands and then repeated after Mother Doreen as she led her to Christ.

"My child," Mother Doreen said, her own eyes filled with tears, "you are now saved. You are now a member of the Kingdom." She threw her arms around Helen, who was shaking and crying. "Now give Him some praise."

"Thank you, Jesus," Helen proclaimed. "Thank you for saving me. Literally, Jesus, thank you for saving me." Helen rested her head on Mother Doreen's bosom and sighed. Sniffing and praises could be heard from some of the other members.

Eventually, Mother Doreen pulled Helen away from her. She stared her in the eyes. "Not only are you a member of God's Kingdom, but you are also a member of this church family. Ain't that right, saints?" Mother Doreen said matter-of-factly, looking over Helen's shoulders at the sometimes feisty divas of the New Day Temple of Faith Singles Ministry.

The women didn't speak a word. Instead, one by one, they got up, walked over to Helen, and put their arms around her. The more the women embraced her, the harder Helen shook with tears. They didn't care about how jacked up she was on the inside or what she looked like on the outside. They didn't care whether her blood pumped the same way as theirs. They coveted her like family. Helen let them in, receiving their embraces. The women's actions showed Helen that she was worthy.

That was not the only thing the women's actions showed Helen. The same way God had blessed Helen with this church family was the same way He'd blessed her with Rakeem and his family . . . her family. The same way Helen was receiving these women was the same way Helen should have received her family—blood or no blood. This brought on the realization that some of her pain had been self-inflicted. She'd allowed her mind and heart to harbor unfounded grudges. She made a mental note to reach out to her family and acknowledge them as being her gift from God. It was a little late, but she was ready to tear off the bow and rip the package open.

As Helen stood in the midst of the women, a foreign object blanketed her very being, an article she would wear internally eternally. Love. Real love. Genuine love. Unconditional love. Unconditional love was what Dino had promised Helen. But she hadn't believed him when he was telling her these things. She'd been afraid, afraid that his little outbursts would turn into bigger outbursts later on, and she wasn't willing to live the life she'd lived with Dub all over again, to have the same stuff, different man. But most of all, she'd been afraid that she really didn't deserved unconditional love, and therefore, it would have been nothing more than part-time bliss disguising itself.

Right now, at this very moment, Helen was certain that what she was experiencing was no masquerade. It was the real thing. A feeling swept over her, whispering to her soul that her life would never be the same. Because for the first time ever, she had truly let love into her heart. God was love.

On that day Helen learned that knowing there was a God wasn't enough. Talking to Him every now and again wasn't enough. Not even believing in God was enough. Simply joining a church definitely wasn't enough. But now Helen had had enough. She'd had enough of pushing around that stroller of hurt and pain, coddling them like newborn twin babies. Today she cut the umbilical cord, weaned them, packed up all their belongings, and kicked them out of the house all in the same day.

Sure, she'd suffer from a case of empty-nest syndrome here and there, but ultimately, that void would be filled with all that God had for her. She feared what her life would be like without having the twins around, but she feared even more how her life would end up if she held on and babied them. She'd grown far too dependent on hurt and pain, and now it was time for her to grow dependent on God.

Turning her life over to Christ would not make Helen a whole different person overnight, but it was a start. Come morning she would be nowhere near where she needed to be in life, but she wouldn't be where she used to be, either. Most importantly, day by day in her walk with Christ, the closer she grew to Him, the farther she would be walking away from who she used to be. Amen!

# Epilogue

"I saw Grandma Daniels today!" Baby D says with such excitement while getting off the school bus and running into my arms. Usually, my mom gets him off the bus, because Baby D is still staying with her. He goes to school from her address. She has a doctor's appointment today, so I've picked him up instead.

"What?" I'm not sure if I'm hearing my son right. Ever since Dub got that extra year in jail because of me, I haven't heard a peep from Ms. Daniels.

"Yes, she came to my school and had lunch with me today. She brought me McDonald's!" Baby D is having the hardest time containing himself.

I guess after almost a year, Ms. Daniels couldn't stand not seeing Baby D anymore. I'm not mad. I would have allowed her to see him, just under the condition that she promised not to allow him to speak to Dub on the phone. But she never reached out to me, and I certainly am not about to reach out to her, not knowing what her reaction might be.

"So she brought you some McDonald's up to the school, huh?" I ask.

"Yep, and she brought you something too." Baby D begins to dig in his book bag as we head to my car. "Here you go."

Baby D hands me a letter. My breath abandons me as I read the envelope. It's not what is written on the envelope that gives me pause. It's how it's written.

*HELEN*

I'd know that handwriting anywhere. It's none other than Dub's.

"What's the matter, Mommy? You okay?" Baby D asks as I stand by my car, immobilized.

"Yes, b-baby," I stammer. "Everything is okay. Let Mommy buckle you in." I get Baby D buckled up in the backseat, then plant myself in the driver's seat. I just sit there, clasping the envelope. Finally, I inhale a lungful of air and remove the letter inside the envelope.

*Hi, Helen.*

*Please don't ball up this letter and throw it away before reading it. It's not what you think. It's not like all those other letters. I was on some crazy, jealous stuff then. But I'm over it. Don't get it twisted. I didn't get over it overnight. I had to go through counseling and anger management. The court ordered the anger management. The counseling was something I requested. I'm understanding the source of my anger. I know I watched my dad treat my mom as bad, if not worse, than I treated you. But I know I can be a better man. Oh, and guess what? I got my GED too. I'm taking English and math courses and stuff. It's pretty cool. When I get out of here next week, I'm coming out a new man. A better man.*

*Anyway, I just really wanted to tell you that I'm sorry for ruining your life. I bet you regret the day you ever showed up over at Rochelle's house to meet me. It's funny because it wasn't even you I was supposed to be meeting. Rochelle had told me that y'all's girl Chelsie was digging me and wanted me to meet her over at her house. That afternoon when*

*I showed up and met you there, I'd been expecting Chelsie, but I just rolled with it. I think she was just trying to get me over there because she knew I hung with Earl Lee and she wanted to get with him. Nonetheless, I was glad it was you there and not Chelsie. I just wish I'd done you better.*

*I miss my son. I know you won't bring him to see me, but would it be cool if my moms brings him? I know that you and I will never be together again, but I'd still like to have a relationship with my son if at all possible.*

*Well, I won't keep you. Just wanted to say I'm sorry and hope you have a good life. God bless you!*

*Dub*

*P.S. My mom's number is 614-555-4321. Call her to set something up with Baby D. Give him a hug and a kiss and tell him his daddy loves him. I'll apologize to him myself when he's old enough to understand.*

"Looks like Dub found God too," I say to myself. "Or God found Dub."

"What, Mommy?" Baby D asks. He is now eight years old and is growing up to be a kind, loving, and respectful young man. Disconnecting himself from the madness that had surrounded him during his earlier years seems to be paying off. That and the fact that God has placed a loving grandmother and great-grandmother in his life to mold and nurture him. I'd been saved for only a couple months, so God is definitely still working on me.

"Oh, nothing, son. Nothing at all." I smile as I start the engine to my car.

I look down at the letter and shake my head. I guess Rochelle ended up getting the last laugh when it came to me. She'd set everything up. This whole thing about Dub liking me had been a lie. She'd lied to him and she'd lied to me for her own selfish and conniving reasons. I can't help but think that a large portion of my life was not supposed to happen—not to me, anyway—and all because of Rochelle. Had I lived Chelsie's life, or had I just been a casualty of Rochelle's interfering with destiny?

It doesn't even matter at this point, and there is no room in my heart to be mad at Rochelle. The old me probably would have hunted down Rochelle and figured out a way to make her life just as miserable as mine had been. But I ain't me no more, and today I know that what God has for me is for me. I'm going to get only what He has planned for me to receive. My portion is mine. And God is such a giver.

I've managed to keep my head above water financially, thanks to the unexpected check I received in the mail from the IRS. That Monday after my last night as a dancer, the IRS notified me that through an internal audit it was discovered that monies, in addition to the refund I had already received for the past three years, were due me. It was almost seven times more than what Damon had offered me that night in the strip club. Talk about waiting on and depending on God to be my provider instead of man.

At first I thought it was some kind of crazy accounting error, but it was all God, and God doesn't make mistakes. And because He doesn't make mistakes, I can only believe that the life I'm living is the one I'm designed to live. At least now I'm not living it how Dub wanted me to live it, or anyone else, for that matter, including myself. Now I'm living my life according to God's plan for me. I know that as long as I trust in God, allow Him to direct my path and order my steps and always be my plan A, I will never need a plan B.

# Readers' Group Discussion Questions

1. If you have ever questioned why someone stays in an abusive relationship, did Helen's inner thoughts and reasoning give you a better understanding?
2. Would you say that throughout Helen's journey she is running from God or He is chasing her?
3. If you have read any of the books in the "Divas" series, do you have a better understanding of who Helen is after reading her story?
4. Do you feel Helen really wants to change?
5. What role do you think Helen's past/childhood plays in her not so nice ways as an adult?
6. Do you think you could be like the women of New Day Temple of Faith and embrace a woman like Helen?
7. Do you think Helen should have left Dino?
8. Do you feel that Rochelle played with destiny by introducing Dub and Helen or that it was meant to be?
9. Do you understand why Helen was friends with Rochelle in the first place? Have you ever been friends with someone who you knew didn't have good intentions toward others?

# About the Author

BLESSEDselling author E.N. Joy is the writer behind the "New Day Divas" five-book series and the "Still Divas" three-book series, which have been coined the "soap opera in print." Formerly writing secular works under the names Joylynn M. Jossel and JOY, this award-winning author has been sharing her literary expertise on conference panels in her hometown of Columbus, Ohio, as well as in cities across the country.

In 2000 Joy formed her own publishing company, End of the Rainbow Projects. In 2004 Joy branched out into the business of literary consulting, providing one-on-one consultations and literary services, such as ghostwriting, editing, professional read throughs, and write behinds. Her clients include first-time authors, *Essence* magazine bestselling authors, *New York Times* bestselling authors, and entertainers.

Some of Joy's works have received honors, such as being named an *Essence* magazine bestseller, garnering the Borders Bestselling African American Romance Award, appearing in *Newsweek,* and being translated into Japanese. Joy's children's story, *The Secret Olivia Told Me* (written under the name N. Joy), received the American Library Association Coretta Scott King Honor. Scholastic acquired the book club rights, and the book has sold almost one hundred thousand copies. Elementary and middle school children have fallen in love with reading and creative writing as a result of the readings and workshops Joy performs in schools nationwide.